Outstanding praise for Kelse[y James]
and *The Woman in the Ca[stello]*

"Kelsey James had me at 'a film shoot at an Italian castle in the 1960s.' Like Jess Walter's *Beautiful Ruins*, the glamour and heady indulgence of the era take center stage in this captivating, multilayered story that will keep you guessing to the end. Silvia and Gabriella are flawed, fascinating characters who will linger in your mind long after the book is closed."
—Susan Wiggs, #1 *New York Times* bestselling author

"From the moment a stunning 1960s Italy kisses your hand and draws you into the opening pages of this novel, you'll be riveted to *The Woman in the Castello*. Mysterious, stimulating, intoxicating . . . a dark, rich *caffè corretto* of a novel."
—K. D. Alden, author of *A Mother's Promise*

"The 1960s in Rome, a crumbling Italian castle on the edge of a volcanic lake, a glamorous aunt she's never met, and a starring role in a horror movie that begins to feel a bit too real. . . . Kelsey James's debut novel is a delicious Gothic filled with atmosphere, twists, romance, and dark secrets. Readers will devour it."
—Megan Chance, bestselling author of *A Splendid Ruin*

"An impressive debut by a writer sure to become a favorite of readers. *The Woman in the Castello* is a tantalizing mixture of romance, mystery, and the Gothic enfolded in a well-crafted plot that pays homage to the long lineage of ghostly tales and romantic suspense."
—V. S. Alexander, author of *The War Girls*

"Cinematic and spooky, *The Woman in the Castello* had me riveted from page one. There is something for everyone in this gripping historical novel that expertly blends a love story with family drama and a twist of suspense. Readers will be swept up in the glamorous—and sometimes grungy—1960s movie scene, and the magnificent setting is sure to inspire many a trip to Italy. A delight for the senses and a truly entertaining story!"
—Nicole Baart, bestselling author of *Everything We Didn't Say*

Please turn the page for more extraordinary praise!

More praise for *The Woman in the Castello*!

"An impromptu movie set in a medieval castle in 1960s Italy provides a fascinating backdrop for this fresh Gothic tale filled with mystery, family secrets, and unexpected romance."
—Lorena Hughes, author of *The Spanish Daughter*

"You'll get lost in the pages of this lush, entertaining story as you follow aspiring actress Silvia Whitford through the dark towers and crumbling staircases of a remote Italian castle, where she uncovers twists and turns around every corner, including shocking family secrets you'll never see coming."
—Ellen Marie Wiseman, *New York Times* bestselling author

"*The Woman in the Castello* has it all—mystery, romance, and an enchanting cast of characters with a plucky heroine at its heart. Against the richly drawn backdrop of post-war Italy, in a castle brimming with secrets, Kelsey James explores the enduring and sometimes destructive power of love, family, and ambition. A page-turner from start to finish, *The Woman in the Castello* is a marvelous debut!"
—Amanda Skenandore, author of *The Nurse's Secret*

"A young actress desperate for stardom agrees to film a horror movie in her aunt's crumbling Italian castle. Then the aunt disappears. What secrets lurk in her past—and in the mysterious lake behind the castle? *The Woman in the Castello* is a thoroughly original blend of mystery, family drama, and sultry romance, all unfolding in the fast-paced world of a Swinging Sixties movie set. A riveting debut from author Kelsey James!"
—Elizabeth Blackwell, bestselling author of *Red Mistress*

SECRETS OF
ROSE BRIAR
HALL

Books by Kelsey James

THE WOMAN IN THE CASTELLO

SECRETS OF ROSE BRIAR HALL

Published by Kensington Publishing Corp.

SECRETS OF
ROSE BRIAR
HALL

KELSEY JAMES

John Scognamiglio Books
Kensington Publishing Corp.
www.kensingtonbooks.com

JOHN SCOGNAMIGLIO BOOKS are published by

Kensington Publishing Corp.
900 Third Avenue
New York, NY 10022

All Kensington titles, imprints, and distributed lines are available at special quantity discounts for bulk purchases for sales promotion, premiums, fund-raising, and educational or institutional use.

Special book excerpts or customized printings can also be created to fit specific needs. For details, write or phone the office of the Kensington Sales Manager: Kensington Publishing Corp., 900 Third Avenue, New York, NY 10022. Attn. Sales Department. Phone: 1-800-221-2647.

The JS and John Scognamiglio Books logo is a trademark of Kensington Publishing Corp.

ISBN: 978-1-4967-4293-3

ISBN: 978-1-4967-4294-0 (ebook)

First Kensington Trade Paperback Edition: July 2024

10 9 8 7 6 5 4 3 2 1

Printed in the United States of America

For Steve, who makes everything better

CHAPTER 1

The striped bass flopped about helplessly in the boat, its belly flashing in the sun. I flinched as the fisherman sliced below its gills in a swift, sure motion and carved off bloody filets of flesh. On our dock, his partner spoke animatedly with the chef and gestured at his catches. In October, it was getting cold to be going out on the water, and our own yacht was tucked cozily in the boathouse, but the fishermen were still at it. What an awful fuss went into feeding us, and the kitchen would be in an absolute uproar right now in preparation for our big dinner tomorrow.

The sand and rock crunched under my feet as I walked down the beach, letting the wind whip my hair and the salt prickle my skin. I liked to come down here to clear my head, but it wasn't working this morning. My mind was full of the party. I was determined it would be an event to remember.

Once, I would have laughed at myself for getting worked up over something so frivolous, but I knew how much it meant to Charles. Somehow we'd become the most talked-about couple in New York after our lavish wedding the year before, and now I had to prove that I was up to the task of being Mrs. Charles Turner; that my taste was sophisticated enough, my house grand enough, my pockets deep enough.

I gazed up the sloping lawn toward Rose Briar Hall, and it was something to behold, with its fresh white limestone façade and its commanding position overlooking the bay. The manor's gabled roofs, balustraded parapets, series of window bays, and decorative friezes made it look like one of the great aristocratic houses of England, plucked up and transported to Long Island's North Shore. We'd only just finished it, and I knew Charles would have preferred us to build in Tuxedo or Newport, but Long Island felt like virgin land society hadn't conquered yet. Here we could set the trend instead of following it too late. I hoped he would come to see it that way.

I spent the rest of the day overseeing preparations, and later that night I struggled to fall asleep; unsurprising, given how nervous I was. I dreamed of a gale and watched in horror as our guests emerged from their snug cars and carriages into the freezing rain and howling wind. Inside, the lights buzzed strangely, and then the generator suddenly failed, casting us all in blackness. A glow emanated from Charles, beautiful and transfixing, while I grew invisible and weightless, drifting above the room like a ghost. Fear gripped me, and I knew there was some sort of danger brewing and that I had to warn my friends. But I couldn't find my voice.

When I finally awoke, my nightgown was drenched in sweat, and my bedclothes were twisted into a great heap at the foot of the bed. I pressed the button in the wall to call for my maid, my heart thumping, and trembled as I poured myself a glass of water.

Outside, it was a gorgeous fall day. The sky was clear and blue, and the morning sunshine was so bright it hurt my eyes, after my restless sleep. The trees were a riot of reds and oranges and yellows, and the abundant maples carpeted the ground with gold. I should have breathed a sigh of relief, but I remained deeply unsettled. The dream felt like a bad omen.

Downstairs, I found Charles preparing to go out shooting. He looked marvelous in his tweed Norfolk jacket, his frame tall and lean and graceful, and he was pulsing with energy. That was Charles for you: always the well-groomed gentleman on the outside, but underneath there was a streak of wildness to him; he was a man who followed his impulses. I always felt so small standing beside him. I was especially petite, but it was more than that; I was often so overwhelmed by him that I felt dwarfed by his presence.

He took one look at me and rushed over to take my hands in his. "Millie, dear. You look like you've seen a ghost. Are you all right?" His green eyes were soft.

I was still shaken, and I clung to him. "I had an awful nightmare, that's all. I'm just so worried about this evening. I want it to be everything you've hoped for."

He stroked my cheek, then my neck, and my skin tingled under his fingertips. "Don't be a silly goose."

I should have been excited. I'd planned every last detail of the event. Our menu that evening would include triplets of oysters, caviar, turtle soup, fresh fish, stuffed young turkey with cranberry sauce, leg of mutton, and prime rib. Every wood surface gleamed, thanks to the ministrations of a small army of maids, and it wasn't hyperbole to say that the house positively sparkled: the chandeliers, the crystal glasses, the mirrors, the gleaming mullioned windows, which sunshine poured through. For some reason it brought to mind the fancy-dress ball at Sherry's where I'd first met Charles, of the lights shining on the gilded walls and the twinkle of jewels. I'd dressed as the Greek goddess Persephone, and when Charles had shown up as Hades, it had seemed like fate.

"I'm going to wear the Bonaparte earrings tonight," I told him, still a little breathless from his touch. He'd given me the precious ruby and diamond pair as an engagement present, and they'd once belonged to Napoleon's wife, Joséphine, or at least so the dealer claimed. Charles had told me that together we'd be the envy of everyone in the city, and he'd kissed me, the type of kiss that was bold even for a newly engaged couple. I may have been inexperienced, but with him I'd understood what desire was.

We'd been married within a month.

"I hoped you would. They can be your good-luck charm," he said, his mustache twitching as he smiled. "Not that you need it. You've outdone yourself. It's going to be splendid."

The compliment made me flush with pleasure. The house was good enough for us, his expression seemed to say: we who deserved the best of everything, who needed a house as glamorous and illustrious as we were.

He took a step back to assess me. "And you're splendid, too. Evanson is going to be green with envy. All that money and somehow he ended up with a woman who looks just like Ajax."

I couldn't help laughing. Charles knew just how to lighten my mood. Ajax was Charles's favorite horse growing up, and the ancient thoroughbred still moldered in our stables in the city. "Don't be cruel."

"How am I cruel? I adore Ajax. Do you suppose Mrs. Evanson is fond of apples?"

"There is to be apple tart among the desserts."

"See? You think of everything. Nothing could possibly go wrong."

He kissed me, a long kiss that made me wonder if he meant to delay his outing, never mind that we had guests in the house. It was the sort of reckless thing he might do. But he did let me go, reluctantly.

The dream lingered in my mind for the rest of the day. A few of our guests not fortunate enough to have a nearby estate were staying at our house for the weekend, and while the men were out shooting, it fell to me to entertain the women. Rebecca Wainwright was older and a terrible bore: straight-spined, proper, and a teetotaler. I liked Gertrude Underhill even less. She'd had her sights set on Charles before I did, and resented that he'd chosen me over her. She still flirted with him shamelessly, especially now that her own husband was engaged in a well publicized affair with a Ziegfeld Follies dancer. There were rumors swirling that they might divorce. I hadn't wanted to invite her at all, only Charles insisted, saying it would look petty if I didn't.

At least my dear Arabella was there, too. Arabella was fiercely loyal, and faster than most of my friends—she cared less about decorum and was more fun than the rest of them put together. With her dark hair—almost black—and dark eyes, her arresting beauty made Gertrude look limp and pale in comparison. Gertrude was a listless, colorless little thing with blond hair and blond eyelashes, and a delicate disposition that meant she always had a head cold. I always thought her little illnesses were just an excuse for her to complain and to draw sympathy and attention toward herself.

"Look how much progress you have made on the house!" Gertrude declared, as we sat down for tea, and I was surprised at the compliment and prepared to be pleasant to her in return. "Why, it looks nearly complete. You'll have to have us over again once you've finished decorating."

I sucked in my breath. I was finished, of course. I'd taken special pride in the drawing room where we sat. Its palette of cream and gold was elegant and understated, and it was swathed in soft velvet, from the sofas to the flocked wallpaper, providing reprieve from the dark woods and imposing stone found elsewhere in the house. Overhead, a crystal and bronze chandelier glittered. The oil paintings I'd chosen provided a vibrant and moody contrast, and the stained-glass Tiffany windows—selected with the help of Louis Tiffany himself, whose estate was near our own—lent the space the reverence of a cathedral.

I made no reply, but Mrs. Wainwright had heard.

"Is the work still in progress, then?"

My lips thinned. There was no possible way to reply that wasn't embarrassing.

Luckily, Arabella came to the rescue. "Well, of course

Charles is such a great collector, he is always looking for new pieces to add."

I exhaled and gave her a grateful look.

But Gertrude was determined. "Naturally, it takes years to really round out an art collection. A house doesn't feel established until it has been in a family for at least a generation, I always say."

She emphasized the word "established," to remind me that my house—and my money—were new. It didn't matter to her that I had spent months selecting the antique table clocks, French armchairs, Qing dynasty vases, and Flemish tapestries. I'd put so much care into everything, building this house from nothing, and in the space of a breath she'd tried to tear it all down. I seethed, my dislike for her growing sharper every moment, blossoming into hate.

I sipped my tea to avoid answering her. I listened to the dogs baying and the guns firing in the distance and watched the weather. I had difficulty concentrating on the conversation as the ladies moved on to other topics, and then I worried my mood might ruin the weekend even if the weather did not. I did my best to pull my attention back to them, to talk of dresses and gossip and decorating.

No storm materialized. That evening, everything looked magnificent: fires roared in the grand fireplaces—one nearly tall enough to stand in—and fresh flowers adorned the tables. Electric lights shined everywhere, and as our guests pulled up in the circular drive, I knew the house would be radiant against the night sky. Even the elaborate greenhouse on the West Lawn was lit up, and I could easily picture it, a jewel box in the dark.

Charles and I looked wonderful, too: grand enough for the house we'd built. I wore a new dress made by Madame Paquin in Paris, a delicate, flimsy, cream and pink evening gown of French silk that fell off of the shoulders, complementing my pale skin and dark hair. I had a small, full mouth, pert nose, and dark brown eyes, and at my debut, society had described me as a classic beauty. Charles once said I reminded him of the heroine in a romantic poem. But it was hard for anyone to stand out next to Charles. With his patrician features— straight nose, strong bones, almost feminine lips, and those striking green eyes—he was the kind of handsome that didn't just turn heads, it dropped jaws.

I hadn't been able to find my engagement earrings, which worried me, but I tried to push it out of my mind.

Everything should have been perfect.

And yet, as I sat in the drawing room in tense anticipation, I couldn't shake a terrible sense of foreboding. I'd never believed in premonitions, but in some dark corner of my mind, I knew that something terrible was about to happen.

CHAPTER 2

I blinked, and the room before me appeared blurry and distorted, as if I were still dreaming. Such strange nightmares I'd had, too. In most of them I'd found myself trapped—in a great underground cavern, in a train car speeding out of control, and worst of all underwater, choking on the briny waters of the Long Island Sound.

But I was awake now. My head ached, and my mouth was dry as a bone. I searched my nightstand for water and gulped it greedily. My stomach twisted with hunger. I stood up, and the room tilted; my legs shook beneath me. I steadied myself on the wall and crept over to my sitting area, hoping to find a breakfast tray.

There was none.

I collapsed on my silk chaise and looked around, my vision clearing. Patterns of roses decorated the wallpaper and the cream pillows, looking oddly forlorn this morning, and I wondered why. My spacious room was French in style, normally cheerful and bright, with its white decorative plasterwork on the ceiling and fireplace, gilded cream wood furniture, and pink drapery around the canopy bed and windows. Something about the room felt different.

The fire blazed fiercely in the grate, but even so, I shivered. The heat wasn't on, I realized. We'd designed the house with every modern convenience—central heating, electricity—but the house was cold.

And dark. That was why the decor looked wrong. The lights were off, and the sunlight filtering through the windowpanes was weak.

Odder still, the windowpanes were covered in frost. I rose carefully, still feeling wobbly, and looked outside. Snow had dusted the estate in a layer of white. In the distance, the water of Oyster Bay was dark and choppy.

I frowned. Snow was unusual for October, and the weather had been perfect for the party yesterday.

Hadn't it been?

I must have drunk too much at dinner, because I could hardly remember the night before. I'd never gotten sick from drinking in the past or lost bits of time from it, as some did, but I must have had more than I realized. It wasn't like me to lose control like that, but I'd been so nervous. That must be why my head throbbed.

I found the knob for the lights on the wall and spun it, but nothing happened. I sighed in exasperation. There must be some sort of issue with the generator. We'd had dual fixtures installed in many of the rooms, at Charles's insistence; he was a bit old-fashioned in some ways. So we had gas, too, and I turned the key in the sconce nearest me. It lit, thankfully, the little flame casting strange shadows.

The door behind me creaked open and I jumped. Charles strode in, looking as immaculate as ever. His trousers were perfectly pressed, his mustache neatly combed, and the sight of him still gave me a little swoop in my belly. He was pale, though. His smooth skin and strong-boned handsomeness made me think, not for the first time, of the marble statues of Greek gods in my father's garden. He wore an overcoat in deference to the cold, but he wasn't trembling, like me. He'd never minded chilly weather.

"Thank God you're awake." He gathered me in his arms, and his closeness warmed me for a moment. The wind snapped the branches of the birch trees outside the window.

"The generator isn't working. The boiler, too, I think."

"I know. There's been a delay in the coal delivery."

I furrowed my brow. Surely we hadn't run out of coal since the party yesterday.

"How are you feeling?" His words were soft, and he peered curiously at me. I paused, confused by the question. Was it because he'd seen me drinking too much last night? But somehow I didn't think that's what he meant. I shuddered, but not only from the cold this time. The prolonged, eerie dreams, the snow outside, the empty crystal vases that were usually full of roses, his sudden paleness, when at the party he'd still had a slight tan from his days out hunting—all of it suggested that more time had passed than a single day.

A wave of anxiety overcame me. "What happened, Charles?" My voice was faint.

He sighed and seated himself in the wingback chair closest to the fire. I sank back down into the settee.

"You don't remember?" He studied me with those striking green eyes, his forehead creased in concern.

"No." I searched my memory, but the last thing I recalled was of the two of us in the drawing room waiting for our guests to arrive. I'd gone to the walnut burr sideboard and poured a glass of sherry, the crystal decanter reflecting in the silvery mirror behind it, and swallowed it in one trembling gulp.

After that, there was nothing.

"The doctor said this might happen. It's not unusual after a shock."

"The doctor?"

"Dr. Wendell. There was . . . an incident at the party, Millie, a very upsetting incident, and you had a bit of a fit. You've been terribly unwell. You fainted, and you've been in and out of consciousness. I've been so worried."

My heart stuttered in my chest. "For how long?" Ice coursed down my spine. And hazy images came to me then, of my maid Briggs spooning soup into my mouth, helping me to the bathroom. I did feel unwell.

"Three weeks."

I inhaled sharply and squeezed my hands together in my lap.

"My God, Charles. Am I going to be all right?" My voice caught. I was terrified. How could I have been unconscious for three weeks? The party had been late October. That meant it was November, nearly Thanksgiving. My heart pounded and my mouth went dry again. I was still so thirsty. I gulped my water, and my stomach churned uneasily. He nodded.

"Dr. Wendell is optimistic. You were hysterical before the—well. He thinks it was your nerves, and perhaps a sleep disorder of some kind. I told him about the nightmares."

This reassured me only a little. I'd never heard of a nervous fit causing someone to lose consciousness for such a length of time. I did often have vivid dreams, and I'd told Charles about some of them, but I didn't understand what they might have to do with my condition. I trembled. I wished my thoughts were clearer, but I was still so tired.

"But I'm going to get better?"

"Yes, there's every reason to expect it. I'll have Dr. Wendell come soon, now that you're awake. He can explain it all better than I can." He smiled reassuringly. Of course Charles would be here watching over me, waiting for me to awake. He was so good, so loving. He was one of the most renowned stockbrokers in the city and he'd been so busy with work lately, so his presence here when he was surely needed in the office meant a great deal.

"Why did I have a fit? What happened?"

"Dr. Wendell insisted I shouldn't upset you when you first

awoke. I will tell you everything, Millie, but first you must get well." He took my hands in his, and the affectionate gesture soothed me.

"Surely you can give me some idea. Please."

Charles shook his head sympathetically. "I know this must be so difficult. Confusing. But your health must be our first concern right now."

"But—"

He put a finger to my lips, stopping my words. "Patience. Patience, darling. All in due time."

I wanted to keep arguing, but I didn't have the strength. And Charles could be so persuasive when he wanted to be. When he pitched prospective clients, it was almost hypnotizing. He sounded so sure, and I wanted to recover.

Just then Briggs sauntered in at her usual snail's pace and set a tray down with a slight smirk. Briggs had never warmed to me—she was all officiousness and pinched lips—but she had served Charles before he met me and he wouldn't dream of parting with her. She stared at me with her watery blue eyes and placed her hands on her wide hips. "Will that be all, ma'am?"

"I'll be requiring a bath soon, if you could draw one."

"Water will be cold, ma'am."

I blanched. It hadn't occurred to me that without the boiler working even the water would be freezing. "Charles, we truly don't have any coal left?"

He flicked an invisible piece of lint off his trouser leg and stood. His expression was tender and concerned. "Cold baths are therapeutic, I've heard," he said gently. "It might be good for you."

"For patients in asylums, you mean. What are you saying?" Something truly shocking must have happened at the party, but I couldn't begin to guess what. I wondered if any of our other guests had been as upset by it as I had. I wished he would explain.

"It will be bracing, after being asleep so long. It might help restore you to your usual self." He smiled. Charles usually doted on me, too much sometimes, calling me his delicate little blossom and buying me extravagant presents without an occasion. My friends always commented how lucky I was, what a catch Charles was, and I'd always tried hard to be the type of wife who deserved him. Normally he would have presented me with a new bath fragrance from Paris, perhaps even bathed me himself. Waking up from my illness to find a cold house, a cold bath—it was all so strange. It scared me.

"If you truly think it will help."

"I do. This is all only temporary, Millie. And once you're feeling up to it, we can pay your parents a visit if you'd like. They've been worried."

I didn't feel physically ready to see my parents just yet, but I did long to see them. My mother, surely, would know what had happened at my party that upset me so much, and she wasn't the type who was capable of keeping secrets.

"All right. Tomorrow, perhaps."

Charles smiled at me, and in an instant his face was trans formed. He was dazzling.

"You're being so brave, my darling." He chucked my chin and strode out of the room. An ember flew out of the fireplace, past the decorative fan-shaped grate, and sat glowing on the rug. It died out quickly, leaving an ugly black smear.

"Let's have your bath," Briggs said, and I didn't think I was imagining the mean edge to her tone. I did want to bathe, so I acquiesced. Her hands when she helped me into the tub were too firm, and her fingers left red stripes on my skin. The water shocked me to my core. "Leave," I demanded. I wouldn't give her the satisfaction of seeing me suffer.

"Mr. Turner says I'm to stay, since you are still so weak, ma'am." She patted her gray-blond hair, tied neatly into a bun. I would have scowled at her, but my teeth were chattering too hard.

Briggs dumped water on my hair without warning and I shrieked. "Let's get you cleaned up nice," she said, and began lathering. I was too feeble to resist. Briggs had never taken this sort of liberty with me before, and her impertinence chilled me almost as much as the bath.

I remembered the nightmare, the one where I'd been drowning, and wondered if this was how it began. I could barely move now, and for a horrifying moment I thought I'd sink under the surface.

My old life seemed to be slipping away from me.

Just like my memory.

CHAPTER 3

After my bath, my veins were still filled with ice. Even the next day, I couldn't shake my chill. I still felt woozy and a bit nauseated when Dr. Wendell arrived early in the morning.

The doctor sat at my bedside and studied me through gold-rimmed pince-nez glasses perched on the bump in his nose. He was gray haired but not old, forty perhaps. He was very well-dressed for a country doctor, and a gold watch flashed at his waist. He felt my pulse, looked into my eyes, and sat back, apparently satisfied. Charles sat near him, and both of them looked too large for the upholstered King Louis chairs.

"You've made excellent progress. I don't see why you can't travel."

"But it's nothing permanent? I'll be back to . . . how I was?" I worried perhaps the diagnosis was more serious than they were letting on. I'd heard of such things happening, women with terminal illnesses being lied to so that their final days would be less stressful. Dr. Wendell considered the question and nodded slowly. He seemed genuine.

"We'll need to consider whether your hysteria and neurasthenia will continue to trouble you. It's possible you'll need ongoing treatment. However, Mr. Turner tells me this is the first incident of this sort he's witnessed, so I'm hopeful you'll be quite yourself again soon." I exhaled, relieved at least that I wasn't suffering from something grave. The question of hysteria concerned me, but I'd never been prone to nervousness or wild outbursts. My thoughts were a bit sharper this morning, and my disposition didn't seem any different to me than it had before the party. I was only physically weak from being abed for so long.

"What caused this to happen? Why is it I can't remember anything?"

Charles pursed his lips, and the doctor just shook his head.

"It would be risky to allow you to revisit the trauma that induced your hysterical episode at this juncture. It could cause a relapse. If you are still doing well in a few days, we can reconsider."

I sighed. It seemed a wholly unnecessary precaution in my view, but then, I couldn't be sure.

The doctor continued. "As for your memory, it's quite normal to suffer amnesia after a traumatic event. I suspect that is what has happened here."

I wasn't completely satisfied by this answer, but he didn't seem inclined to say more. I hadn't the slightest notion of what I might have witnessed, and why it should have upset me so much. It was useless to conjecture.

After the doctor left, I rose from my bed and let Briggs dress me and fix my hair. I dismissed her and sifted through my jewelry box, looking for the pearls my mother had given me for my last birthday. Even though I still didn't feel my best, I was determined to look well. My fingers grazed a piece of paper, and I picked it up, puzzled, and unfolded it.

It was a note.

Don't drink the tea.

My lips parted in astonishment. The words had clearly been written in a great hurry, but even so, I recognized the writing as my own.

I didn't understand it. I must have written it sometime during my illness. I couldn't remember the party, or the weeks after, which must have been why I couldn't remember penning the note. Perhaps I'd had a nightmare and been confused.

Unless I'd meant it as a warning.

My heart kicked up. Briggs brought me my tea every day. She'd played nursemaid to me during my illness. Had she been giving me something to keep me sick?

It was an outrageous thought, and I sighed. Briggs didn't like me, but there was no reason to suspect something so dramatic. My imagination could run wild sometimes. I hoped it wasn't a sign of the hysteria the doctor had mentioned.

My hands were shaking so badly I dropped the note back in the box, just as Charles strode in, his greyhounds Prince and Duke loping at his heel. They were beautiful beasts, sleek and graceful, all ribs and muscles and long legs, but they were a bit standoffish.

"Charles. I need to speak to you about Briggs." My voice caught. "I want to replace her. She was far too forceful with me in the bath yesterday. It was completely out of line."

Charles knelt beside me, his face sweet and troubled, and I relaxed a fraction. "What did she do?"

"She grabbed me too hard. I have a bruise on my arm, here." I couldn't show him since I was already dressed, but he kissed the spot I indicated. Briggs's daughter used to work for us also, a sweet, compliant girl with freckled cheeks, and I wished I could have had someone like her instead.

"All right. Of course. You should have whatever maid you want. I won't fire her—you know she's like family to me—but I'll find something else for her to do. Just as soon as you are better." He smiled.

"But surely I am better. Dr. Wendell was so encouraging."

"I hope so. We will have him come again soon."

The tension in my body eased. I'd expected him to fight me harder on this. In the meantime, I'd be on my guard around Briggs, just in case.

"McDonough is readying the car," he said in his cultured accent, his vowels smooth as silk.

"What? We should take the train," I protested. Driving that distance in winter was madness, even if our landaulet was enclosed.

"I don't want us to be seen." Charles looked pained. He screwed his jaw shut, its hard line growing more pronounced. My surprise stole my words. My fit must have been quite a scandal. My stomach clenched. Despite all my careful planning, I must have humiliated myself, and him. I supposed a fainting fit that left me incapacitated would have caused plenty of gossip, and he probably didn't want to try my nerves so early by running into anyone.

He saw my astonishment. "Don't fret. We'll have more privacy this way, that's all. It will be an adventure. I'll make sure you stay perfectly warm." I didn't miss the innuendo in his words, or his sly wink. And I let myself be carried away by the vision of the two of us snug under a blanket as the engine rumbled beneath us.

I followed Charles and his dogs out. I'd spent the prior day convalescing in my own rooms, and I was shocked by the transformation in the rest of the house. In the gaslight, the once-bright and sumptuous hallway looked shadowy and uninviting. The oil paintings on the walls of Greek and Roman tragedies had once struck me as dramatic and romantic, but now they looked threatening, violent. And as cold as I'd been before, now that I was away from the meager warmth of my fire, I was freezing. The air was almost damp, and it seeped into my bones.

The Gothic cast-iron chandelier suspended in the center of the mahogany, slightly dizzying circular staircase was electric, so it was almost entirely dark as we descended the red-carpeted treads to the front hall, and I squinted in the gloom. The front hall was cavernous, like all the rooms, with highly polished white and beige marble floors, carved wooden wall paneling from England, and oak Corinthian columns stretching elegantly toward the distant coffered ceilings. Usually the effect was impressive, but right now it only magnified the house's emptiness.

"We don't need much staff for just us," Charles said, as if reading my thoughts.

I frowned as I digested this. The reduction in staff was a dramatic choice, especially without discussing it with me. We would probably both be returning to our city house soon, but even so. Charles did have a tendency to make hasty decisions; it was also the reason he could be so spontaneous and passionate, but the downside was occasional situations like these. "We could have given them board wages to stay."

"We won't be entertaining anyone here for quite some time, I'm afraid," he said, gently. "It seemed the more prudent course."

My heart drummed in the hollow of my throat. It wasn't the season for being in the country, but he made it sound as if we wouldn't be returning to Rose Briar Hall at all, or at least not having friends come here. Had whatever happened tainted the house so irrevocably?

"Who did you keep on?"

"Briggs, Terry, McDonough, Hannigan, and Petit," he recited. My maid, the groundskeeper, the chauffeur, the gatekeeper, and the cook. It was the absolute bare minimum. At the party we'd had a staff of twenty-five.

"What about Sanders?" Sanders was our housekeeper, and we depended on her to manage the other staff.

"In town. Briggs has agreed to take on some housekeeper duties here. Payments and that sort of thing."

A taxidermic zebra stalked along the wall near the base of the stairs, one of many souvenirs from Charles's hunting expeditions, and it stared at me with glassy-eyed fear, frozen and helpless. I swallowed. The strangeness of the house unsettled me. I was disturbed and disoriented.

We passed the drawing room, and I hardly recognized it.

It was usually so lavish, with its gold wallpaper and intricate gilded plasterwork on the ceiling. But the soft velvet sofas had been covered in dust cloths, looking forlorn and ghost-like. The feeble sunlight filtering through the stained glass dappled the cream rug red, making me think of blood. The back of my neck prickled, and something floated on the edge of my thoughts, a memory just out of reach. I stared into the room, as if it could provide answers. Charles pulled my hand.

"Come along, dear."

As much as I wished I could remember the party, in that moment, I dreaded knowing as much as I longed for it. I wanted to believe that everything might soon return to normal again.

Even if I knew in my heart it was a lie.

The drive to New York rattled my teeth and my nerves. We put hot water bottles at our feet, but it made little difference. By the time we arrived at my parents' house on Fifth Avenue, my insides felt like pudding and my hands tingled painfully. I let McDonough help me out, and stepped onto the pavement with shaky legs. Poor McDonough's seat in front wasn't enclosed like ours, and even stoic as he was, he looked well and truly miserable, his nose red as a winterberry and his hands clumsy as he covered the radiator with a horse blanket. My hatpins had come loose; my hair was probably a fright. My breath formed a little cloud in the cold.

"They'll be thrilled to see you." Charles took my hand in his, and I squeezed it back too hard. Even after our drive, he still looked perfect, not a hair out of place. He was always perfect.

My parents' house fronted Central Park, a giant French chateau-style mansion that dwarfed its neighbors. It made exactly the impression my mother had hoped it would when they built it, its size and grandeur astonishing all who beheld it. In 1908, the fact that we were new money didn't matter as much as it used to, and it brought her the notice she sought.

Across the street, a couple in warm furs promenaded beneath the bare trees. I could just make out a group of boys curling in the distance on a patch of frozen lake.

We walked through the front garden, the neat gravel path lined by privet hedges and bare magnolia trees, which would be covered in splendid pink blossoms in the springtime. The front steps were wide and shallow, easy enough even for elegant older ladies. A butler greeted us after we rang, and as well trained as he was, I could tell by the subtle widening of his eyes how I must look.

He showed us in, and I didn't have time to excuse myself to fix my hair before my mother swept in, a whirlwind of distress and perfume.

"Darling. What on earth happened to your *hair*!" She hugged me close, and I smelled the cloves on her breath. Her voice echoed in the marbled reception room. From my mother's perspective, looking unladylike was the worst of affronts, probably far more concerning to her in that moment than my health.

"We drove." I patted my head ineffectually. My mother did not behave like the restrained Knickerbocker set she was determined to emulate, for she was too frank, and I loved that about her, her lack of pretense in that regard at least. But she was determined to dress better than everyone else in the city, to be ahead of every trend, and she usually had something to say about my appearance.

"I'll go and freshen up." I excused myself and headed to the guest bathroom. It was as opulently decorated as the rest of the house, with vibrant wallpaper depicting peacocks and flowers, and I took in my appearance in the gilded mirror. I looked exactly as wild as I feared, but at least the excursion had brought an attractive flush to my cheeks. I turned on the tap and let the warm water run over my chilled fingers. I lingered longer than I should have, suddenly afraid of what gossip my mother might tell me.

When I reemerged, looking presentable again, my parents and Charles had already sat down for tea in the drawing room. The space always struck me as too large for intimate gatherings such as this, the giant mirrors on the walls and vast expanses of Turkish rugs making me feel small in comparison. That was probably my mother's intent: to make her guests feel insignificant in her presence. The room reflected my mother's flair for excess, with its busy red and yellow wallpaper, heavy red curtains, bronze pots filled with palms, and surfaces crowded with trinkets: an antique Persian oil lamp, a heavy gold plate with intricate arabesque engravings, a bronze figurine of a stallion. In a smaller room the effect would have been oppressive, but here it created the impression of a Near Eastern palace.

"Everywhere I go, I see hats with those enormous black osprey feathers you helped popularize, Georgina. Whatever will you think of next?" Charles smiled warmly at her.

My mother shooed away the compliment but was obviously tickled by it. She beamed.

"They cost a pretty penny, too. You can tell a great deal about someone's finances by the size of their wife's ospreys. It can be very helpful, I'll tell you," my father said, and Charles laughed loudly. I smiled to see the camaraderie between them. Their relationship was not always so warm. My father hadn't approved of the speed of our engagement, and I suspected he never fully approved of Charles, either, though I never understood why. Everyone else hadn't been able to stop congratulating me on the coup of securing the city's most eligible bachelor, slightly awestruck by my conquest. He was astoundingly handsome; he was an only child who had inherited his parents' vast fortune while still at Princeton; he had an eminent lineage; he was the most charming man in New York City.

The day before my wedding, my father pulled me aside, frowning, and told me, "Never forget that he is the lucky one, Millie."

But it had never felt that way.

I sat on the sofa beside my mother and she clasped my hands in hers. "It's so good to see you. Charles has told us you've been unwell." Her mouth tightened. I accepted a cup of tea from the maid. I thought fleetingly of my note, but the tea here, surely, was safe.

"What are people saying? Charles told me I had a bit of a fit. I can't remember anything. It's so strange, isn't it?" My mother, normally never one to hold her tongue, didn't answer right away. She and my father exchanged a look.

"You shouldn't worry yourself over the specifics. It's all just a lot of idle talk anyway."

My mother loved idle talk; it was strange to hear her dismiss it. My father's face had turned stern, and whatever brief warmth there had been in his attitude toward Charles seemed to cool. He turned away from him. I watched them, bemused, my heart sinking.

"How are you now? Are you feeling better?" My father leaned forward, true concern on his face. And shrewd appraisal. Very little escaped my father's notice. I wondered what he thought of the circles under my eyes or how my hand trembled when I lifted my teacup. My father and I had always been close, even closer than me and my mother. Most people found him formidable. He was a large man with a large personality, white haired, with bushy side whiskers, and stern around the mouth. Even Charles was never at ease in his presence, but he was only ever affectionate with me.

"I'm quite recovered," I said. I hoped it were true.

"The doctor says she is still very frail," Charles cut in, warningly.

No one spoke for a minute, and I could hear the clock ticking on the mantel. I stared at my gold-rimmed teacup, featuring hand-painted roses on the side; it reminded me of one I had played tea party with as a child. That one had been chipped, though, and the porcelain less fine. Charles shifted in his chair.

"Harold, I've actually been meaning to get a chance to speak to you privately, if the ladies don't mind sparing us. A little bit of business I'd like your advice on."

My father frowned. I looked down to hide my disappointment. I knew Charles well enough to understand that he wanted something, even though my father had made it very clear he didn't like to mix business and family. Charles had taken it personally that my father had never become his client, especially when so many of his friends were. The maid poured more tea into my half-full cup, and I watched it swirl and turn dark. Maybe he really did merely want advice. I just wished that he would discuss his business in front of me. My father, who had risen from a humble dry-goods store owner to department store magnate, often solicited my mother's opinion on fashion and what to carry in his stores, and I envied her.

"Just a few minutes." My father's voice had a hard edge, but Charles was unabashed. "I'd like to spend time with my daughter."

They rose and headed toward the library. At least I'd get some time alone with my mother. She loved gossip the way a fish loved water. She was the type who got impatient if her tea took too long to arrive, and was bored by any party that lacked a society doyenne of standing that impressed her. She fit more social engagements into a day than many women fit into a week. She may not have been at my dinner, but she would have heard exactly what had happened, and what our friends thought about it all. The doctor's warning nagged at me a little, but I was sure I could handle whatever she told me without losing control again.

"Oh, darling, I really am so glad to see you. You look a little pale. Are you hungry? I can have Fournier make you whatever you like. You need to get your strength up."

I shook my head. The idea of eating her chef's decadent creations made me queasy. "Tea is lovely. And how are you?

I'm sorry to have interrupted your plans for the day. I know you love Mrs. Walsh's bridge parties."

She waved the comment away. "I'm sick of them. And I'm sick of all the nonsense they talk. I was glad to have a reason not to go."

It was the sort of polite comment I would have expected her to make, but she spoke so forcefully that I suspected she was sincere. It was unlike her, and my queasiness increased. "Please. You have to tell me what's going on."

Her eyes flicked toward the pocket doors where Charles and my father had just disappeared. "Charles made us promise. I don't like to disappoint either of you, but we all agreed it would be for the best for now, while you get better."

"I'm perfectly fine. Whatever it is, you can tell me." I sat straighter and raised my chin.

Without Charles's interference, I was sure I could get the truth out of her. She wouldn't be able to hold back.

"Well . . ." She sipped her tea while she assessed me. "But you can't tell Charles I was the one who—"

She never finished her sentence, because just then Charles threw open the pocket doors, his face flushed. "We have to go."

"Now? But—"

"Now, Millie."

I was dumbfounded. Even my father, always unflappable, was decidedly flustered. His lips were thin. He looked at Charles disapprovingly, a look that made many men shrink in his presence. My mother looked as startled as I must, her teacup paused midair on its way to her mouth, which was as open and round as her eyes.

"I-I'm sorry," I stammered, and kissed my mother briefly on the cheek before rising to follow Charles. He was already out the door.

Chapter 4

I considered refusing to get back in the car until Charles explained, but he was still too angry to speak. I got in, and I didn't notice the cold at first, as if Charles's hot anger radiated off him and filled the space.

"What happened?" I guessed it had something to do with work. We'd done well in the Bankers' Panic the year before, but some of our friends hadn't. It had made it slightly more difficult for Charles to find new clients, even though his returns were unrivaled. His business was still growing, just not as quickly as he'd hoped.

"Not now."

Soon the engine roared, filling the silence.

I waited a few blocks for his anger to dissipate a fraction before pressing again. "You can tell me." We'd been married March before last, but after over a year of marriage I still sensed there was a part of himself he'd kept from me. He was usually so wonderful and romantic that it hadn't mattered much, and I'd still hoped that we'd grow even closer in time. His air of mystery had intrigued me at first, but now I wished he would confide in me.

"It would be quite beyond you."

The insult stung. I could hardly believe he would speak to me in such a way, and tears threatened. I turned away from him, huddling deeper into my sable coat.

"Was it about work?" I guessed he'd wanted my father's help with some business dealing, and I knew my father had refused him. I just didn't know what, or why. He complained often that my father didn't have enough confidence in him where money was concerned. Though Charles had his own fortune, it irked him that I had separate assets—a trust that I would gain access to when I turned twenty-five the following August. Rose Briar Hall was mine, too, a gift from my father and the deed in my name, another point of contention. I secretly loved that it was my house, and mine alone, but Charles thought it proved that my father didn't trust him.

Perhaps he didn't.

"It doesn't matter." He sighed. "Your father already turned me down flat. You won't change his mind."

I knew this to be true, and I also knew that I didn't want to try. I'd always taken Charles's side, telling my father what a brilliant stockbroker he was, but my father had been unmoved. He'd been right, as usual. Whatever Charles had wanted, I was suddenly fiercely glad he hadn't gotten it. The way he was behaving was unconscionable. He'd never acted like this before.

The car jolted to a stop, and I looked out in confusion. We'd arrived at our city house, a handsome brownstone nowhere near as grand as my parents' house, but still very fine. The sight filled me with relief. So we would be returning soon to our normal lives, after all.

I reached for the door.

"No." Charles reached over to place his hand on mine, and his grip was firm. "I'm staying in the city, Millie. I have some urgent business to handle. I'll be back out to Rose Briar Hall this weekend."

My mouth opened in surprise. "Surely we can both stay."

"It's better for you to keep away from society for a time. I promise I'll explain everything soon."

"Charles, this is all so extreme."

His eyes, closed off only moments before, softened now. He sighed exuberantly. "I can't imagine what you must be going through. I know it doesn't make sense now, but I promise it will soon. Can you trust me, Millie? Please? You know I wouldn't ask something like this if it weren't terribly important." He caressed my cheek. "I love you, Millie."

Love. His words ignited something inside of me, reminding me of everything we'd shared, of how when he looked at me like I was the only woman in the world the earth seemed to stop spinning. A kind word or look from him was like the first sip of a glass of wine, heady and intoxicating, making you eager for more.

I had to do something to make things right.

I reached to one of the windows and pulled the little curtain closed. Then I did the rest. We'd had them specially installed; Charles liked his privacy. Charles watched me, and his face relaxed a fraction, a crack in the marble, while the rest of him hardened. I used my free hand to stroke the bodice of my dress, trailing fingers along creamy skin, and his mouth opened, suddenly hungry. And then his hands were on me, on my breasts, my waist, pushing me down onto the cushioned seat. His teeth grazed my earlobe and then moved to my neck, while he roughly pulled up my dress, his fingers grasping my thighs painfully hard. He yanked down my lacy French drawers and I reached for his trousers. He had taken me like this before, and also up against a wall, or bent over furniture, or on the floor before we reached the bed. No soft cushions and feather blankets for us; our lovemaking was hard angles and wildness and impatience and bruised skin. The car shook as he thrust into me. His teeth and tongue were on my collarbone and I tried to breathe, my corset still on and constricting, my lungs empty as I cried out with air I didn't have. It was exquisite. Finally, Charles groaned and went still. I gasped, my whole body shaking, and we stayed there for a moment, locked together as one.

Then he climbed off of me and straightened himself. "God, you really are beautiful."

I sat up slowly, pulled up my drawers.

McDonough probably knew what we'd been up to, but Charles, growing up rich, thought of servants the way one thinks of the furniture, and McDonough was always the soul of discretion.

"I need you to return to Long Island. Just for a little while, while I set things right here. And you can rest and get better. We'll get through this, Millie."

I swallowed. I'd thought offering myself like this might change his mind. I still didn't have the air to speak. My chest rose and fell, and I was still trembling all over. Before I'd drawn enough breath to argue, he stepped onto the gray November sidewalk. He slammed the door behind him and the engine rumbled to life beneath me.

"Wait—"

But it was too late. McDonough had already slipped into the traffic.

I turned in disbelief and saw Charles climb the steps to our house, seemingly unperturbed. Meanwhile, the bottom had fallen out of my stomach. This was the same man, I reminded myself, who usually doted on me like a queen and fulfilled my every whim. I didn't understand what could have changed things between us so dramatically. A dark thought weaseled its way into my mind that our marriage might never be the same again. I tried to push aside my disquiet, but I couldn't.

I watched the city slip away, my blood turning colder with each passing block. At the Brooklyn Bridge I stared at the skyline behind me, cloaked in a fog that swallowed the city's lights, and bustle, and people, and suddenly I felt terribly alone.

The brownstones soon faded away into farms and forests. The quiet and peace of Long Island, which not long ago had so appealed to me, now filled me with foreboding.

When Rose Briar Hall appeared in view at last, a little shudder coursed through me. It looked imposing, especially with the gray sky above and every window dark. The groundskeeper's bullmastiff sped into view, a blur of brindle coat and black snout and white teeth, and his master, Terry, lumbered behind him, thick-bodied and strong. They made a menacing pair. The dog barked viciously and I flinched.

I was struck again by how different the house seemed from before, when I'd had a large staff to command and guests to entertain. I still couldn't believe Charles was abandoning me like this, with nothing but my confused thoughts for company. Suddenly the idea of returning to the empty, freezing manor terrified me.

It may have been my house, but I no longer felt like its mistress.

CHAPTER 5

Briggs was nowhere to be found when I entered the house, weary from travel. I was both annoyed and relieved. I didn't miss her sour presence, but when I returned to my room I found the fire was out, the grate coated with ash. I sighed. Without Charles around she would be next to useless. I kept my fur on.

Out the window, a light snow started to fall, and I watched as it dusted the estate with a layer of white. The late-afternoon sun peeked out, causing it to glisten. My thoughts swirled like the flakes, round and round. The encounter with Charles in the car had been so strange. I determined to call him later, once my mind had settled; hearing his voice would soothe me. I was sure if I could only understand what had happened at the party, I could find a way to set things right again. Somehow, I had to remember.

I wished I could get warm. If I couldn't have a fire, maybe I could thaw a little in the greenhouse. I headed back outside and the wind bit my cheeks and chapped my lips. My boots made soft outlines across the frosty grass as I crossed the West Lawn. In the distance, the waters of Oyster Bay churned, black and forbidding, and the skeletal branches of the birch trees stretched against the gray sky. The bright flora of the greenhouse was visible through the glass, a spot of color against the bare landscape. I loved the greenhouse, and had insisted upon it when we drew up the designs for the estate. The massive gabled complex had multiple sections with different plants emphasized in each, and a gravel pathway ran through it, widening in places to allow for statues and reflecting pools.

I savored the slight warmth inside and took my time as I strolled down the central pathway. Even the greenhouse had boilers to warm it, but without any coal, Terry had to rely on the sun and the barrels of water in the corners to keep away the frost. There were some mums that still looked hearty, and some potted lilies and orchids that had survived. The camellias looked a little leggy, and I made a mental note to remind Terry about them. Normally we had more gardeners to help.

The stars of the greenhouse, though, were always the roses. I shared my mother's love for them, and we had a number of varieties; it was the reason we'd decided to name the house Rose Briar Hall. I located shears in the gardener's potting bench and cut some tea roses, with the idea of putting them in a vase in my sitting room.

That's when I noticed the stalks of delicate blue flowers growing in one of the beds. I furrowed my brow. I didn't recognize what they were. They shouldn't have been here. I knew every flower, every variety of plant that grew here, and Terry wouldn't have taken the liberty of a new addition without consulting me. It was strange. I brushed my fingers against the delicate petals, inspecting. I had gardening books in the library and would try to identify them later.

I wrapped my roses in paper from the potter's bench and started back toward the house. I was distracted, still puzzling over the origin of the blue flowers, and almost didn't notice the figure of a man in the drive ahead. I stopped abruptly, startled. It wasn't the groundskeeper, or the gatekeeper, or the chauffeur. My heart thudded against my ribs and my hands trembled, sending a few rose petals trailing softly into the snow.

I stood still and watched him, studying his distant outline as he strolled closer to the house and examined its elegant profile. He could be a trespasser. Or a thief. I looked around for Terry. He must have taken his dog for a walk in the woods.

Our gatekeeper, Tom Hannigan, had been serving my family for years, and normally he'd call the house for approval before opening the gates for a stranger. I wouldn't have heard the phone ring in the greenhouse, but it surprised me he would make a decision on his own. Charles didn't like Hannigan's Irish heritage and also thought he had gotten too old for his work. I'd known Hannigan since I was a little girl. Once, he and his wife had been my parents' only servants, and I still had fond memories of his wife singing Irish folk songs while she washed dishes, and of him telling me scary stories by the fire. Charles pestered me about him nearly as often as I complained about Briggs. I'd thought him still able to do his duties, but perhaps—

My thoughts stopped as the man crept closer to the house. Rang the bell.

I crept closer, too. A thief wouldn't ring the bell, surely? Once I could see him more clearly, it was evident he was almost respectable looking. He wore a tweed coat, and he was clean-shaven. He was on the shorter side and stood with his feet slightly apart, a pugilistic stance that gave him an air of energy and a whiff of danger. Perhaps he was a scoundrel, after all; he looked like he could hit someone in the jaw without breaking a sweat.

"Can I help you?" My voice wavered. He turned around and his brown eyes examined me in a way that felt almost indecent. His nose was slightly squashed—so he was a boxer then, or a brawler—but his face didn't suffer for it. If anything, it added a bit of rakish appeal. He was handsome, I realized, but that didn't mean he wasn't a threat. Perhaps it would have been wiser to hide until he left. I took a careful step back. "Did Hannigan let you in?"

He smirked. "Something like that."

This didn't reassure me. In that moment I felt a flash of anger for Charles, for leaving me so vulnerable here. If we had a full staff, I would be safe.

"You wouldn't remember me, I suppose. I'm Tom's son."

"David." The name tumbled out instinctively, too quickly, for of course I remembered him. "Mr. Hannigan," I said, correcting myself, my use of his Christian name, and he smiled at my lapse. We had played together as children, roving over the grounds of my first house, collecting sticks and scraping elbows. And we had spent time together later, too, after my father became rich. The summer when I was twelve and he was thirteen. I wondered if he remembered it. By the way he was looking at me, I was sure he did. That summer my parents were busy with society functions and I hardly ever saw them; neither had paid attention to how much time I spent with the gatekeeper's son.

"Miss Munroe. Or I suppose Mrs. Turner now." The way he said Turner, he made it sound like something unsavory.

"So you came to visit your father? Are you living nearby?"

David—I couldn't help but still think of him by his Christian name, which I'd called him by as a girl—turned his hat around in his hands, suddenly uncomfortable. "I live in the city. And that's part of why I came here, yes." He cleared his throat. "I'm a journalist now, has he told you? I write for *The World News*."

I frowned. *The World News* published politics and that sort of thing, but also vicious little gossip columns. They had written about Emily Post's divorce, James Hyde's two-hundred-thousand-dollar ball . . . more scandals than I could count. I wondered if he had heard something about my party.

"I'm very happy for you."

"You held a dinner here a few weeks ago, is that correct?"

I fought to keep my hands and voice steady. "I did. But I'm

afraid I don't remember anything about that night." I decided I may as well be honest. It seemed safest.

"Why's that?" He widened his stance and crossed his arms against his chest. It was hard to imagine a man like him hunched over a typewriter. I could easily picture him haranguing sources, however, and I wondered idly which of them had punched him. His nose hadn't been like that when he was thirteen.

"The doctor said it's not unusual after a shock."

"I see. Was Gertrude Underhill a close friend of yours?"

I blinked, paused a beat. So Gertrude had something to do with all of this. I supposed I should have seen that coming.

"I've known her for years. Why, did you speak to her? What did you say about the party?" I wouldn't put it past her to leak something unsavory about me. David looked at me strangely.

"You mean you really don't know? No one's told you?"

The blood rushed to my head, and I grew dizzy. I felt a little queer. My fingers tingled where I'd brushed the strange flower, and I could feel every beat of my heart in my throat.

"No one wanted to upset me. I was unwell, afterward." I put a hand to my head, worried I might faint. David's expression grew concerned, and his brown eyes were piercing and direct.

"You do look unwell. Can I help you inside?"

I waved him away. "I'll be fine. Please—just tell me what happened." I was desperate to know. I forced myself to stand up straighter.

"I'm sorry to say that Gertrude Underhill died. The coroner's official report said she choked to death on her tea." He emphasized the word "official" slightly and I caught a hint of a sneer on his lips. As if he didn't believe it. My mouth dropped open and I pulled the collar of my coat up higher. The tips of my fingers turned numb. I stumbled backward, and the world around me turned blurry. He caught my arm, steadying me. "I'm very sorry for your loss, Mrs. Turner. Please, let me help you." I didn't resist as he offered his elbow, and I leaned on him as we headed toward the door. My mind reeled. I could hardly believe what he'd just told me. It was too shocking to comprehend.

I'd known the party had been disastrous, but I thought maybe I'd embarrassed myself in some way. I never guessed it was as serious as this. Gertrude, dead. No wonder Charles wasn't quite himself. He had nearly gotten engaged to her before he met me.

I should have been grieved by the news, but I found I wasn't. I was horrified, but not mournful.

I needed to speak to Charles. I had to know what he was thinking, and why Gertrude's death had made me so unwell. I could believe that I'd fainted, but it didn't explain my illness, or why Charles didn't want me to see our friends.

Just then, Terry and his dog finally appeared. Charles had picked out the dog as a puppy and named him Cerberus before giving him to Terry as a gift. Protecting estates was bred into Cerberus's blood, and he instinctively would attack anyone he deemed a threat. Most men reacted at the first sight of Cerberus, backing away or jumping, but David didn't budge.

"It's all right, Terry," I called. "It's an old friend."

Terry whistled and Cerberus trotted back to him and heeled, about twenty feet away now. But they both continued toward us, and Terry's stride was purposeful, his expression almost threatening. I shivered.

"I must be going. Thank you, for—well, it was nice to see you again, despite the circumstances." My voice shook. I hoped he'd interpret it as grief.

I moved past him toward the house, its white stone shining like frost against the freshly fallen snow.

"Mrs. Turner." He spoke at a normal volume, but his voice carried. "I feel I should warn you. There's something not right about this business." He handed me his card and replaced his hat with a swift, sure hand. "If you remember anything, you'll let me know, won't you?"

By the time I opened my mouth to reply, he was already walking away.

CHAPTER 6

My heartbeat slowed to a dull throb. It seemed like I could hear each beat thudding in my ears. I truly wasn't well, and I stumbled into the drawing room and collapsed on a dust-cloth-covered armchair. I'd probably just exerted myself too much for the day, after my extended bed rest.

But the tingling of my fingers was odd.

Briggs appeared suddenly in the doorframe, and I jumped. She hadn't made a sound.

"Where have you been?" she demanded, as if she had a right to know my whereabouts. Her tone was completely out of line. She didn't approach, but hovered just outside of the room, as if something about it disturbed her.

"The greenhouse. Not that it's any of your concern," I added, archly. "Please, get these some water. And bring some for me as well."

She didn't move. "Who was that man, here? Mr. Turner won't be pleased." I bristled at her words. She acted as if I were a prisoner in my own house. And she were my jailer.

"I can do as I like, Briggs, and your questions are impertinent," I snapped. I wondered what exactly Charles had told her about the dinner party that night. I understood, suddenly, that she thought she held something over us. That's why she'd been pushing boundaries even further than before.

"He'll be hearing about it from me, you can count on it."

I didn't have the energy to keep arguing with her. I felt too queer.

"Water," I said again, handing Briggs the bouquet. She shifted her weight and eyed the chair where I sat with a strange gleam to her eye.

Suddenly I understood. David had said Gertrude choked to death on her tea. She must have been in the drawing room. Perhaps even in this very chair. I stood as quickly as I could in my condition. Briggs smirked, but finally she turned to go.

I couldn't bear the idea of staying in the drawing room, and I made my way slowly back upstairs to my sitting room. I was pleased to see that Briggs had relit the fire, and sank onto the chaise beside it gratefully.

I'd tell Dr. Wendell about the strange tingling on his next visit. I was sure it was nothing. Yet my thoughts lingered in the drawing room. I didn't believe in ghosts, but the specter of Gertrude haunted me all the same.

I didn't wait for Briggs to bring me my morning tea. I seemed to have recovered from my episode the prior day, but I didn't mean to tempt fate. Remembering my note, I headed to the kitchen myself, dressing as if for a blizzard.

Jacques Petit was a dough-faced, fiftysomething man and a bit hard of hearing. He was used to having more help in the kitchen, and I wondered how long he'd be willing to stay in these new circumstances. If he was surprised to see me instead of Briggs, he hid it well.

"Good morning, Petit. I'd like soft-boiled eggs, toast with jam, a rasher of bacon, and hot coffee, as quick as you can make it." I was gratified to see him turn promptly to his task.

I waited while he cooked. The kitchen was huge, with two stoves and two large wooden work tables in the middle of the room, and it looked a little preposterous with only him to manage it. It did get warm, though, once the stove was on, so he wouldn't freeze down here. I chatted with him while he worked. He, Terry, and McDonough stayed in the building near the garage housing most of the servants' quarters, and he assured me they had plenty of firewood for their grates. Hannigan kept to the gatehouse, so it was only Briggs and me in the main house at night. I couldn't remember the last time I'd been so isolated. I hadn't been able to get a hold of Charles when I rang him last night; Sanders had informed me he was out. I wondered where he'd gone, who he'd seen.

I devoured my breakfast right there in the kitchen, not caring about protocol, and afterward felt like a new person.

When I returned to my sitting room, Briggs was there, looking put out. "You should have rang," she said, and I scoffed.

"I was hungry. I didn't feel like waiting."

Usually Briggs resisted just about every request. It was unlike her to mind me excusing her from some of her work.

"It's my job to bring you your breakfast. My duty," she emphasized, fiercely.

My heart beat in the hollow of my throat. I'd been right, then. The note had been a warning to myself. She'd been putting something in my tea these last weeks.

I could scarcely believe such a thing to be true, much less understand why she would do it. Perhaps I was mistaken, but I could no longer ignore that something was very wrong. I hugged myself and took a careful step back.

"After you make the fire, you can go."

She grumbled and acquiesced, to my great relief. I had to tell Charles. I had to turn her out, at once. I was scared. I waited until I heard her heavy tread disappear, and hurried down the stairs to the phone. I regretted my decision to install only two in the main house—a smart silver candlestick model we kept on the console table near the stairs to the kitchen and another in Charles's study.

Luckily, it was early enough that Charles was still at home.

When I heard his deep voice crackle over the line, I nearly sobbed in relief.

"Charles, you must come home at once. I've discovered something awful."

I expected him to agree instantly, but I heard only silence. "Charles? It's about Briggs. I think she's been dosing me with something. That's why I slept so long."

I thought I heard his heavy sigh. "I'll be out tonight."

The call ended and my pulse slowed. Charles would fix everything. As much as he cared for Briggs, he couldn't excuse this.

I hung up the earpiece with shaking fingers, and that's when I noticed it—the painting above the console table was missing. It had been a particularly valuable piece. Had Charles moved it for some reason?

Another, darker thought entered my mind. Maybe Briggs had stolen it. Normally I would chastise myself for being preposterous, but not anymore. I couldn't imagine why Charles would have taken it down, given how uninterested he'd been in decorating the house, and if not him, then who? She was the only logical answer. If Charles had gone to the city while I was incapacitated, she could have easily robbed us. She could have wrapped it and arranged for a carriage to take her to town, or even asked McDonough. Charles gave her so much leeway no one would have questioned that she was performing an errand for us. It was brazen, but I didn't doubt she was capable. Perhaps that had been her plan all along, and the reason she'd drugged me.

If one painting were missing, there could be others. I decided to investigate.

The house was still dim with only the sporadic gaslights, but after spending hours poring over the ink drawings before construction began, I could have walked through every room blindfolded. I knew how many paces exactly from the front door through the front hall to the rosewood Rococo table near the mouth of the staircase, a blue and white Qing dynasty vase balanced on its marble top. The drawing room was to the left, the dining room to the right, and toward the back of the house were the library, billiards room, and ball-room.

I combed through each of them. The dust cloths hanging off the chairs in the library and the ballroom fluttered gently, even though I couldn't feel a draft. There shouldn't have been one, in a new house. I checked the windows and they all sat snugly in their frames.

Nothing appeared to be missing. Shivering, I moved on to the music room in the east end of the house. We had the latest model of Victrola, a grand piano, and a series of paintings of harp-playing satyrs. I didn't stay long; to combat the cold, I had to keep moving. Even the blue and cream sunflowers in the room's William Morris wallpaper looked chilly, as if blue from frost.

If only Rose Briar Hall weren't so silent. The mounted heads of Charles's many trophies—elks, rhinoceroses, and even an elephant—watched me as I stalked about the house. The white eyes of the figures in the oil paintings seemed to follow me.

I shook my head. I was being ridiculous and fanciful.

I reached the hallway that led to my room, and was just about ready to give up when I stopped short in front of a Flemish tapestry. It showed a unicorn on its hind legs, with wild eyes. Beside him, there should have been a painting of dancing maenads.

I ran my hand over the burgundy wallpaper where it used to be.

It was gone.

CHAPTER 7

The crunch of tires on the gravel made my heart leap into my throat. McDonough had arrived back from the train station. With Charles. A woman shouldn't be nervous about seeing her own husband, but sometimes Charles left me a bit off-kilter. True love, my dear friend Arabella had said.

But this time, I wasn't sure that the twist of anxiety in my gut was due to passion. I hadn't seen Charles since he'd taken me in the car. He'd been a different man after the fight with my father. I hoped that our short time apart had thawed the chill between us, and that he'd have returned to his usual self.

I sensed Charles's presence the moment he entered the house. I hadn't heard the door—always elegant, he wasn't the type who barged—but suddenly the house seemed to pause. I could no longer hear the clocks ticking, and in the distance Cerberus stopped barking from his kennel. Briggs stood in the foyer still as a statue. She looked tense.

I wore a smart midnight-blue winter suit, silk-lined with ivory trim and jet buttons on the fitted jacket, and a white fur stole. I wasn't as warm as I would be in my coat, but I wanted to show off my figure. I shivered as his trouser leg appeared in the doorframe, his polished shoe clacking. He went stock-still when he saw me, his lean figure immobile in front of the drawing room, like one of his taxidermic beasts.

"Mr. Turner. Welcome home. Mrs. Turner—"

But whatever Briggs was going to say was cut short by a wave of Charles's hand. Good, so he was angry with her. As he should be. Briggs poured him a glass of his favorite claret without being asked. She knew he liked a drink when he got home, but I sensed she was buttering him up. Perhaps she'd overheard my phone call and knew her position was in jeopardy.

"You can go," he told her. She didn't hesitate, and the pocket doors glided shut behind her soundlessly. I stroked my fur stole, wishing it bestowed more warmth. He came and sat beside me, his face twisted with concern, and I exhaled in relief at the display of affection. He sipped his claret, and it glinted in the gaslight. I got the impression that he was preparing himself to say something difficult. "We'll get to the issue of Briggs in a moment, Millie, but first there's something else you must hear." He was as somber as I'd ever seen him, and I sat up straighter, my breath bated. "I'll just get right out with it. Gertrude is dead. She died at our party. In this room." He released my hand and stood to light the wood in the grate. I guessed he was doing it for my benefit, since he never seemed to mind the cold, or perhaps he only needed an excuse to turn his back to me and hide his expression. He was upset. Shameful as it was, the idea of him mourning her provoked a twinge of jealousy. Even dead, the woman wouldn't cease tormenting me.

I arranged my features into an expression of surprise. I already knew, of course, but I had no intention of explaining to him how.

"How terrible. Shocking." The fire blazed to life, and I scooted closer to its radius. It didn't do much. My stomach was a block of ice. "Was she ill? I hadn't any idea."

Charles continued as if I hadn't spoken. "The coroner was summoned. He's a bloated, rheumy-eyed fool. I promised to donate to his next campaign. His is an elected position, you know." He spat the words, suddenly bitter.

I frowned. I didn't understand what he was getting at. "Why should you need to do that?"

"Because, darling, Gertrude was poisoned. Officially, of course, she choked to death. I saw to that." He picked up his claret and finished it, and he gripped the stem so hard I thought the glass might break. His features contorted in apparent anguish.

The ice spread from my stomach to my limbs. I was frozen with astonishment. I'd understood that her death would have caused a scandal, but something like this had never entered my mind. *Poison.* The word reverberated through me, painfully, as if it were my own insides that were being destroyed by a hidden agent.

"My God. How do you know? Who would do such a thing?"

My mind reeled. Gertrude hadn't been especially popular she was self-important and known for her sharp tongue. Her husband, Richard, had been here that night. Perhaps—

"Millie, don't pretend you don't know." Charles ran a hand over his face.

"How would I know? I've told you I don't remember the party." My snug little jacket seemed to squeeze my rib cage. He looked so handsome in the flickering gaslight, so beleaguered and heartbroken. And suddenly I understood exactly what he thought. "You can't believe—"

"Everyone knew you disliked her. Jealousy, they're saying."

"Who is?" Everything began to make sense. My parents' reticence. Charles's insistence that I stay away from our friends. His determination that I stay on Long Island was because of this, because a foul rumor about me had ruined our glittering reputation.

"Everyone thinks it was you, Millie. The two of you had a little spat over dinner. Something about her earrings. And then you were the one who poured her tea for her. Right before it happened." He put his hand over his face again, as if the memory were too much to bear.

"I would never do such a thing. You can't believe it." My voice shook and tears pricked my eyes. It was true I detested her, but I wasn't wicked.

And yet, the fact that my memories eluded me, and the doctor's diagnosis of hysteria, caused doubt to coil in my breast. Was it possible I could do something so horrible in a flash of rage? Had something provoked me that night that made me lose my reason?

"I saw you, Millie. I saw you put something into her cup."

I gasped. He spoke with such conviction. I was astounded. Charles wouldn't say such a thing if he didn't think it were true, and yet his belief in my guilt knocked the wind out of me, like a physical blow. I could easily believe some of our friends would be swift to judgment, and could picture them as all too eager to witness my downfall after my swift social ascent. But Charles—I would have expected him to defend me. He could have misunderstood what he saw.

It certainly explained his recent behavior, at least. I picked apart the last few days in my mind swiftly, like ripping out stitches. His gentle coddling after I'd awoken took on a new form. It hadn't only been because of my physical ailment; he believed I was mentally unsound.

I understood, too, the slight frostiness in his attitude toward me that hadn't been there before. He thought I'd killed a woman. I was only surprised he'd been as kind as he had been. I wondered if it were born of love, or pity.

"What did you see exactly? Perhaps it wasn't what you thought. Maybe I was pouring the cream." My certainty grew that there must have been some terrible error. I shook my head, as if I could dislodge the suspicion that had twisted its way inside. I wouldn't have killed Gertrude, no matter how irksome I found her. Made snide comments behind her back certainly, but murder?

"No, it was something else." Charles looked momentarily confused that I'd questioned him, as if he were so sure in what he'd seen that it never crossed his mind he might be wrong.

"Why should I have poured tea for her? We have servants," I insisted, my voice increasingly shrill. It wasn't completely unusual to top up one's own cup from the tea tray, or even do it for a friend, but I didn't like Gertrude. I would have let the footmen attend to her.

"She didn't want coffee with the rest of us, after dinner, and insisted on her own pot of tea. You were annoyed. You made a show of pouring, to make a point." I frowned and furrowed my brow. He spoke with calm certainty, and it rattled me. He remembered everything with such perfect clarity. But I knew he must be mistaken. Somehow Charles had misinterpreted what he'd seen.

"We must learn what really happened. I swear it wasn't me, Charles. Maybe Richard, he hated her enough." My hands trembled in my lap. Suddenly my throat was very dry. I crossed to the sideboard, where we kept a decanter of my favorite Oloroso sherry, from Sierra de Montilla in the south of Spain. Charles disliked it, finding it too sweet.

"He'd retired early."

I pursed my lips. I splashed the sherry as I poured, because my hands were still trembling, but Charles didn't see.

"I had nothing to do with it, Charles. How could you believe otherwise? I must go back into society at once and show our friends I have no reason to hide."

I was his wife. His distrust hurt me, deeply, and I had to fight to suppress a sob.

"They won't receive you, Millie." He spoke so coldly that I flinched. Surely he was exaggerating; my closest friends wouldn't hesitate to see me. Arabella, certainly, wouldn't believe I was responsible.

But then, Charles had.

Still, my involvement was only speculation. It wasn't as if I'd shot her, like when Harry Thaw shot Stanford White over that sordid Evelyn Nesbit business a couple of years ago. I didn't care as much about what other people thought of me as my mother did, but I didn't relish the idea of being a social pariah.

"You should be grateful that I spared you from even worse scandal. At least there won't be an investigation."

I returned to sit across from him, pinching the sherry glass tightly. It was very fast thinking, bribing the coroner, but it was just the sort of impulsive thing that Charles would do.

"But it might have exonerated me." Of course, the coroner could have easily taken our friends' view of things, and I could have ended up facing criminal charges. Even the electric chair. No, Charles had been right to do what he'd done. I squeezed my eyes shut. The only thing I knew for sure was that I couldn't remember anything from the party or for weeks afterward.

Then I remembered the reason I'd summoned him here, and the answer to the mystery of Gertrude's death presented itself, so obvious that I scolded myself for not realizing it at once.

"Briggs could have done it. She's been drugging me. As I told you. She could have done the same to Gertrude."

I expected Charles's eyes to widen in shock, but he only sighed.

"Briggs was following Dr. Wendell's instructions. He prescribed a rest cure. I've called him here so that he can explain it. He'll arrive later tonight."

I stared at him, uncomprehending. Then I let out a strangled cry. "You kept me asleep on purpose?" I thought of my scribbled note, written in haste. In panic.

Charles's green eyes were pleading. "You murdered a woman. You were out of your senses. He said it could cure you." He went and stood by the fire, his athletic form as straight as the fire poker, his fingers stroking his mustache.

Charles was a problem solver, always looking for the quick fix, the sure shot, and it wasn't difficult to imagine him leaping at the doctor's treatment recommendation. It was an easy way to handle things.

"And am I? Am I cured, Charles?" I demanded. A traitorous tear slipped down my cheek. I couldn't blame him entirely, given what he'd thought I'd done, but I was angry at him anyway. He should have questioned such an extreme medical recommendation. He was supposed to protect me.

"The doctor will be here soon. We'll see what he says." His tone was tender and apologetic. He was still so handsome, but when I looked at him now, the usual swoop in my belly was gone. I felt only confusion, anger, and a twinge of wrongness.

I wiped my cheek and swallowed my sherry in a single gulp.

CHAPTER 8

My first thought when I regained my senses was that I didn't know where I was. It was so dark, I could have been anywhere. My fingers were red and raw from the cold, my head was full of wool, and my tongue felt like sand. I sat up abruptly and then lay back down, holding my head. I felt weak, faint. "Oh no." Gradually the contours of the room began to take shape as my eyes adjusted. I was still in the drawing room. The sky outside was pitch-black; hours must have passed.

Tentatively, I wriggled my fingers, trying to regain feeling. I stood slowly and lit the sconces, which blazed to life, penetrating the dim. I looked at the antique gold clock on the mantelpiece, but its hands were stuck at a little past six. No one had wound it.

"I'm telling you, she's completely insensible. We should move her upstairs." It was Charles's voice echoing in the foyer. He sounded businesslike and a little impatient. His concern from earlier had fled. The forbearance he'd shown must have only been to spare my feelings, and now I realized he was even more upset at me than he'd let on.

My thoughts moved sluggishly. And then understanding dawned: I'd been drugged again. But how? By whom?

"An institution would be more appropriate for a woman in her condition. You shouldn't keep her here too long." The man who replied had a high, reedy voice I recognized. Dr. Wendell.

"Her father will be damned difficult about that."

A shiver coursed down my spine. His tone was as icy as the house. And the word "institution" jolted me, conjuring images of women with matted hair and hollow eyes. I was sure Charles would never send me somewhere like *that*, but the idea of any institution horrified me. That he would want to send me away at all seared into me, the pain so hot that for a moment I didn't notice the cold.

I drew a shuddering breath, unsure what to do. There was no time to consider before they both appeared in the drawing room, and the look of surprise on their faces would have been comical if I weren't so scared.

"Millie, you're awake." Charles's words grew soft and gentle now. Not sharp, like when he'd spoken about me to the doctor. "You had another fit. Just like at the party. Do you remember?"

"What did you give me?" I must have drunk something. Sherry, I remembered. I'd had it the night of the party, too, before our guests arrived. Briggs could easily have slipped something in it.

"No one gave you anything. You got excited, and anxious, and started speaking a lot of nonsense. It was incoherent. Then you collapsed." Charles sounded worried and a little weary. I pressed my fingers to my temples, willing myself to remember. The first time, witnessing Gertrude's death had triggered an episode. Tonight, I'd learned that my husband thought I killed her. It was gut wrenching, but had that been enough of a shock to cause me to have a fit? Had I ever really had one, or had I only been drugged?

"No. There was something in the sherry," I insisted. I didn't know it for sure, but the explanation appealed to me. It was much better than considering the alternative. The doctor and Charles exchanged a look. "Briggs must have done it. She's been stealing from us, you know. There are paintings missing."

"Millie. Listen to yourself. You're delusional." Charles turned away from me, as if he couldn't stand to look at me, and it felt as if my very soul had fissured.

The doctor looked somber. "Paranoia could be a symptom of your condition."

"And what condition is that, exactly?" He'd mentioned hysteria before, but now that I understood more of what had happened, I wasn't sure I believed it.

Dr. Wendell and Charles seemed comfortable with each other, familiar even, and I wondered how often the doctor had come to examine me while I was asleep for three weeks. The doctor cleared his throat. "I've told your husband that you may be experiencing a form of somnambulism. You are able to walk, even speak while you are asleep. But there's another, more concerning possibility." He cleared his throat again.

"Please have a seat," I said in my best hostess voice. I looked around for a servant out of habit, someone who could offer him refreshment. "I'm afraid we are short-staffed at the moment, but I can pour you a glass of sherry if you'd like." I smiled wryly. "Charles says there's nothing wrong with it, so I'm sure you won't object."

The doctor looked startled.

Charles cut in, smoothly. "This isn't a social visit, Millie."

I studied them both. Charles looked beleaguered, the way he got over work sometimes. I was a chore to him, apparently. The doctor rearranged his glasses nervously. He chose a spot on the sofa, keeping his coat on. Charles and I sat across from him, and Charles's physical nearness confused me. Normally I'd be tempted to place a hand on his knee, or curl my finger around his, but now everything had changed.

I longed for a sign from him that he still cared, that he really did still love me in spite of what he thought I'd done.

"I'm worried you may still be experiencing hysteria. The rest cure I prescribed previously was meant to be a reset of sorts. To calm your nerves and your mind. It appears not to have been effective, based on this recent episode."

I scoffed. A rest cure—what outdated nonsense. He was probably one of those men who abhorred society's New Women, the ones who rode bicycles and talked about the right to vote. I still struggled to accept that Charles credited the doctor's assessment. Did he truly believe I was a hysterical madwoman, a murderess?

"What did you give me, during this rest cure?" I forced myself to use my most imperious air, even though inside I was falling to pieces. But I wanted him to understand that I didn't value his opinion just because Charles did.

"Chloral hydrate, mostly. Some trional, some Medinal." He spoke matter of factly. I blanched. I knew women who took chloral to help them sleep, but I knew, too, of it being used by thieves at saloons in the Bowery to immobilize unsuspecting marks before they picked their pockets. Knockout drops, they called them. Afterward, the victims often lost their memory. It had actually happened to an acquaintance of mine when he'd gone slumming in the Bowery, which some of the faster set liked to do for laughs.

"And no one thought to consult me?" My uncertainty over what had happened gave way to indignation. I'd deserved to be at least informed of what I was being medicated with, and why, no matter what had occurred. I went to the window and stared at the dark outlines of the forest, pale and ghostly in the moonlight. In the distance, Cerberus howled from his kennel, and a shiver ran down my spine.

"You weren't in your right mind, Millie," Charles said, imploringly.

"Tell me, Doctor. If I'd had chloral *before* the party, could that have caused this 'fit' Charles has described? It would explain the memory loss, would it not?" I spun around, eager to examine their reactions. Surprise flashed across Charles's face, and it was clear such a possibility had never occurred to him. The doctor readjusted his glasses again.

"There have been other symptoms as well, Mrs. Turner. Charles has told me that you have yet to fall pregnant." He smiled without showing his teeth. "Hysteria could be responsible for that. It can lead to immoral behavior. It can make you—ungovernable."

I gasped, appalled that he should speak to me in such a way. I expected Charles to reprimand him, but to my even greater shock, he did not. He only looked sideways at me. Was he thinking about our encounter in the car? Would he discuss something so personal with Dr. Wendell?

I knew most men expected women to hide beneath the bedclothes and do their duty, but it had never been that way for Charles and me. But he was responsible as much as me, more so even, for the nature of our encounters. And it was cruel to blame me for our childlessness; I longed for a child, and ever since our marriage I'd carefully monitored my moods and eating habits, waiting for a sign, my chest tight from the pressure.

"Thank you for your perspective, Doctor," I said, emphasizing the last word to show how little I thought he deserved the title. "As I mentioned, we don't have footmen at the moment, but I trust you can show yourself out."

"Millie, be reasonable." Charles crossed toward me and touched my hand, tentatively, as if unsure how I might react. Moments ago, I had craved a gesture of affection from him, but now it only unsettled me. The cracks inside me widened and deepened.

"Me? Me, be reasonable?" I didn't care that my voice raised in pitch, that I sounded like the hysterical woman they were accusing me of being.

"I don't want to do anything drastic yet. Dr. Wendell says we can try another rest cure." The flickering gaslight cast Charles in shadow, and his figure loomed ominous and large on the wall.

"I think I've had quite enough rest."

A clock in a distant part of the house chimed the hour. It was so silent I could hear every gong. Eleven. Someone must have remembered to wind that one. The house seemed to reverberate in response, or perhaps it was only the thudding of my heart.

I wouldn't let them put me to sleep again. Charles couldn't force me. This charlatan had persuaded Charles of his ideas, but I'd get another diagnosis and prove to Charles just how wrong they both were. And I'd find out what really happened to Gertrude. If I could make Charles see that someone else was responsible, perhaps everything would be all right again.

I blinked back a wave of tears. I didn't want to cry in front of Dr. Wendell.

"If you'll excuse me." I swept out of the room, not wanting to risk making a bigger scene.

I went to my rooms, but I already knew I wouldn't sleep. After the rest cure, it was the last thing I wanted.

Someone had poisoned Gertrude. I'd find out who it was, and why.

CHAPTER 9

I worked out a plan while the rest of the house slept. I sat on my window seat and stared out at the black sky as I made a mental list of all the questions I should ask. I covered myself with a thick blanket and drew it to my chin, shivering; there was no chance of a fire after my accusations against Briggs.

First, I'd solve the problem of this delayed coal delivery. It was hard to think when I was so cold. My mind moved slowly, like a river freezing over.

Then I'd find out the addresses of our old servants. I owed them letters of reference, anyway; I'd assumed Sanders had done it, but I had to make sure. And they'd be grateful for a personal note from me. I'd ask the footmen and the maids if they'd noticed anything strange.

And then I'd visit Hannigan in his cottage. He might have heard something from the other staff, or noticed something useful about the comings and goings of the guests that night.

I didn't know if it would lead anywhere, but it was a place to start.

I fiddled with the card David had left me, flipping it over between my fingers. I wondered what his life was like now. I hadn't noticed a wedding ring. Not that it should have mattered one way or the other to me. I hadn't seen him for over ten years, and he was practically a stranger. Still, I was curious. I liked picturing him in a little room somewhere, scribbling his columns. Even when we were younger he'd wanted to be a writer and carried a notebook everywhere. He'd liked watching people, too, and as a girl I'd reveled in the intensity of that gaze.

Maybe I'd call the number on his card. Just in case he'd learned anything.

I didn't wait for dawn to dress. I struggled with my corset without Briggs's help, but I managed, its S-curve thrusting my bust forward and my hips back. I buttoned the endless buttons on my boots and dress, my fingers clumsy. Even if no one would see me yet because of the hour, I refused to drift about the house in a nightgown like a wraith. For one thing, I'd freeze.

It was even more frigid than my room in the dim hallway, and dark, even once I'd turned on the gaslight. I was up even before Briggs or the cook, and my skin prickled in the eerie quiet.

I descended the narrow servants' staircase, to Sanders's tidy little office near the kitchen. Briggs's now, I guessed. Somewhere in her papers was surely the name of the coal company. I sat at the desk and was surprised to see everything still carefully organized. I hadn't expected such conscientiousness from Briggs. The ledger book was open helpfully to the most recent page of expenses and payments.

Only it couldn't be right. I frowned at the spidery handwriting, and the neat little columns of figures.

Not only was there no payment to a coal company listed, there were *no* payments listed for over a month.

I groaned as I understood what must have happened. Whatever Charles has said, Briggs hadn't actually taken on Sanders's work. She hadn't paid anybody. Maybe the coal order had never even been made. I slammed the ledger book shut in frustration.

A perusal of the drawers didn't reveal a list of the former servants' addresses, so I determined to call Sanders about it later.

As I returned upstairs, I heard the crunch of gravel on the driveway. McDonough with the car. The quality of the light had changed. Peering down the length of the hallway, it no longer dissolved into blackness, but into gray shadows. Morning had arrived. The noise was probably Charles going back to the city early. I knew he had work, but even so, I'd hoped he'd want to say goodbye. Heartbroken as I was by what had transpired between us, I thought maybe in the light of day he'd see reason. Apologize. Tell me that he was wrong not to trust me, that he could have misunderstood what he'd seen that night. Allowing the doctor to administer a rest cure was deeply upsetting, but it was even worse that he didn't want to try to make things right. I hated leaving things so fraught between us.

I sighed and then jumped at the sight of Briggs only a few feet away from me, beside the telephone. Had she been there the whole time, or had I just not heard her arrive? I placed a hand on my heart, feeling its thump against my palm. It looked as if she'd been about to make a call. "Mrs. Turner. You're awake early."

I frowned. Briggs probably knew that I'd accused her of drugging me, but I wasn't sure if she'd known that I thought she was stealing from us as well. I didn't know what Charles had told her. It didn't matter.

"Briggs, I'd like you to go to town today. Charles has new duties for you."

I considered dismissing her outright, but I knew Charles wouldn't stand for it. But that didn't mean she had to stay *here*.

Briggs's face was a picture of insincere astonishment. "I thought Mr. Turner explained. I was only giving you what the doctor ordered. Please don't be upset with me, ma'am."

"You are supposed to work for me, not the doctor, Briggs. I need a maid who is loyal." My words were crisp.

"I would go to town, ma'am, only Mr. Turner says I'm to stay. He told me he needed someone he could trust to look after you. He made me promise. So I won't go unless he says so." Her voice dripped with syrupy sweetness, and her watery blue eyes widened. I huffed.

I could hardly believe she was fighting me on this. I hadn't expected her to. A bubble of anger swelled in my chest. This was my house, and my household.

Next time I saw Charles, I vowed to get this resolved. I'd make him see how deceived he was in her. For now, I'd have to handle things a different way. "If you are to stay, Briggs, I expect you to be useful. We are over a month behind on payments. I expect this business with the coal to be sorted out today. And I noticed several paintings missing—for dusting, perhaps?" I studied her reaction for a sign of guilt. She blinked a few times but remained impassive. "Replace them. If you weren't the one to remove them, and can't locate them, I'll need to call the constable and file a report. They're very valuable."

It felt good to put her in her place and assert myself as mistress. Even if she didn't actually follow through on my orders, which I expected, at least I'd made them. It would be more ammunition against her when I spoke to Charles.

I expected the mention of the constable to rattle her, but it didn't. In fact, she smiled. "I'll have a good look for those paintings, ma'am. But I don't think Mr. Turner will want the constable coming. Not after what happened to Mrs. Underhill."

I sucked in my breath. The threat had been implied ever since I awoke, with every ignored order, every cheeky remark. So she knew what Charles believed I'd done; perhaps all the servants did. I still suspected her own involvement, although it was only a hunch. Her smug expression made me boil.

"I *will* call the constable, Briggs. We have nothing to hide."

I spoke forcefully, willing steel into my spine and my voice, but my words wobbled.

"Of course, ma'am," Briggs said, her smirk never wavering.

CHAPTER 10

The wind was up outside, and I clutched the front of my coat as if I could pull it tighter around me, even though it was already buttoned. Hannigan's cottage sat tantalizingly near. It was a bit early to call on him, but a curl of smoke drifted from the chimney, so he was up. I walked as briskly as I could without breaking into a run.

Then Cerberus sprinted toward me, barking furiously, and I did run. I expected his barking to cease once he got nearer and recognized me, but it didn't. I was astounded he would come after me, the lady of the house. My mouth dropped open and a strand of hair whipped against my cheek.

I'd find Terry later and insist he keep the beast in the kennel if he couldn't be controlled. But just then, I was frightened. I banged on Hannigan's door and he opened promptly, looking startled, and I tumbled inside.

"Forgive me, Hannigan, for intruding upon you like this." I paused to catch my breath, and took in the spare but homey surroundings: a living room with—thank goodness—a roaring fire, a couple comfortable sofas, end tables with framed photographs. I'd seen it before, of course, after construction, but not since Hannigan had moved in. "Your home is charming."

"Thank you, ma'am. It's a pleasure to see you. Please make yourself comfortable."

Hannigan himself was in his sixties, but still hale and hearty. He looked so much like his son, especially around the eyes. If he was surprised to see me, he hid it well.

"Friendly dog you've got. Really makes a fellow feel welcome."

I jumped. The voice had come from an armchair near the fire. David Hannigan stood and turned to face me, and for some reason I blushed.

"I'm so sorry. I didn't realize your son would be visiting today. I should go." I may have been Hannigan's employer, but I still clung to some of my youthful deference for him.

"Nonsense. Tea is just ready." Hannigan gestured toward the sofa, and I hesitated a moment before sitting.

David smiled at me a little mischievously. "Well, well. How serendipitous. You've spared me from braving the beast out there to come call on you."

I suppressed a smile. "A personal call, or professional?" I arched an eyebrow. I was being silly. I shouldn't care which it was, but I found that I did. Of course, it wasn't quite appropriate for him to call on me in a social sense, given the difference in our circumstances. David would never have been part of a shooting party with Charles, or attended one of our dinners. The son of our servant, becoming a friend—Charles would have laughed at the idea.

"Can't it be both?"

He smiled, and I admired how at ease he was. Most of my friends were always affecting something or other. He gave the impression that he didn't care what anyone thought. And his roguish charm was quite effective. I bet he got women to admit all sorts of things for his stories.

"I suppose."

Hannigan joined us and proffered a teacup. "Thank you." I flicked my eyes up at his son.

Hannigan sipped his own brew, the mug chipped and familiar. I'd seen it before, as a girl, and it brought on a wave of nostalgia so powerful that I lost my train of thought for a moment, thinking instead of the summer Hannigan returned to work for us at my father's new summer estate in Saratoga, after Mrs. Hannigan had passed. He'd been quieter than I'd remembered, his eyes tragic.

I hadn't recognized David at first, with his mop of curly hair and lean muscles. He'd become a young man, no longer the boy who'd once swallowed an earthworm on a dare. While the servants had been busy unpacking the china and my mother's endless trunks and opening windows, David had shown me the house, the gardens, the blackberry bushes, where we picked fat, ripe berries that stained our fingers and tongues. We spent almost every day in each other's company after that, and if my father noticed at all, he hadn't minded. He still saw me as a little girl, and thought our playing together was entirely innocent.

It mostly was.

Until one afternoon when we'd explored my father's old boathouse, and David had given me my first kiss. It had tasted of blackberries and left my lips buzzing. I'd been a tangle of emotions, nervousness and excitement and happiness.

Maybe my mother had seen something, sensed the shift in me. I was never sure. All I knew was that the next summer David wasn't there. He had secured a position as an errand boy at one of the grand hotels in town, and we saw each other rarely, exchanging meaningful glances the few times we did.

He glanced meaningfully at me now, drawing me from my reverie. "It's for the best we meet here anyway," I said. "There's been an issue with our coal delivery and the house is freezing."

"Probably would have been a little cramped in there, too," David said. It took me a moment to understand that he was teasing me. I laughed uncomfortably.

"It is all a bit much, I know." That was the whole idea, of course. But now I saw it through his eyes, rather than that of our friends. I'd lost that sense of wonder some time ago. I hadn't mourned it until then. I was reminded of the first time I'd seen my father's mansion in Saratoga, when we were newly wealthy, and how it had felt a little bit like a fairy tale.

I sipped my tea, which was earthy and rich. It was quality stuff, better than I would have expected from someone in Hannigan's position.

"This is excellent, thank you, Hannigan."

"David bought it for me." He beamed, clearly bursting with pride for his son. The idea of David spending his hard-earned wages, which couldn't be terribly high as a journalist, on this fine present for his father touched me. I'd noticed that the cuff of David's gray suit was worn, and I glimpsed the strong bones of his wrist when he moved his arm. I felt almost indecent, as a man might feel when spying a lady's ankle. He probably bought his clothes ready-made—I doubted he could afford a tailor—but somehow they suited him better than the finest worsted wool.

"How very kind." I shifted in my seat. For the first time in ages, I was warm. "I actually came to ask you about the evening of the party, Hannigan. I thought perhaps you could tell me something that might help me make sense of things."

Hannigan nodded somberly. He seemed almost to expect the question, as if he'd already guessed the reason for my early-morning visit. "I'm happy to help, if I can. Though there wasn't much out of the ordinary. Until it happened. Then the doctor arrived, to see if she could be saved. And then the coroner." He wore the tragic mien I remembered from my girlhood.

David leaned forward. "Did you remember something?" He put his hands on his knees, and I marveled that such large, masculine instruments could create precise and intricate columns of text. His dark eyes were intent.

I shook my head. "No. In fact, I believe I may have been dosed with chloral hydrate before the party."

David and Hannigan both exclaimed in surprise and concern. I scolded myself for my admission; David was a journalist, after all. I needed to be more careful. I laughed lightly, to ease the tension, although there was nothing funny about it. "I'm probably being silly. I'm sure I just had too much wine. If I'd had chloral I would have fallen asleep, wouldn't I? And I didn't. Charles thinks I'm being paranoid. It's only—it's so strange, what happened to Gertrude."

I sipped my tea again to avoid David's stare, but I could feel it on me like a touch. I squirmed.

"Knockout drops," David breathed. I glanced up and saw that he looked pensive and troubled. "For some people the drops work quickly, for others it might take a little longer. Maybe even a couple of hours. Depends on the dose. You probably would have seemed very drunk at first. Slurred your words, stumbled, that sort of thing."

An image flashed in my mind then, of me knocking over a wineglass at dinner, and a deep red stain seeping into the white tablecloth. I gasped. It was the only scrap of memory that had come to me so far, and I clung to it.

"I see."

"What makes you think someone gave you chloral hydrate, Mrs. Turner?" David's voice was quiet and serious.

"No—I was mistaken. Please forget I said anything."

I was embarrassed and distracted, and the hot tea scalded my tongue.

David seemed to read my thoughts. "You should know that I'm not a gossip columnist, Mrs. Turner. I'm a financial reporter. But sometimes . . . the business and the personal become intertwined." He looked meaningfully at me, so I understood he wasn't only talking about Charles. He meant us, too. "So when the former paramour of one of the city's richest stockbrokers dies at his dinner party, it catches my attention. When not long afterward he is seen at parties with a certain state senator and his daughter, without his wife present, it catches my attention, too."

He paused, letting me absorb this. I was utterly mortified.

"The Applebees." I hadn't meant to say the name out loud, because I didn't need him to tell me who he meant. I knew. There was only one state senator in our acquaintance.

Suddenly I wanted very badly to be away from the warm little room, away from the directness of David Hannigan's brown eyes.

Lily Applebee was younger than me, no more than twenty, and had soft, baby-pink skin and blond ringlets. The last time I'd seen her had been nearly a year ago, and she'd been wrapped up like a present in a snow-white ermine coat. I disliked her nearly as much as I'd hated Gertrude. She was so mocking and self-satisfied, her snide remarks always frosted with a layer of sugary sweetness. She was single, motherless, heiress to a vast fortune, and by all accounts had loose morals. Her father had influence, and was rumored to be vaguely corrupt. Charles was probably only associating with them for business reasons.

I didn't like to consider what other motives he may have had.

Hannigan shifted uncomfortably and topped up my tea. "I've told my son not to be bothering you, Mrs. Turner. You don't need to answer his questions."

His son looked a little shamefaced. I took a shaky breath. I was reminded once again of the social gulf between me and David. Poor Hannigan, proud of his son's career but scared for his own future. "Think nothing of it." I wanted to reassure him that I held him in the highest regard, and that his position was quite safe, but I couldn't make that promise. If David did publish something about us, Charles would be ruthless.

Of course, David was interested in Charles and not me. People usually were. It shouldn't have surprised me. It bothered me more than it should have. I supposed I should be grateful that the rumors about me seemingly hadn't reached him yet.

"I know it's been some time, Mrs. Turner, but I still think of you as a friend. My instinct tells me that there's a bigger picture here." David gave me a rueful smile. "I'm sorry if any of this has distressed you."

"It's quite all right." I didn't mean it, of course, because nothing was remotely all right. How could it be? Someone— and I still wanted to believe it was Briggs—had drugged me and poisoned Gertrude. It was terrifying. And my own husband was out on the town with an heiress known for her easy virtue. A knot formed in my throat. I set my tea down. The fresh betrayal, on top of what I'd learned last night, was almost too much to bear. I had to hold it together in front of David and his father, but my stomach churned. I scooted closer to the fire. "I want to know what happened. I'll do whatever I can to help."

David spun his teacup around in his fingers; it looked almost like a toy in his hands.

"I'm glad to hear it." I met his gaze now, and it was so straight and honest. I knew he believed he was doing his duty.

I only hoped I could trust him.

CHAPTER 11

The memory of Lily Applebee's pink cheeks taunted me as I headed back toward the house. Cerberus had disappeared, thankfully; it felt eerily like the beast only minded me leaving the house rather than returning to it.

It didn't mean anything that Charles was spending time with her. He likely wanted to woo the senator regarding whatever business dealing he'd approached my father about. I knew women admired Charles, of course I did, but before the party he'd never given me any reason to doubt his loyalty or affection. In private, he laughed off the attentions of other women and mocked their attempts at flirtation. "As if I could notice another woman when you are in the room. You outshine them all," he'd say.

But that was before. Now he thought jealousy had turned me into a murderess. He was a handsome, virile man, now saddled with a mad wife. He wouldn't be completely immune to the charms of Lily Applebee.

Upset as I was at him, I still loved him. Our marriage was still fresh, and we hadn't had any trials to test it yet. I wanted to believe we could overcome this. And I knew how much he disapproved of divorce, how much he cherished the sterling polish of the Turner name. He wouldn't want to jeopardize his reputation through scandal. My father's views on divorce were just the same; he had ended friendships and business relationships with those who'd pursued it, believing it a recourse for the immoral and weak. I couldn't bear the thought of his disappointment, and the humiliation of having failed so spectacularly, and so quickly, at matrimony. I was twenty-two when I'd married, and had turned down several proposals before then, much to my mother's chagrin. I'd waited longer than many women did to make a decision, because I'd refused to settle.

Charles had been worth waiting for.

I tried to see things from his perspective. Whatever he'd thought he'd seen that night had clouded his judgment. Maybe someone wanted to make it seem as if I had killed Gertrude, to drive a wedge between us.

I veered off my course and headed toward the greenhouse, hoping seeing some greenery might soothe me.

I paused inside the door, my pulse jumping at the sight of Cerberus in the gravel path. He bared his teeth at me and let out a low growl. Giant and ugly, he really was more monster than dog, and bore no resemblance at all to the sweet terrier named Topsy I'd had growing up. He wasn't just another breed, he was another species. I spotted Terry a moment later, attending to the camellias. He stopped when he saw me and nodded in acknowledgment.

Terry made me almost as uneasy as Cerberus. I didn't know much about him. He'd worked for Charles before our marriage, and he'd hired him. I found him too rough around the edges, with snaggled teeth and unkempt hair. Dogs are often very like their owners, I've found.

"Thank you," I said, in reference to his work. He eyed me a bit warily, as if he'd been expecting me to reprimand him instead. His reaction reminded me that, in fact, I had. "Your dog attacked me earlier. He's wild. I must insist you keep him contained." My voice rose. It was inexcusable that he'd allowed his pet to endanger me. I considered dismissing him for it, only I knew Charles would want to be consulted, and I had to save my arguments for Briggs.

"My apologies, ma'am." He didn't sound sorry, and I frowned. "Mr. Turner wanted him out. Not many of us here and it's a big house. Said he wanted us to be safe."

I'd had the same thought the first time I'd seen David, about how vulnerable we were here. So I understood Charles's instinct, but neither of us had realized how ungovernable the beast was. "I could have been injured. I'm afraid I must insist." I squared my shoulders. Cerberus growled again, louder than before, its dark eyes fixed on mine.

"Of course, ma'am." But Terry made no move to corral the animal.

"At once."

Something menacing flashed in Terry's eyes. He whistled, then connected Cerberus to a lead. "Can't work while I'm holding him."

"Then you'll finish later." Terry moved toward me, and I stepped back, alarmed, before I realized he was heading for the door. "Also, I noticed a strange blue flower here the other day. Did you plant it?" I walked toward the spot I remembered and gestured. Maybe he'd know what it was.

"No, ma'am." He looked at me strangely, as if my question confused him. "I figured it was you who planted it. Odd choice, I thought, when I noticed it."

"Why's that? Do you know what it is?"

He nodded. "Wolfsbane. Very poisonous. Be careful not to touch it without gloves."

I inhaled sharply. I remembered clearly the strange tingling in my fingers and my unsteadiness after I'd brushed its petals. Thank God I'd experienced nothing worse. I opened my mouth to ask him more, but he'd already turned his back and was headed out the door.

Once he was gone, I let out a small shudder. The conversation had unnerved me, especially his assumption that I'd planted the flower.

I closed my eyes and groaned as I processed the full implications. If Gertrude had been poisoned, as Charles said, it wasn't impossible that this flower could have been responsible. Terry must have heard the rumors about Gertrude, as Briggs had. And he, too, blamed me.

I didn't understand who could have planted it, if not Terry. It was a mystery. Perhaps learning more about the plant could provide some answers. I didn't know if the plant was deadly enough to kill someone, but at least now I knew its name.

I rushed to the library, eager to investigate. It was one of my favorite rooms in the house, with its soaring mahogany shelves lining the walls, thousands of elegant tomes, and deep window seat overlooking the water. The fireplace, unfortunately, was coal burning, so there was no hope of a fire, even if I'd been able to persuade Briggs to light one.

I skimmed the spines of the books with my fingers until I found the *Cyclopedia of American Horticulture*. My hands shook as I pulled out one of the volumes. The entries were in alphabetical order, and when I found wolfsbane I was redirected to *Aconitum*. I finally located the appropriate page, but I learned only that *Aconitum napellus* would provide color from July until frost. There was nothing useful. Nothing about its poisonous properties. I shoved the book back onto the shelf, my chest heaving.

The book may not have had the answers I sought, but the flower itself was a clue. It was something concrete, when my memory still betrayed me.

And if it had been what poisoned Gertrude, it meant that her poisoner wasn't among our guests.

It was someone here. In this house.

I paced in the hallway in front of the telephone, gathering the courage to make the call. The wall above the console table was still conspicuously bare.

If the poisoner was someone in my household, it changed everything. But I could be wrong. The flower could be a strange coincidence, and Richard still could be responsible. Or possibly another guest. Arabella might know. At the very least, she'd be able to tell me more about how the evening had unfolded. But it was a terribly awkward call to make, even to a close friend, considering we hadn't spoken at all since Gertrude's death.

Finally, I picked up the silver receiver and made my request to the operator. I tapped my foot impatiently while I waited for Arabella's butler to answer. Finally, his wheezing voice crackled through the line.

"Donahue, it's Millie Turner. I'd like to speak to Mrs. Burton."

There was a long pause. "I'm sorry, but Mrs. Burton is out."

I huffed. I wasn't sure he was being truthful. Sometimes she feigned headaches when she wasn't in the mood for company, as we all did. "Can you make sure? Please, it's urgent."

I waited some more, and finally was rewarded with Arabella's husky register. "Millie. What a surprise." She sounded strange. It was probably due to the distance. Besides, Arabella was terrible at speaking on the phone, never directing her words into the receiver properly, and I often lost some of them to slurring and whistling.

"I'm so glad to hear your voice. How are you? I hardly even know where to begin, there's so much to discuss."

There was a long pause. I heard Arabella coughing. "I'm well."

I waited a moment, expecting her to say more. Arabella wasn't the type to mince words, and such reserve was completely unlike her. I was momentarily at a loss. Perhaps she wasn't feeling well.

"I'm so sorry for what you must have gone through. At the party."

I let the silence stretch on, growing more uncomfortable with each passing second. Finally, Arabella spoke.

"It was shocking. And so sudden. I've never seen anyone—well." Arabella coughed again, and I heard a whooshing noise. I wondered if she was smoking.

I decided I should cut straight to the point. "Listen, dear, I don't have time to explain everything, but this is terribly important. Did Richard go to bed early that night?" He'd been staying over at our house as a guest, and anyone could have noticed his departure upstairs.

"He did. Full as a fiddle, per usual." She sounded a bit livelier now, more like her usual self.

I frowned. If Richard had been drunk—and he often was, Arabella wasn't wrong about that—it did make it less likely that he'd had the capacity to poison his wife. Of course, he could have pretended to be drunk to provide cover.

"So were you, for that matter," she continued, and I squeezed the receiver tighter between my fingers. David had said I would have seemed drunk, if I'd been drugged.

"How is Richard handling all this?" I wanted to ask outright if he could have been responsible, but it wasn't the sort of question one could just ask, even of a close friend.

More whooshing. "Millie, please. I know what you're getting at. He"—I lost a few of her words—"no reason when she wasn't going to contest the divorce." There was another pause. She'd understood me, at least. "I really must be going. I'm sorry you've been . . . unwell."

"Arabella—" But she'd ended the connection. My mouth opened in surprise. It hadn't been my imagination that she'd seemed cold. After everything that had happened, I'd expected her to be eager to hear from me. But there'd been no friendly concern in her voice, no curiosity about the last few weeks.

Charles had said my friends wouldn't receive me and that everyone believed I was guilty, but I hadn't believed him. I swallowed. My cheeks flushed. I was absolutely mortified.

I reassured myself that I could repair things with Arabella

next time I saw her. Telephones were so impersonal, and conversations could be tricky even in the best of circumstances.

At least I'd learned something useful; if Richard and Gertrude had agreed to divorce, he wouldn't have had as much reason to do something so extreme. And I had to admit it was hard to picture Richard, with his perpetually red-rimmed eyes and blotchy complexion, always the buffoon of the party, planning something so calculated.

I huffed. No one was going to be able to give me the answers I sought.

I simply had to find a way to *make* myself remember.

CHAPTER 12

⁂

The library proved more useful during my second visit that day. My father had instilled his love of books in me, and our library was excellent, with tomes on every subject. I was vaguely familiar with some of the theories of Freud, and I knew his psychoanalysis discipline dealt with memories. I located a work by him and Josef Breuer called *Studies on Hysteria* and my eyes widened. I hadn't paid much attention to Dr. Wendell's diagnosis, but it could also prove illuminating to better understand the condition he thought had stricken me.

I spent over an hour poring through the pages. I wasn't sure I believed all of the theories, but there were some helpful tidbits. It turned out the repression of traumatic memories could cause hysteria, and that such memories could be awoken in a hypnotic state. I still thought it more likely that I'd forgotten the night of Gertrude's death because of taking chloral, but I had to consider all possibilities. Maybe what I'd witnessed was so horrifying that my mind had swallowed it deep into its recesses, protecting me from information that would be too much to bear.

Unfortunately, I didn't have a hypnotist handy to lure my reminisces to the surface. But the book did also say that memories could be provoked by "the laws of association," or through a similar experience that recalled the original experience. And something called "ab-reaction," or giving vent to

a repressed experience through words and action, would un-
burden me of it. It was possible that the party would return all
at once with the "undiminished vividness of a recent event."

I pondered this for a time as I stared at the bay, which was
cloaked with a fog so dense I couldn't see the opposite shore.
It felt oppressive, suffocating, as if it were trapping me here.
But it would have to clear eventually. Could the same be true
for the murkiness enshrouding my own thoughts? Perhaps if
I relived the parts of the evening I did remember, more would
come back to me.

I returned to my room and sought out the dress I wore that
night. If I was going to do this, I may as well do it properly. I
found it hanging askew in my closet, and saw that the front
was flecked with red wine. So the flash that had come to me
in Hannigan's cottage had been real.

I paused only a moment before deciding to put it on. I
knew it would seem eccentric, but it wasn't as if there were
anyone to see. I didn't even consider calling Briggs to help,
but I managed decently without her. I added my sable coat,
even though it ruined the effect a bit, but I didn't want to
freeze.

Then I headed to the drawing room. What was it Charles
and I had spoken of, before our guests had arrived? I'd been
worrying about the menu and Petit's preparation of the mutton. Then I'd asked whether we really ought to have placed
Gertrude beside Charles and Mr. Wainwright.

"She's a reliable flirt, and he'll like the attention," Charles
had told me.

I mouthed the words to the conversation as I replayed them
in my mind. I ripped the dust cloths off the furniture, not
wanting them to interfere with my picture of the night, and
sat in the same place I'd sat in then: a nineteenth-century
French armchair with needlepoint upholstery depicting flowers and birds, and a carved walnut frame. I mimicked walking to the sideboard for the glass of sherry.

What had happened next? I closed my eyes and rubbed my temples, searching for the answer.

There was nothing.

A wave of frustration so powerful overcame me that I flung one of the little crystal sherry glasses to the floor, past the rug, and watched it shatter on the wood. It wasn't like me to lose my temper, but I was so angry with myself for forgetting, when everything depended on me to remember.

Then an image came to me, sudden and visceral, of another cup shattering. A teacup. My breath hitched, and I walked toward the broken shards. Gertrude had dropped her teacup, I was certain. And I'd seen it happen.

Had it also fallen here? The nearby chair was the same one I'd sat in when Briggs had stared at me with that strange gleam in her eye. Yes, it had happened here. It had been sudden, Arabella said, so sudden Gertrude had dropped her teacup after she drank the poison.

I laughed out loud at my success.

I'd remembered something. It proved that I might be able to remember more.

"Mrs. Turner, what happened?"

I whipped my head up. Briggs stood in the doorway, a look of horror on her face. I wondered how long she'd been standing there. She might have seen me throw the glass, and I was sure she saw me laughing.

She took a careful step backward, as if I were dangerous.

"I dropped a glass, that's all. Clean it up, when you get a chance." I didn't care much what Briggs thought.

She turned pale. "Of course, ma'am. At once." She disappeared, perhaps to find a broom. I laughed again. It was freeing, acting this way, and it had actually scared Briggs into being helpful.

I walked across the hall to the dining room and sat in my customary place at the head of the table. I decided not to rush myself and sat for at least thirty minutes, willing something—

even the tiniest echo—to come back to me. I moved the silver candelabras to where they'd been that night—we'd planned for soft candlelight for dinner instead of the electricity. I went over in detail every decoration, and the moment when I'd spilled the wine. I was so absorbed that I didn't even hear the rumble of the car, or the heavy thud of the front door closing.

"I'm telling you, she's gone and lost her mind, Dr. Wendell. I don't know what she might do."

I jumped. The doctor's footsteps clacked closer and I stood abruptly, knocking over one of the candelabras. My heart raced faster, but I reassured myself that he'd understand, once I explained. He might even be impressed that I'd acquainted myself with Freud's theories. And I hadn't really done anything so unusual, besides wearing the dress. I truly hated Briggs in that moment.

I hoped the doctor wouldn't mention this to Charles.

"Mrs. Turner." The doctor appeared in the dining room, looking far too dignified for a small-town doctor. I wondered where Charles had found him. His appearance was nearly as fastidious as that of Charles himself, only his age and gray hair gave him extra gravitas.

"Dr. Wendell. I don't believe I called for you." I held my head high and stared him in the eye.

"Your maid here is worried about you, Mrs. Turner, and I must admit I quite understand why." He eyed the décolletage of my evening dress and the visible stain down my front. "You were right to call, Mrs. Briggs."

I righted the candelabra and turned my back to him. "I must ask you to leave, Doctor. I have no need of you."

He would tell Charles no matter what I did, I decided, so there was no point in politeness.

Dr. Wendell cleared his throat. "I'm afraid that's where you are wrong, Mrs. Turner. I do apologize about this, but I'm afraid it's necessary."

I jerked my head back up, confused. "What is?"

"I'll handle it, Doctor. Easier if it's just one of us," Briggs said, and I stared at her in bewilderment as she approached me with a determined expression. Briggs was more than twice as wide as me, and a head taller, so there was little I could do as she grabbed me, hard, and wrapped her arms around me.

"Let go of me this instant! This is outrageous."

She ignored me and then tossed me over her shoulders like a sack of potatoes. I kicked and screamed, but to no effect. I was completely helpless as she carried me up the stairs and tossed me on the bed, her expression fierce and satisfied. She obviously despised me and was reveling in this. I was too astonished to be scared at first, the shock of her attack creating a sense of unreality. Was this truly me, being pinned down in the bed by my maid, or was this happening to some other woman? Everything around me continued normally: my sitting area looked just as I'd left it, with the chair nearest the bare fireplace slightly askew, and outside a sunbeam sliced through the gray sky. Dust motes floated lazily in the air. The world around me seemed to pause, and the stillness of the house mocked me, as if the violence happening within it were beneath its notice.

Briggs hovered above me, her arms pressing me down into my soft mattress, and I stopped squirming. I'd never be able to physically overpower her. My heart beat fast in the hollow of my throat.

The fear that had paralyzed my thoughts shifted into a different gear, and suddenly my mind sped forward. Briggs and the doctor thought I was crazy. Charles must have told the doctor enough of what happened at the party that he believed me to be dangerous. They would never behave this way if they thought Charles would disapprove, which meant he'd given them both permission to subdue me, if they deemed it necessary. To trap me here.

Either that, or they were in league together. I thought again of the missing paintings.

Dr. Wendell approached behind Briggs, unhurried and almost unconcerned. That the two of them should have so much power over me infuriated me.

"Mrs. Turner, you're having a hysterical fit, and I'm going to need to enforce another rest cure. I'm sorry it had to be this way. Trust me when I say I'm doing this for your benefit." The doctor's doleful eyes were persuasive. He either believed what he was saying or he was a terrific actor.

"I was only trying to remember the party. I'm not hysterical."

The doctor seemed not to hear me, and I watched as he tipped out a measure of liquid from a little brown bottle and stirred it into a glass of water. The spoon clanked. I could just make out the word "poison" stamped on the label. I started wrestling with Briggs again, but her grip was firm.

"What is that you're giving me?"

"Just chloral hydrate, Mrs. Turner. It's perfectly safe."

"You can't force me. I'll have you arrested for this."

The doctor sighed. Briggs laughed. Her eyes shone, and I wondered if maybe she were the insane one. Then she pinched my nose and squeezed my jaw open, as if I were a horse or a dog, and the doctor tipped his potion into my mouth.

I sputtered, and gagged, but in the end was forced to swallow.

"Stay here until she falls asleep," the doctor ordered, and Briggs dragged a chair around near the bed. I was breathing hard, but I was still awake. I debated whether I should try to run, but already I could feel the drug hitting my bloodstream and the slowing of my heart. My limbs grew heavy.

For some reason, I thought of my father. He was the strongest and most powerful man I knew. A fighter if there ever was one. He would know what to do in such a situation. He wouldn't be so terrified that he could barely move.

But then, he was a man, and when he spoke, the doctor would have listened.

I hiccupped a sob and closed my eyes. I heard the door close as the doctor left, and I tried to remember the many lessons my father had taught me. He didn't mind discussing his business with me, as Charles did. He often read to me from academic texts, from the newspaper, from anything, really. My mother didn't care for that sort of learning, so it was something just the two of us shared.

A snippet from a book he'd read to me once floated into my head, a treatise on animal behaviors. Some creatures feigned a state of apparent death, he'd told me, to trick their prey. I remembered him chuckling as he snapped the book shut. "Occasionally we must pretend to be weak when we are really strong. It gives us the element of surprise." He'd taken his own advice. His competitors had underestimated him, and he'd used that to his advantage.

Maybe I could do the same.

I fought to keep my mind active and to prevent myself from slipping into unconsciousness. The drug had calmed me, at least, so I wasn't quite so frightened. I evened my breathing, as if I were already sleeping. I had to count on Briggs's laziness to come to my aid.

I was in luck. The chair scraped a minute later, and I listened to her heavy tread and the door closing.

I sat up. The room swayed and tilted, but I managed to get unsteadily to my feet and stumble to my little roll-top desk beside the window.

I didn't know if the drug would make me forget again, so I hurriedly scrawled a note.

> *Gertrude dead*
> *Poison flower*
> *Don't trust Briggs*

I wouldn't be able to resist the drug long enough to escape, but at least I'd left myself a clue. I stumbled and collapsed onto the chaise, the paper balled in my fist.

CHAPTER 13

Charles's voice sliced into my consciousness. Awaking felt like rising to the surface after being underwater. I thrashed, and gulped oxygen, and clutched at the blankets around me.

Paper crinkled against my palm, and all at once I remembered: the doctor, and Briggs, and my rushed note. I hadn't forgotten this time.

Charles was still in the hallway, his deep baritone contrasting with the nasally voice of the doctor.

I stopped stirring. I decided to listen instead.

"I can't thank you enough for taking care of this situation. I'm so grateful for your discretion. You'll be handsomely compensated, of course."

The door opened, and I heard their footsteps stop. They were probably both staring at me, appraising my condition, and I kept perfectly still. My chest rose and fell steadily. So Charles had paid the doctor for his silence. Maybe it explained his flashy watch and the fine clothes.

"Of course, Mr. Turner. A woman like her doesn't belong in prison. An institution, though. I'm afraid it's become necessary."

I heard Charles's long sigh. "Are you sure?"

"Quite. She's a danger to herself and others. It's abundantly clear."

There were more heavy footsteps. "I found this, Mr. Turner. I showed the doctor already." Briggs sounded excited.

"Your groundskeeper helped us identify it. It's a tincture of wolfsbane. A very deadly poison, and a very clever one. If Mrs. Underhill had taken this, it would have caused the effect you all witnessed. The vomiting, the paralysis, the quick death. It leaves virtually no trace. Mrs. Briggs found it on Mrs. Turner's vanity."

It took considerable willpower not to sit up and protest. There'd been no poisonous tincture on my vanity. Briggs must have put it there. And suddenly I was seized with certainty that she must be behind all of this. I'd suspected it before, but now it was obvious it could only have been her. She had the access to plant the flower, to drug my sherry. She was far too old to have designs after Charles or any of that sort of nonsense, and I didn't understand her motive, but no one else made sense.

Maybe she had poisoned Gertrude merely as a means to place the blame on me. It seemed outlandish, but I was increasingly persuaded Briggs might not be in her right mind.

"My God. So there's no doubt, then." Charles's voice cracked. He let out a shaky breath. It was unlike him to get upset in that way. I'd seen him exuberant, or angry, but rarely dejected. I squeezed the blanket a little harder. "She'd seemed so sure there was some mistake. I almost thought . . ." Charles let the sentence trail off.

"I know it is difficult to accept. But she may not even have been aware what she was doing. The fact that she can't remember the evening might indicate she was in a hypnoid state."

"It just doesn't seem real. I never thought her capable of something like this." Charles sounded so grieved and I wished I could go to him. As complicated as my feelings for him still were, it soothed me a little to know that he'd at least been struggling with the doctor's diagnosis.

"She is due for another dose soon. We can keep her medicated for as long as you need to make the appropriate arrangements. Both the chloral hydrate and the Medinal can be lethal, if too much are taken, so you'll need to make sure she can't access the bottles in case she should begin suffering from melancholia."

Briggs's firm hand wrapped around the back of my neck and she pushed my head upward. I fluttered my eyelids.

"Charles? Is that you?"

"It's me, darling." Charles sat beside me on the bed and took my hand in his. "You've had another episode."

Charles didn't look well. He seemed tired. His eyes were bloodshot, and his normally perfectly pressed suit sported creases. It startled me. I'd never once seen Charles appear as anything less than flawless.

I frowned. My inclination was to try to explain what had happened, to argue, but I knew before I drew breath that I would fail. He trusted Dr. Wendell. He was completely persuaded I was mentally unsound. "I'm scared, Charles. I don't know why this is happening." I allowed a tear to leak out of my eye.

"I know. I know." He paused, his green eyes flashing. "Dr. Wendell thinks you may need more help than he can give you. A . . . hospital. It would just be for a little while."

"A hospital?" I sat up slowly. Briggs had changed me into a nightgown. I exhaled slowly. "I want to get better, Charles. I'll do whatever you think is best." I smiled lovingly at him.

I saw the tension in Charles's body ease. He was relieved I wasn't going to fight this.

"Here's your next dose, Mrs. Turner." Dr. Wendell looked pleased and a little proud, as if my sudden compliance were because of his treatment. I obediently swallowed the drink.

"Thank you. If you don't mind, I'd like a few minutes alone. This is a lot for me to process."

Charles shooed the doctor and Briggs out of the room and

kissed my forehead. "Sweet dreams, love." Then he turned off the gaslights and followed them out.

I waited one minute, two. Then I swung my legs out of bed and rushed to the bathroom, where I stuck my fingers down my throat until I gagged. I tasted my own bile as I heaved up the medicine, and I kept going until I had nothing left. My insides were scraped clean. My other hand touched the cool porcelain and it grounded me, keeping me tethered to reality.

I felt wrung out, weak, exhausted.

And free.

I had no intention of letting them lock me away.

As soon as the clock on my mantel ticked to eleven, I crept into the hall. Charles and Briggs had likely retired already, but I'd be quiet, and careful, just in case. I needed to get to the phone. I could so clearly picture it in my mind, shining like a silver beacon in its spot on the mahogany console table with the cabriole legs. I'd call my father, and tell him Charles's plan, and surely he'd know what to do. How to stop it. In the morning, I'd find a way to get to the train station and go stay with my parents until I could find a way to make Charles understand he was wrong.

The hallway was so dark I could barely see my hand in front of my face, but I didn't dare turn on the lights. I didn't need to. I knew this house better than anyone, and my muscles guided me toward the stairs. My feet dragged clumsily in my fur-lined bedroom slippers, and my sable coat seemed to weigh a thousand pounds. The previous dose of the drug hadn't entirely left my system, or perhaps I hadn't rid myself of all of it when I'd vomited.

Someone had left a sconce lit in the front hall, and the weak flickering light guided me as I neared the circular stairs. I peered into the semidarkness as I descended slowly, placing one foot in front of the other, grasping the rail tightly for support.

The windows suddenly rattled in their frames from a strong wind, and the skies erupted. Rather than shielding the noise, the house magnified the pounding rain, and the sound assailed me, making my ears ring. Wind whistled in the chimneys. I was reminded of my nightmare about a gale before the party, and I pulled my fur coat tighter around me. It felt like a warning.

Through the din, I heard a low rumble. It wasn't thunder; it was something animal. I paused, thinking wildly of fairy tale beasts, and to my horror the shadow of a monster appeared on the wall before me, its snout enormous and gaping. I blinked and bit back a scream. Once my heart stopped thudding so fast and reason prevailed, I peeked carefully over the railing.

I could just make out the figure of Cerberus pacing across the hall. I exhaled, although I was still on my guard. After his near attack outside of Hannigan's cottage I didn't trust him. I was shocked Charles would allow Terry to bring him in the house. Perhaps he had finally believed me about the missing paintings and decided extra safety measures were needed.

I continued on bravely, but Cerberus's growling grew fiercer as I made my way down. Then he barked, and it startled me so much that I stumbled, and my heart was in my throat as I fell. I tumbled down a few stairs, and when I stopped, my leg was beneath me at a painful angle.

I winced and slowly straightened it, suppressing a cry of pain and fury. I may have ruined my chance for escape out of sheer clumsiness.

I allowed myself a moment of self-pity and then forced myself to my feet. I couldn't give up now. I could barely support myself and hunched over the railing, dragging myself down the next step, and the next. I could just barely tolerate it.

Cerberus waited for me at the bottom of the stairs, still snarling and barking. "Shhh," I said, but I knew it was pointless. He'd wake Charles and Briggs if he kept at it. I neared him tentatively, assessing whether he'd really attack, and as my foot hit the last stair he lunged. I yelped and flailed backward. I crawled back up the staircase, crying and confused. It really did seem as if the dog were containing me rather than protecting me.

Perhaps he was. Had Charles seen through my lie? Maybe he suspected I didn't plan to go quietly away.

Crawling was more manageable than hobbling. I didn't care if it was undignified. When I reached the second floor, rather than head back to my room, I continued to the other side of the house, through the gallery and to the servants' stairs. This set let out right near the stairs down to the kitchen, and console table. I should have thought of them straightaway.

The servants' stairs were narrower, and steeper, the wood hard without a rug to soften it, but by the time I reached the hallway, I felt like an Arctic explorer must feel when he finally reaches his destination. The tears I'd been holding back disappeared, and laughter bubbled up like champagne.

I pushed myself up, using the wall for support, and my laughter died as quickly as it came.

The telephone wasn't there.

"No." A sob rose up and I ran my hand over the top of the wood, knocked it into the crystal vase, empty of flowers. "No, no, no."

It had to have been deliberate. Either Briggs, or perhaps Charles, didn't want me making calls. Perhaps Charles was worried I'd make the scandal worse by contacting our friends. Or perhaps he knew I'd tell my father about the institution. I remembered how unfeeling he'd sounded when I'd overheard the doctor first mention it. *Her father will be damned difficult about that.*

He wasn't wrong.

"Mrs. Turner. You know you're not supposed to be out of bed." I jumped. Briggs appeared in the hallway before me, Cerberus at her heel. I could only make out the bulky shape

of her in the shadows, and she stalked toward me purposefully. I backed away, as quickly as I could with my foot. "I
was just going to the kitchen. For a bite to eat."

I stumbled again, still so clumsy and slow from the drug,
and fell hard on my backside. I was crying again, hiccupping
sobs. The situation was so surreal.

"And now you've gone and hurt yourself." Briggs reached
me and dragged me up, her grip so hard that her fingers dug
into my flesh even through the fur. "Come on, now." She
hoisted me up again and carried me upstairs, but this time I
didn't protest. My ankle throbbed.

"What's going on?" As we approached my room, Charles
emerged from his, still fully dressed. Briggs deposited me on
my bed, and Charles followed close behind.

"Mrs. Turner, sir, was out of bed, having another fit. She
hurt herself. I think it's the melancholia the doctor warned
us about." Briggs's voice was cloying, and I couldn't believe
Charles didn't see through it. Briggs could have been on the
stage, one of those vulgar, overacted shows downtown with
the dim lights and stiff seats.

"Gracious. You'll need to be extra careful to keep the medicine away from her." Charles frowned, and his green eyes
darted back and forth as he looked me over. "And perhaps
we should keep this door locked. To prevent any more acci-
dents." He spoke as if I weren't right before him.

"I was hungry, that's all. I fell."

Charles cupped my cheek. "In time you'll understand that
I'm just trying to keep you safe. I'm sorry about this." He
kissed my forehead, and his lips were dry and cool. "I have to
go back to the city in the morning, but I'll be here in a couple
of days with some men from the hospital. You're going to get
better, Millie. It's all going to be okay."

Once he left, Briggs poured several teaspoons out of a
brown bottle into a glass of water. "I'm making the dose a
bit stronger this time. The other one didn't work as well as it

should have." Her eyes gleamed. Her comment about melancholia finally permeated my consciousness, and all at once I understood the greatness of my danger.

Briggs could give me a lethal overdose, and no one would question it. They'd think I'd done it to myself. Charles thought I'd killed someone else, so why shouldn't he think I was also capable of killing myself? Guilt, they'd say.

"Why, Briggs? Why are you doing this?" The words scratched my throat. I watched as she stirred the medicine into a glass. She wouldn't attempt the overdose now, not while Charles was here, and she hadn't put in much more than the doctor had. But I sensed that she was laying the groundwork for it. Maybe she planned to accompany me to the institution and do it there. It was clear she hated me, but I didn't know why. I hadn't been the kindest mistress, but only because she was so contrarian, and even so, it hardly seemed like a reason to kill someone. Her anger toward me had become more and more apparent, and it struck me as deep and personal.

"Poor Mr. Turner. To be stuck with a woman like you. A murderess," she hissed. "He deserves so much better. Drink up." She pinched my nose without waiting to see if I'd comply, and once again I gagged and swallowed. I watched through hazy eyes as she turned the key in my door and pocketed it, before closing it behind her.

I was her prisoner.

CHAPTER 14

I stared at the locked door through bleary eyes. I'd managed to throw up most of the medicine again, but I could feel some of it coursing through me anyway, making me drowsy and slow. It was pitch-black outside, the middle of the night. I had limited time to act before Charles left.

Before it was just me and Briggs.

Charles kept a phone in his study, and I decided he probably would have left it there for his own convenience. I never went in there; it was his sanctuary, and it wouldn't have occurred to him that I would violate his space.

But I didn't have a choice. I needed to call my father. And right after Charles departed for the train, I'd do the same. It wasn't too far, only a couple of miles; our servants walked it often. It might be difficult with my injury, but I'd have to manage as best I could.

The trouble was the lock.

I pushed myself out of bed, walking gingerly, and turned on the gaslights. I located my hairpins and palmed a few. Then I bent over and peered at the doorknob. It wasn't particularly sturdy, designed for guarding my privacy rather than my valuables. I'd picked one other lock before, the summer when I was twelve. David had read about lock picking in a dime novel detective story and become enamored with it, so when we encountered a locked door on the derelict boathouse on my father's estate, it had seemed like the perfect opportunity to practice. We'd spent the better part of the afternoon learning the skill, and I still remembered his gentle grasp as he'd guided my hands, and how the thrill of his touch awakened a powerful infatuation in my young breast.

I didn't know if I quite remembered how it worked, but I had to try. I did recall that two tools were needed: the pick and the lever. I bent one of my pins to make a little handle—the lever—and inserted it and the pin I was using as the pick into the lock. I grappled with my makeshift tools for the better part of an hour, my forehead growing damp with sweat. My fingers were awkward and I struggled to hold the tools with the precision needed.

But finally, probably more due to the flimsiness of the lock than any special skill on my part, I felt the seized pins pop. The doorknob turned.

I laughed in triumph.

I dressed simply and comfortably in a navy gored skirt, matching jacket, and white blouse, topped with my sable coat. Then I packed a purse with some money and jewels, as well as the pins. I might not return upstairs before I fled.

We had three sets of servants' stairs, and I headed toward the set on the west end of the house, letting out on the first floor nearest the library, billiards room, and study. I moved slowly and quietly, limping, but luckily Cerberus must have still been stationed at the base of the main staircase. I made it into the study safely, astonished at my success.

A blast of icy air assaulted me when I opened the door. The study was even colder than the rest of the house, and its sturdy English furniture hulked in the dark. I fumbled to turn on the gaslights. The room was paneled in dark mahogany, and a white elaborately carved stone fireplace lightened the effect a little. An eight-point buck above the mantel overlooked the room with shining black eyes. Near the windows, facing the doorway, was Charles's massive Tudor-style walnut desk.

A silver candlestick telephone sat proudly on top of it. I let out a whoosh of air and hurried as best I could toward it. I put the receiver to my ear and waited for the operator to answer.

I heard nothing. I waited; it was very late, after all, and the operator might have dozed off.

I waited some more. I pressed the switch hook up and down a few times, dread gathering in my stomach. The line was out of service.

It had worked when I'd called Arabella recently, and I huffed in frustration as I realized what may have happened. Briggs hadn't paid the bill. Either that, or the storm had caused a problem with the line. I sat in Charles's chair and placed my head in my hands. I could still leave for the train in the morning, but alerting my father to my situation would have provided extra assurance, in case I should be apprehended leaving the estate.

As an additional precaution, I decided to write my parents a letter instead. Charles had left a couple of outgoing letters in a tray atop his desk for Briggs to post for him, and if I slipped another one in, she might not notice.

I pulled open the top left desk drawer in search of stationary.

Instead, I found bank statements. I pawed through them, surprised at Charles's disorganization, and then paused, picking one up with a quaking hand.

The balance couldn't possibly be right.

I rifled through the next drawer and discovered dozens of angry letters from creditors.

And all at once everything clicked into place: the delayed coal delivery, the reduced staff, the dead telephone, the missing paintings.

Charles was ruined.

I didn't know how long I sat and stared at the papers before me, the hard chair pressing into my back. My eyes swam with numbers and letters and my head ached. Charles had lied to me. When I'd mentioned the missing paintings, he'd called me paranoid. When I'd asked about the coal, he'd said it was delayed. The servants had to go because we wouldn't be entertaining for a long time, he'd told me, because I was in disgrace.

He'd had an answer for everything. What scared me was how self-assured and persuasive he'd been. There'd been no ring of falsehood to any of it. But now the truth was in my hands.

I wiped away a tear. He had deliberately deceived me. Even if he'd been embarrassed, he could have confided in me. Instead he'd blamed me and made me doubt myself. It was cruel.

I searched for a way to explain his actions that made sense to me, but I came up with nothing. If I confronted him with it, what would he say? Probably that his financial situation was beyond my understanding, that I was wrong.

But I wasn't. I knew I wasn't.

The most obvious answer was that he wasn't the man I'd thought he was. Maybe that version of Charles had only ever been a figment of my imagination. I'd loved him so desperately that I could hardly accept the evidence before me, but I had my father's rational mind, and even through my heartbreak I recognized the reality of the situation.

I pawed through some of the papers again for more clues. I wanted to understand just how deeply his deception ran. How long had he been facing financial hardship? Since the Bankers' Panic?

Since he'd asked me to marry him?

My insides felt hollow.

I thought of his recent disastrous meeting with my father, and now I had a better idea what it had been about. He'd wanted money. Either for my father to invest with him, or to gift us money outright.

A half-formed theory sprouted deep in the recesses of my

mind, dark and shadowy, but I couldn't quite make out the shape of it. David's voice came to me, rumbling through me. *Sometimes the business and the personal become intertwined.*

I couldn't bear to confront my own thoughts. I was afraid.

Instead, I busied myself with activity. There were six drawers in all, three on each side, and I went through the first five thoroughly, reading everything until I'd acquainted myself with the full scope of Charles's financial predicament. Not only were his personal finances a disaster, but his business seemed to be in serious trouble, too. On impulse, I stuffed some of the more incriminating papers into my purse.

The sixth drawer was locked.

I pulled it harder, just to make sure it wasn't merely stuck, but it stayed firmly in place. I frowned. It was strange that Charles had bothered to lock it, in a room almost no one but him ever entered. A little brass keyhole caught the light and I traced it with my finger.

I'd already had some practice with lock picking that evening, and hairpins in hand, I returned to my task. My fingers turned numb in the cold air, and it took me as long as it had to escape my bedroom, longer even. But finally—finally—the lock clicked.

A revolver rested against the wood grain. Wood handle, nickel reflecting dully, the words "Smith & Wesson" engraved on the barrel. I groaned. All that, just to find out where he kept his handgun. I wasn't surprised he kept a revolver in his desk, not in the least; after all, he also kept Cerberus to guard the estate. I picked up the gun carefully and let it rest against my palm. It was heavier than I expected.

It didn't explain why he kept the drawer locked, however. If there were an intruder, surely he would want ready access. I set the gun on the desk and turned back toward the drawer. I wanted to learn *something* after my effort. I jerked it open farther than it was meant to go, and reached my hand in, feeling the back corners. But there was only wood and a small ball of dust.

I scraped my fingers against the wood once more and this time they closed on something hard and cold. When I opened my palm, I saw a flash of red against my pale skin, a sparkle of white. Two exquisite ruby and diamond earrings. They were the Bonaparte earrings that Charles had given me for our engagement, the ones I hadn't been able to find the night of the party.

Dr. Wendell had said my amnesia was likely temporary, and Freud and Breuer had written that certain objects and sensory experiences could trigger recollections. But I still wasn't prepared for how quickly my memory returned to me. In a rush, the dinner party unfurled itself before me, fresh and vivid as the night it had happened. I gasped and balled my fist, clutching the jewels tightly against my flesh.

I knew who had killed Gertrude.

Chapter 15

⁂

The glass of sherry had gone straight to my head, and the sweet liquor coated my mouth. I'd glanced at my reflection in the mirror over the sideboard and saw that my cheeks were flushed.

"Did you just have a drink?" Charles crossed over to me and plucked the sherry glass from my hand. He looked alarmed. "Our guests will be here any minute. You normally have your sherry after dinner." His tone was sharper than I was used to, accusing. It was true that my usual habit was to have it later.

"I'll be fine." But the truth was I didn't feel fine. The sherry seemed stronger than I remembered.

Still, I made it through the usual pleasantries well enough, even if I wasn't at my quickest and wittiest, and my words rolled too slowly off my tongue. I told Mr. Carter that I'd make sure to save him some of his favorite claret before Mr. Evanson drank it all. I told Mrs. Wainwright that her Worth gown was the most beautiful I'd seen that season. Everyone was gay and comfortable within minutes of arriving, and glasses of claret helped warm our guests after the crisp autumn chill and loosen their tongues. Gertrude and Richard, despite only having to travel downstairs from their guest rooms, were among the last to arrive. Arabella rolled her eyes at me behind their backs and whispered a comment about how it was no wonder Richard had sought out a mistress when Gertrude always looked like she'd just swallowed a lemon. It was mean to laugh at Gertrude's expense, perhaps, but she made it hard to feel sorry for her.

It was about thirty minutes into the party that I noticed Charles's absence. I'd assumed he'd gone to speak with the butler about something, the wine selection for dinner, perhaps. But then I saw that Gertrude had disappeared, too, and I couldn't suppress a twinge of annoyance. He'd reassured me before that I had no reason to be jealous, but I knew what a determined little minx she was. I made an excuse to go check on the dinner preparations and went in search of them.

Of course, they might not be together. I hoped that they weren't. But the timing was too coincidental. She probably would have lured him away somewhere under the pretense of wanting to see more of the house. I was angry that he'd fallen for it.

It didn't take long to find them. In the ballroom, I spotted them through the floor-to-ceiling arched windows, out on the veranda. They appeared to be deep in conversation.

I knew I shouldn't snoop and that I should trust Charles, but I couldn't resist. I slipped outside through the French doors on the opposite end of the ballroom, small and quiet. In the distance, the moon shone on the water of the bay. The veranda's tiles, balustrades, and beamed ceilings were all clad in white limestone to coordinate with the house's façade, and the space was lit only by candelabras on the torchères, their dancing flames lending a soft and romantic atmosphere.

That had been the intention. I hadn't meant for them to enjoy it.

It was dark enough, and their conversation animated enough, that they didn't notice me. The wind carried their words toward me so that I caught everything.

"I'm going to tell her tonight, Charles. I swear I will, if you don't." Gertrude was crying. My mouth opened in surprise.

"I'm just asking you to be patient for a little longer. You know how I feel about you." I watched in horror as Charles cupped her cheek. He'd done that to me a thousand times, his touch featherlight and his eyes suggestive. The night around me grew blurry and I collapsed against the wall, clutching the stone as if it could anchor me to a different reality. "She's bound to find out eventually. I gave you her engagement earrings, for God's sake. Because you admired them and I wanted you to have them. It's only a matter of time before it all comes out. But you know my business will take a hit from the scandal and I can't afford that right now." He grasped her wrist, and I backed slowly away, escaping back to the ballroom. I couldn't bear to hear any more.

He loved her. He'd loved her before he met me, and maybe he'd never stopped. I was more beautiful, and that wasn't vanity on my part. But she was refined. Maybe Charles regretted his new-money wife who didn't want to build in Tuxedo or Newport, never mind that President Roosevelt's summer residence was just down the road. I wasn't enough. My taste, my looks, my money, none of it had ever been enough for him.

I wiped away the tears coursing down my cheeks. Maybe I should go back to the veranda and confront them. I wanted to scream, to make Charles admit to my face that he'd betrayed me. But Gertrude would love that. I could just picture her smug little smile. I would only embarrass myself in front of her and give her exactly what she wanted: for everything to come to a head, and for Charles to leave me.

She'd taken enough from me. I would at least salvage my dignity.

Besides, making a scene would only prove to him that he'd been right about me. Gertrude had never caused a spectacle of that sort, no matter how often her husband embarrassed her. No, the best thing to do was to show him I was better than her and make him regret what he'd done. I'd thrown this party to please him and I wasn't going to let it fail now. I wanted to rub his face in its grand success.

And then I'd wring his mistress's fragile little neck.

I stumbled as I made my way back to the drawing room, then dabbed my face and put on a bright smile before I entered, steeling myself. Fortunately, the butler came in moments later to announce that dinner was served, so I was spared from speaking to anyone, and we all made our way to the wood-paneled dining room. Charles and Gertrude appeared at the tail end of the group, having apparently left the veranda only minutes after me. Charles was as composed as ever, but Gertrude still seemed slightly shaken.

The dining room was too dark without the electrolier on, and I chastised myself for my mistake. I'd thought the candles and flowers were elegant when I'd planned the decorations, but now the atmosphere struck me as funereal. The stone fireplace had been shipped here from one of the great houses of England and dated to the reign of Henry VIII, but its size suddenly struck me as ostentatious. The blaze would be a nuisance to anyone seated closest to it. I'd labored over so many details, all to please Charles. It had been for nothing.

None of the guests complained about anything, and the food at least was delectable. They were all too rosy with drink themselves to notice if I slurred my own words. I glared at Gertrude for most of the meal, furious that she was seated next to Charles, and suffered through conversations that held only a fraction of my attention. With every glance Gertrude directed at Charles, every covert touch, my dedication to the party's success dwindled. I could be the best hostess in New York and it wouldn't change the fact that he'd bedded my rival. By the dessert course, I no longer cared about impressing him to make a point. I wanted to punish him. And her.

During a brief lull in the conversation, I couldn't stop myself from provoking her. "I love your earrings, Gertrude. They look just like the ones Charles gave me for our engagement. Did you have the style copied?" I smiled viciously at her, daring her to speak the truth. If she did, Charles would never forgive her for it. My consonants had grown slippery in my mouth and Gertrude appeared blurry at the end of the table, so that I couldn't make out her reaction. Was I drunk? I'd had only the sherry and one glass of Burgundy.

"I hadn't noticed yours," she said. "We must have similar taste."

"We certainly do. You seem to like a great many things that belong to me."

There was a sudden hush at the table. The mood grew tense, and Gertrude's husband Richard coughed. I'm sure most of our guests knew what I was insinuating. I stood to announce that we would be serving coffee in the drawing room, but my elbow bumped my glass of wine, and a deep red stain seeped across the pristine white tablecloth. The commotion was swift and immediate—everyone exclaiming, a maid at my elbow, dabbing ineffectually. I might have been able to recover the evening if I'd cared to, but anger and alcohol coursed through me, turning my thoughts toward revenge instead. The wine I'd already drunk soured in my stomach, and the world around me appeared hazy and warped.

We did head toward the drawing room soon after, and Charles pulled me aside in the front hall. "You have to do something to smooth this over," he demanded, and his jaw ticked. "I know you don't like Gertrude, but everyone is going to talk about this."

"You know what, Charles? I don't give a damn what your friends think."

He'd grasped my wrist, just as he'd held Gertrude's on the veranda, and I yanked it away.

"What's the matter? What's gotten into you? I've told you so many times that you have nothing to worry about." He acted exasperated and put-upon, as if my jealousy were irrational. He was so convincing that if I hadn't witnessed the little scene between them, I would have believed him. What a fool I'd been.

Just then, a footman passed with a tea tray. Coffee was more customary after dinner, but Gertrude abhorred the taste, so I knew this brew likely had been requested by her.

"Wait." Charles stopped the footman. "Darling, I can't imagine what's gotten you so upset, but here's your chance. Why don't you pour her tea for her? She'll appreciate the deference of the gesture." He sounded so sincere. I was so angry at him but even angrier at myself. I shouldn't have fallen for his lies. I watched him rearrange the teacup, and something silver flashed in his hand. Maybe a teaspoon. I didn't think much of it.

"Lord it over me, more like." I gestured for the footman to continue in, but I did follow him and seated myself across from Gertrude. Maybe I would pour for her, and spill the scalding liquid on her dainty little lap. I felt drunk enough to think it seemed like a good idea.

Impulsively I did begin to pour but thought better of staging a little accident at the last moment. I didn't want to give her the satisfaction of knowing how much she'd upset me. I noticed some sediment swirling in her cup, probably some of the tea leaves that had escaped, but decided not to mention it. She'd only make a fuss.

I sat back, scowling, and watched as she took her first sip. Then she choked. Everyone was slow to respond, thinking she just needed to cough and not wanting to embarrass her. But she didn't cough. She vomited, and yellow bile dripped down her chin. Her eyes bulged, and she looked at me, terrified, her hand clutching her throat. The teacup fell and shattered beyond the rug, against the wood floor.

I stared at her in confusion and horror. I stood, thinking I should try to help her, but my legs gave out beneath me. Then the room around me tilted and turned black.

Chapter 16

The hard jewels of the earrings cut into my skin. My whole body convulsed. I couldn't breathe.

My husband, a man I'd cherished, was a monster.

My stomach was still queasy from being sick earlier, and I gagged, then threw up on the thick green Turkish rug. My mind raced as I went over the memory again, picking it apart, trying to make sense of it all.

Had Charles killed Gertrude because she was going to expose their affair? That he would murder a woman over that was hard to comprehend. But he'd touched the teacup before it was delivered; he'd told me to pour. He was guilty. Not Briggs, not Richard. My own husband. I thought of all the times he'd spoken honeyed words to me, and understood that they'd been lies. The man I'd loved had been a carefully constructed façade.

I pictured him leaning over Gertrude's dead body, a woman he'd taken into his bed, and discreetly prying my earrings from her lobes with his long, elegant fingers. I stared at the jewels in my palm, shining and cold, and shuddered. How many times had he touched me with those same fingers?

I gagged again and vomited until I felt wrung out.

Then I stuffed the earrings into my purse and pushed the bag securely into a pocket of my sable coat.

There was so much more I needed to try to understand,

but there was no time. The sky outside had lightened. Charles would leave soon and I needed to be ready.

A dog bayed in the hallway and I froze. It wasn't Cerberus; it was Duke or Prince. One of Charles's dogs. He could be headed here for some final business before he left for the train.

I had to hide.

Beside the fireplace was a concealed door in the wall paneling, with a bar behind it for Charles's private liquor stash. I slipped inside and waited with bated breath.

I heard the door open and Charles enter. I couldn't remember if I'd shut all of the desk drawers, or if I'd put the receiver back on the telephone properly. Would he see my vomit on the rug? I couldn't bear the idea of facing him, knowing what I now knew. He was dangerous. Briggs seemingly wanted me dead, but I understood now that he did, too. If I appeared to have committed suicide, few would question it. Perhaps not even my own parents.

Utter terror overcame me, seeping into my bones, and I stood completely still. I wondered if the deer whose head hung above the fireplace had frozen like this before Charles shot him.

The wait was interminable, but to my shock, I heard Charles leave. His step was unhurried, but there was no way to know if he'd noticed my interference. I didn't emerge for thirty minutes, to be sure he was really gone, and crept carefully out into the hallway.

I clamped a hand over my mouth to stop the scream. Briggs stood in the hall five feet in front of me, and her back was to me. She hadn't noticed me yet. I retreated into the study as quietly as I could, but not quietly enough.

She spun around. "Mrs. Turner. There you are." She followed me into the room and I backed away from her slowly, as I would from Cerberus, anticipating the attack. "If you're thinking of calling out, don't bother. Mr. Turner's left for the train already. And he'd understand what needs to happen now, I think. He'll be glad to be rid of you."

Her words ricocheted inside my skull. She really meant to kill me. I scanned the room, looking for something that could be used as a weapon. There was the fireplace poker and a heavy vase on the mantel. It was expensive and exquisitely beautiful, and once I would have been devastated to see it broken. Now I visualized its shards scattered on the floor, stained red with Briggs's blood. I didn't know if I was strong enough to deliver a blow that would render her unconscious, but I had to try. I edged toward the fireplace.

Briggs held a glass in her hands, and I watched as she fished in her pocket for the little brown bottle and tipped its entire contents into the water. Then she pulled out a second bottle. She didn't mean to leave this to chance.

I grabbed the fireplace poker, which was within easier reach than the vase, my palm slick with sweat. Briggs only smiled at me, as if my attempt to defend myself was a joke. She wasn't the least bit frightened. Briggs knew she could overpower me. We both knew it.

Then I swung. She jumped back and dropped the second bottle onto the plush carpet. It rolled toward me and I grabbed it and shoved it in my pocket, beside my purse. I'd had the element of surprise the first time, but now she was ready for me.

She pocketed the other empty bottle and sprang forward, pushing me back into the desk. She set the glass beside me and leaned me backward so that I was sprawled on top of the wood, then pinched my nose.

I squeezed my eyes shut. I was going to die.

I swept my hand out to the side in a last desperate attempt to grasp anything that might save me, and my fingers brushed the chilly metal of the telephone. I reached out with my last strength and clasped my fingers around its base. Then I slammed it against Briggs's head.

It stunned her. Her grip on me loosened, and I wriggled free. I ran for everything I was worth, ignoring the pain in my ankle, and kept going until I reached the front hall. I was winded, and the drug still pulled at me, slowing me down, but my mind was sharp. She'd expect me to go out the front door. So instead I changed course, moving toward the kitchen.

I hurried down the crowded wooden stairs and found Petit slicing into a bloody hank of something. He dropped his knife in surprise. Outside, a peal of barking echoed, and I realized what the meat was: horse steak, for Cerberus's breakfast.

"I'll take that to Terry, thank you, Petit." I reached for the steak, breathing heavily, and he stared at me in shock, as if I'd told him I planned to eat it raw.

Upstairs, I heard Briggs's tread. She didn't hurry; with Cerberus loose, she probably thought she didn't need to. I grabbed the steak off of Petit's cutting board and headed toward the servants' entrance. The meat was slick and blood dribbled between my fingers.

The door barely budged, and I shoved it harder, creating just enough of a gap to squeeze through. It had been blocked by snow. At some point last night, the rain had turned, and at least five inches of pristine white powder blanketed the ground. The wind stung my fingers and face as I trudged forward, making my eyes water, but the outline of the gate was fixed in my vision. It was only fifty feet away now, but each step was a struggle. My coat offered insufficient protection against the bitter air, the bottom of my dress and stockings grew heavy and wet. The snow coated everything—the tree branches, the hedges, the gatehouse roof—smothering them, and it seemed intent on trapping me, too. Somehow, I continued on. The cold numbed the emotions swirling inside me, and my only thoughts were for survival.

Blood from the horse steak dripped onto the ground, leaving a trail of red. And then Cerberus appeared before me, lean muscles bunching in his thick, stocky frame and white teeth flashing in his black muzzle. He barked.

I prepared to throw the steak, but I knew it wouldn't delay

him for long. Pure instinct guided me and drove my fingers into my coat pocket to retrieve the brown bottle. The label read "Medinal." I uncorked the top. Inside were white crystals, and I poured them liberally over the meat. Then I folded the steak and hurled it as far as I could—not far, it turned out, and it landed neatly at Cerberus's feet. He devoured it in a few wolfish bites and licked his mouth while he stared at me, dripping saliva into the patch of blood before him.

I edged forward. I didn't have time to spare. Cerberus continued barking, and I knew it would be only minutes before Briggs or Terry appeared, or both.

Another step.

Did sleeping medication even work on dogs? I had no idea. I'd acted on impulse. The barking rang in my ears, and my heart beat in my throat.

And then the barking stopped. Cerberus started panting heavily and licked his mouth. It wasn't out of hunger; he seemed suddenly ill. He licked it again.

I moved quickly sideways, and he didn't follow. I zigzagged my way toward the gate, keeping the beast in my peripheral vision, and at long last pushed open the wrought iron barrier. Hannigan hadn't chained it, perhaps because McDonough hadn't yet returned from the station. I laughed and wept in relief as I dragged myself toward the train.

CHAPTER 17

❦

The town of Oyster Bay was nearly desolate. The storm had driven everyone inside. There was a lone horse at a hitching post outside of Snouder's drugstore, and one more outside of Moore's grocery store, which had become somewhat famous for housing the summer executive offices of President Roosevelt upstairs.

It was the most beautiful sight I'd ever seen.

I was wet and miserable and couldn't feel my toes in my boots. But I was alive. I was free.

The train platform was also empty. I looked surreptitiously around for Charles, but the two-mile walk had taken me ages with my ankle and in the cold. He was long gone. The adrenaline that had propelled me forward dissipated, leaving me exhausted and shaking. I longed for the warm, plush armchairs of the first-class carriage and the weak train tea more than I'd ever longed for anything.

I secured a ticket from the window, and the agent took in my bedraggled appearance with wide eyes but no comment. It occurred to me hazily that perhaps I ought to have gotten second class, now that Charles was destitute. But I'd never ridden in the second-class carriage before, and after my escape, I needed a little comfort.

After the train arrived and I finally boarded and settled into my seat, I actually sobbed in relief. I looked around for a sign

of Charles again, fearful. It wasn't impossible he'd had an errand in town and gotten a later train for some reason. But the
carriage, so far, was empty. I watched the door closely, waiting to see if anyone else would board, ready to hide my face
or run for the door at the other end of the carriage should he
appear. I also didn't relish the thought of seeing any friends in
my current state, petrified and looking like a wet ragamuffin.
What would I say? How could I even begin?

My fingers and toes thawed slowly as the train dawdled in
the station, and a porter brought me scalding tea that heated
my insides. I moaned in pleasure.

And then Laura Hatfield stepped onboard, and my breath
hitched. The door closed behind her, and a minute later the
train rolled forward. At least I had avoided Charles, and the
train suddenly struck me as the coziest of havens. I would
have been content to stay in that armchair, safe, forever.

Well, if not for Laura Hatfield, anyway. I was out of danger, and the annoyance of seeing her was nothing compared
to that, but it didn't change the fact that she was an awkward,
graceless little waif with a sallow face who always managed
to say the wrong thing. There was no way she wouldn't recognize me, and I had no doubt she would pester me for all
kinds of details about the night Gertrude died. I couldn't
bear the thought.

I huddled into my seat and put my head down. She moved
down the aisle with her usual mincing gait, and I sensed her
still as she passed me.

But then she surprised me. She kept walking and found a
seat at the other end of the carriage. I was astonished. Had
she recognized that I wanted to be alone, and done the tact-
ful thing for once? No, that wasn't it. She didn't understand
what tact was. And I could sense her discomfort, the way she
studiously avoided my gaze.

Laura Hatfield had snubbed me.

It confirmed what I'd already guessed. She blamed me for

Charles's crime, and if she did, then all of my friends did. Laura was a follower, eager to adopt whatever trend or opinion society dictated. If Briggs had succeeded this morning, everyone would have accepted it as suicide. A fit of shaking overcame me as I confronted the narrowness of my escape.

Had that been Charles's plan all along? To rid himself of two women with the same crime? It was conniving on a level I could scarcely believe. I fervently didn't want to accept that it could be true, and I homed in on that moment where he'd touched the teacup over and over until I doubted the memory was even real. Maybe someone else had poisoned it already. It could have been coincidence.

But no coincidence could have placed those earrings in a locked drawer in his study. I fingered them inside my purse, reassuring myself that I hadn't imagined them.

At least my ignominy had spared me an hour of listening to Laura Hatfield. To be knocked low by her, of all people! I'd always been kind to her, half pretended to listen to her boring stories while other ladies simply tittered and walked away. I wondered if Charles had further stirred up suspicion among our friends while I was trapped on Long Island. I pictured Lily Applebee hanging off his arm, cooing sympathetically, and I wanted to scream.

Was her fortune large enough to save him? Gertrude's wouldn't have been, because Richard had squandered it, and in any case she'd have needed a divorce first. Mine couldn't save him, even if I were dead, because it was controlled by my father. The only asset that was truly mine was Rose Briar Hall, but valuable as it was, I doubted even its sale would be enough to staunch the bleeding. And finding a suitable buyer could take time, which he didn't have.

I pondered his plan from every angle as the train clattered over the tracks. I stared out the window, letting the passing landscape lull me into a sort of stupor. I knew he wouldn't want the stigma of a divorce. Men like my father would never invest with a divorcé, and Charles himself would have hated his name being dragged through the muck. He wouldn't have wanted the public spectacle of a trial and me going to prison, either.

But a disgraced wife who committed suicide? His business probably wouldn't suffer. His visit to my parents had been one final attempt to get the money he needed, and my father's refusal meant I was no longer useful to Charles.

Still, it was hard to fathom that he killed someone merely to spare his reputation. Perhaps there was something I was still missing.

I was so absorbed in my thoughts that the lurch of the train pulling into the station caught me by surprise. Outside was the chaos of Long Island City, the horses and carts and crowded pier, where I'd take the ferry across the East River. Boats chugged along the water, their smokestacks billowing black clouds, and after the too-still quiet of our country house, I was momentarily overwhelmed. I wished the tunnel to Pennsylvania Station were already complete.

Once across the river, I hailed a hansom cab and gave the address for my parents' house. I hadn't given much consideration yet to what I'd tell them. I was physically and emotionally spent, and my own terror of the morning had faded into a sort of emptiness.

I settled back into the cushioned seat and listened to the familiar clop of the horse's hooves, which I missed whenever McDonough took me somewhere in the car. I studied the city out the window as we trundled along Fifth Avenue, the buildings getting grander as we headed north, the sidewalks crowded with men in well-cut suits and women in furs, the roads loud with the roar of engines and the clatter of carriages. Piles of dirty snow were pushed up against the side of the road.

I paid the driver using the money I'd stuffed in my purse before my flight, and stood on the sidewalk studying the mansion's gray limestone façade and large gleaming windows.

I braced myself and rang the bell. Perhaps it was foolish

to come here, where Charles might know to look, but I still viewed my parents as my protectors. Surely under their roof no harm could befall me.

However wild I'd looked when I showed up for my last visit, it was certainly nothing compared to how I looked now. I probably appeared like a woman who had been through a battle. But then, I had. The butler coughed to hide his shock and showed me inside. My mother arrived only moments later, greeting me with her usual overzealousness, a frenzied mixture of anxiety and affection.

"Darling, I was so terribly worried I wouldn't see you for ages, after Charles and your father had that silly row. But it was nothing too serious, I'm sure—after all, here you are." Her perfectly manicured eyebrows rose into her forehead as she took in the wet and muddied hem of my dress. "Good heavens. What's happened?"

The last of my fortitude abandoned me and I collapsed into tears, as if I were a little girl again.

"Oh no, oh honey." She wrapped me in her arms.

"Is it all right if I stay here for a little while?" I finally managed. My tears eased and I sniffled.

She sighed. "Are you and Charles having problems?" I only nodded. Her eyes were shrewd. "You must have left in a great hurry. Why don't you go upstairs and change. There are some old dresses in your room—I keep meaning to send them to Paris to have them made over for you, but they'll do for now. We'll talk about this more once you've had a moment to calm down."

I plodded up the stairs, dreading my mother's questions but utterly relieved to be here. I'd survived. In my parents' house I felt safe. My journey from Long Island felt like a great odyssey, like something out of a Greek myth.

I passed through the gallery, lined with marble columns and sculptures and potted plants, before reaching the room

I'd nicknamed the Blue Room. It had been mine for several years before I'd wed Charles, and upon entering I was surrounded by the color: even the plaster ceiling was painted mostly blue, a sky accented with some fat cherubs and garlands and clouds. The last time I'd slept here had been before my wedding, when I'd been overcome with excitement for my future life. So hopeful and naïve. What would I have thought if someone had told me then what Charles really was?

I changed into one of my old tea gowns, happy to be rid of my corset for a while, and joined my mother reluctantly in the drawing room.

My mother wore a stylish, loose-fitting blue tea gown of crepe de Chine with a gold fringe, and I saw a copy of *Les Modes* spread open on a table, from which she was likely already getting ideas for her wardrobe next season. It lay next to a novel with its pages still uncut, which I knew she would never get around to reading. I sat on a cushioned red velvet chair, its artful fringe brushing the floor, and prepared myself. I helped myself to some finger sandwiches and tea—I was famished—and waited for her interrogation.

"What did you fight about? Does he know you're here?" she demanded, without preamble. I ate another sandwich and considered how to reply. I decided on the truth. It would be liberating to talk about what I'd endured and I pictured her horror, followed by her indignant fury. I could use her comfort. My mother could be a fierce ally.

"Charles and Gertrude were having an affair. She was going to expose it. So he killed her. He's a dangerous man." It came out too rushed, too high-pitched and desperate. My mother's teacup paused on its journey to her mouth.

"What on earth are you saying? Charles adores you. He's been sick with worry while you've been ill." She looked alarmed. I saw the wariness creep into her expression as she assessed me, as if I might be the dangerous one. "No one was killed. Gertrude choked. It was a horrible tragedy. I don't know how often I've had to say it to people." She huffed. I gaped at her. It hadn't occurred to me she wouldn't believe me. But I knew the stubborn set to her mouth so well. My mother was as obstinate as they came, and impossible to persuade once she'd made up her mind about something.

"I know what I saw." My cheeks grew hot. I hadn't seen him actually pour the poison but close enough. "And I wasn't ill; he's been giving me sedatives." She stirred her tea and I watched her struggle with her emotions. I guessed she'd already spent considerable energy trying to convince her friends that Gertrude's death had been an accident and she wasn't ready to accept a different narrative. I knew, too, how much she admired Charles and how proud she'd been of my marriage, which helped her status as well as mine. She hadn't been accepted by her circle easily. I remembered all too well going calling with her when I was younger and leaving cards for women who never responded with a visit. But she'd been remarkably persistent.

"Charles told us about the rest cure. He said you haven't . . . quite been yourself. I know when I'm upset I don't always see things clearly." She spoke gently.

I snorted. Of course he had tried to bias them against me as well. My father wouldn't have been so easily persuaded by Charles's lies, or at least I hoped not, but my mother had always been so susceptible to his charm. She nodded to herself, pleased with her own explanation of events, now the definitive one in her mind. It wasn't the first time my mother had been determined to live in her own reality.

"I've never seen things so clearly," I snapped, my frustration mounting.

"This is coming from a place of anger. Truly, Millie, I won't listen to these outrageous accusations." Now her own voice rose. I sighed, the fight leaving me. Painful as it was, I needed sanctuary here more than I needed her to agree with me. And I knew how insidious gossip could be, and had witnessed how that when rumors were repeated often enough they morphed into established fact. Apparently my supposed instability had become so widely accepted as truth that even my mother hadn't doubted it.

Maybe I shouldn't be too hard on her; after all, I was still struggling to understand what Charles had done.

"I just need to stay here for a while until I figure out what I'm going to do next. Please." I didn't have any kind of plan. My only object had been escape. Refuge.

"It's a good thing your father's not home. Let me handle him, darling. You know he won't like this."

It was true. Even though my father and I were close, I knew how strongly he felt about the sanctity of marriage. He wouldn't like me and Charles living apart, and I'd need to tread carefully. I traced the pink-threaded outline of a rose on my dress.

"You should call on everyone soon, now that you're back in town. Of course the George Daltons won't receive you, you know how they are, but there's no harm in at least trying. You must act as if nothing at all has happened."

"Aside from one of our friends dying at my dinner."

"Yes, well, as I said, that was a tragedy. You have an excellent cook, no one could blame the meal, at least."

I had to suppress the urge to laugh. My mother could be so unwittingly absurd. "Very true. The roast in particular I thought turned out quite well."

We finished our tea, and the normalcy of the ritual seemed strange given how my morning had begun. Even though I still had to worry about convincing my father that my marriage was over, I felt liberated. I had a hot bath and a large supper, and applied a mustard plaster to my twinging ankle. As it turned out, I was spared speaking with my father, as he had to work late in the office.

That night, for the first time in a long time, I wasn't afraid to go to sleep.

CHAPTER 18

❦

I awoke thrashing and panicked, and it took me a minute to remember that I was at my parents' house. Briggs wasn't there, nor was Charles. The blue wallpaper around me soothed me, and bright sunshine poured through the windows.

A young maid called Duffield helped me dress, a gentle girl with a shy, lilting voice, and I'd never been so grateful for a servant's help. I'd missed breakfast downstairs—and my father, thankfully—so she brought me a tray. I glanced at the clock and saw it was actually closer to lunch than breakfast.

"Whenever you're ready, ma'am, there's a gentleman downstairs waiting for you in the drawing room." She smiled shyly and my heart plummeted into my stomach. Had Charles found me already? With the phone out, I'd hoped Briggs hadn't told him what had happened yet. But it was only a matter of time. "Mr. David Hannigan, the butler said."

My heart slowed. David. What on earth could he be doing here?

When I found him seated in the drawing room, I half expected he would be hunched over nervously, as visitors often were in the opulent space. But his legs were spread wide, and he was tapping his homburg on his knee distractedly. He was so completely at ease in his own skin that I envied him. I supposed he was the sort of man who could make himself comfortable anywhere, whether he was at a Bowery saloon or, well, here. Perhaps it came from being a reporter. He was used to the world of high finance, roving between boardrooms and clubs and, I'm sure, the occasional rowdy dance hall.

"Mr. Hannigan. What a pleasant surprise. How on earth did you know I'd be here?"

I sat down across from him elegantly and deliberately to show off my figure to its best advantage. A silly little pretense that I hadn't bothered with since before I'd been married.

"I'm a journalist, Mrs. Turner. I'm rather good at finding things out." He tapped his hat, as if deciding whether to say more. "I visited my father yesterday. He mentioned he'd seen you running out of the estate like it was on fire." He peered at me, giving me time to elaborate, but I didn't reply. I only blushed.

"Did you learn something?" Perhaps he'd caught wind of Charles's financial woes. His personal finances might not merit an article, but if his business were in trouble, that would be another thing entirely. It seemed like it might be, if I'd understood all the details correctly.

He paused a beat. "I debated for a long time whether or not to involve you. I'm still not sure it's the right thing." He looked pained. My pulse raced a little quicker.

"Please. I want to know. Whatever it is."

He nodded, his face grim. "All right. Are you up for a little outing?"

The redbrick apartment building fronted Washington Square Park and had pretty cast-iron bay windows. David hadn't explained our errand, saying only that I would understand soon enough. He said it was better for me to see it for myself. We stood across the street from the building, and it seemed he was waiting for something. Finally, a man I didn't recognize took out his latchkey and opened the building's front door, and we darted quickly across the pavement; it was lucky there was a pause in the traffic just then. David followed the man, tipping his homburg hat at him as he held the door open for us, as if we were also residents. I hesitated a moment and David grabbed my hand.

"Come along, dear."

I was shocked by the intimacy of the gesture, and his presumption that I'd play along. But I did, and the man eyed me appreciatively and winked at David. Then he headed for the elevator and we headed for the stairs, our shoes clacking over black and white tiles.

"That man winked at you. He must think . . . something vulgar."

"Yes, well."

"I don't understand, Mr. Hannigan. Do you live here?" If he did, he was more prosperous than I'd imagined.

"I think it's about time you start calling me David. And no, I don't. That's why I needed someone to let us in."

"You mean we're trespassing?"

"Not exactly."

I clutched the iron stair railing with a gloved hand, trying to decide whether or not to continue without more information. David might have been used to this sort of thing, but I had never done anything remotely illegal. Whatever people thought. But my escape the day before had emboldened me. I followed him up the slippery marble steps until we found ourselves in front of a door on the third floor.

"Take out your hairpins."

"What?" I touched my hat, which sported several large peacock feathers. And then I understood what he had in mind. I could have laughed.

"Just two will be enough."

I obliged, taking off my hat first and then retrieving the hairpins with careful fingers. I watched as he bent one of them open and then bent the end of the other one to make a little handle.

"Still up to your old tricks, I see." If only he knew how much this skill of his had meant to me. I swallowed. It had saved my life.

His hands seemed far too large to manipulate something so small, and he squinted at the knob, so focused that he didn't even flinch when someone slammed a door upstairs. I eyed the hallway nervously, sure someone would happen upon us. Within a few minutes there was a series of little clicks, and he twisted the knob open. He was much more adept at lock picking than I, but then in his line of work, he'd probably had more practice.

The door creaked forward, revealing a sliver of dark hall-way.

"You know, I can still do that, too." I wondered if the memory of that day meant as much to him as it had meant to me. Perhaps he'd forgotten all about it.

"I remember you had a light touch." He smiled at me, his eyes twinkling.

"Well, you should try lacing a lady's boots sometime without a buttonhook handy."

"Oh, I have."

My cheeks tingled with heat as I tried not to picture when David might have had that opportunity. "You're not short on life experience, are you?"

"I guess I'm not."

We stepped into the apartment and closed the door behind us. I noticed there was no art on the walls, not even a print.

"Who lives here? Will he be home anytime soon?" It could only be a man's apartment, with such spare decor.

"The cleaning woman told me that he hasn't been here in some time. More than a month."

I peered through several of the doorways and discovered a library without any books and a sitting room with a single settee. The occupant seemed to spend little time at home. It occurred to me as we wandered through the space that I had almost never been entirely alone with a man besides Charles since our marriage, and that being alone with David now would have risked my reputation, were anyone to know of it. But I trusted David. "I should be nervous to be alone with a man with so much life experience, I suppose."

I said it lightly, as we arrived in the bedroom, my tone teasing and a little provocative. I used to love saying things that shocked people, and I hadn't flirted in ages. It never meant anything when I flirted at tedious dinner parties with tedious old men, but it occurred to me too late that David might not be used to society repartee.

"I hope you know that you're always safe with me." He said it casually, but his eyes were serious and they lingered on mine. I wasn't sure what he meant. Maybe that he wasn't interested and would never make an advance of that sort, or maybe he was just saying that he was a gentleman. I turned away, unsettled.

"You know, this apartment has no kitchen. That's strange, isn't it?"

"The building has maid service and a morning breakfast provided, I believe. It caters to single men." He paused a beat. "And unofficially, married men who . . . desire a second abode."

Whatever the reason we were here, I got the sense that he wanted me to discover it for myself. I went over to the closet and started pawing through the clothes.

"There are some women's things here, too." His comment about the married men suddenly made sense. This was where someone had met his mistress. My hand paused. I recognized a charcoal gray sack suit, finely tailored. I also recognized a single-breasted burgundy vest. A pair of striped trousers.

"These are Charles's things." My voice was soft. Even though I knew now about Gertrude, the apartment made it clear that their affair had gone on for some time. The intimacy of their things, mingled together in the closet, made his heartlessness even harder to comprehend. He'd cared for her enough to arrange this love nest for them, and then he'd killed her. And perhaps it was shameful, knowing now what kind of man Charles was, but his betrayal hurt, too. I'd never suspected my feelings weren't returned, and it was humiliating that I'd been so blind to his true nature. I'd loved him, really loved him, and despite my revulsion and horror over what he'd done, there was a small part of me that maybe still did. It sickened and confused me.

David didn't try to comfort me, which I appreciated; I was embarrassed enough without hearing empty platitudes. He just stood a few feet away with his legs apart, looking sorry for me.

"I hope I did the right thing. Bringing you here."

"Yes, thank you." I wasn't sure whether I meant it. He was a journalist, after all, and he could have brought me here as a test of sorts, to gauge my reaction for himself. Maybe he was trying to ascertain whether I'd already known about the affair and had in fact killed Gertrude in a jealous rage. I wandered over to the vanity, curious to see more clues about their liaisons together. I fingered a pretty silver rouge pot, a silver hair brush. I picked it up, imagining Gertrude sitting here, lazy and satisfied while she smoothed her hair. Her initials were inscribed on the back: "G.L.U."

"I didn't kill her, if that's what you're wondering." I considered for a brief moment revealing exactly how much I really knew about that evening, but I still wasn't sure I could trust him. I wanted to. But my own mother hadn't even believed me, and if he didn't, either, he might publish something awful that would make things even worse.

"I wasn't. I just wanted you to see, in case you didn't know."

I nodded, but couldn't find my voice.

"Come on. You look like you need a stiff drink."

CHAPTER 19

David steered me out of the apartment as someone might direct a friend who had just been in a fight. As if he wanted to get me away quickly before the apartment could hurt me further. It was too late, though. My insides felt bruised.

"Where are we going?" It occurred to me hazily that he might be taking me to a saloon, and that I should protest. We weren't too far from the Bowery, with its gin-soaked dives, dance halls, cheap theaters, beer gardens, and whores. Before I met Charles, I did socialize with a faster set, but not that fast.

"Not sure yet. Somewhere close by."

"Is it—will it be respectable?"

When we emerged from the building it was nearly dusk, which came so early now in the winter. David continued to, steer me forward, and we walked along the damp sidewalk, lined with piles of dirtied, slushy snow.

"Watch your step." He looked at me out of the corner of his eye. "Is it important to you, to go somewhere respectable?"

"Yes, of course." I knew that Café Martin near Madison Square Park would serve ladies alcohol when accompanied by a gentleman, as Charles and I used to have pre-theater drinks there often. I opened my mouth to suggest it, but closed it again. I wasn't dressed for it, of course. I was still in a morning outfit designed for errands, a long, narrow champagne-colored skirt with matching long, fitted coat, the hems patterned with brown braid. I sported sensible pearls in my ears. Besides, some of my supposed friends might be there, and it would be uncomfortable to run into any of them. "Actually, no. No, it isn't important."

"Excellent." We were on a street near the park featuring a few saloons and restaurants. David chose one on the corner, and we went in through the side ladies' entrance together. Inside, it was decked out in dark woods, and the ceiling was cheap stamped tin. Even though it was early, there were several men clustered in front of the long bar, and they all turned to stare at me. They wore suits—this was no dive, at least—and no one would mistake me for a whore or a working-class girl, not with what I was wearing. Still, I was self-conscious as David stepped up to the bar and asked for two whiskies. I hung back and waited. I was grateful for my fine clothes, and I straightened my back, wearing them like armor. I watched one of the men gulp his beer, and pick up a mustache rag from a hook to wipe his face. Another perched a foot on the bar's brass foot rail and never took his eyes off of me. But David got our drinks, and we went together to one of the tables in the back room, where I was relieved to see another couple sharing beers and a plate of oysters.

David slid the whiskey to me. "You've earned this, I think."

I took a tentative sip, and the drink burned as I swallowed. I didn't like the taste, but I liked that warm tingling, the feeling of blood rushing to my cheeks and thighs. I took another sip. "Thank you."

"So. Did you know?" David considered me over his own glass.

I paused, unsure how to reply. I had known the night of Gertrude's death, but afterward that information had been buried in some crevice of my mind. Until yesterday.

"Not until very recently. I suppose you think I had motive." I kept my voice light, but my heart rapped a fast, whiskey-fueled melody. The alcohol had made me bold. It was so much better than the dulling effect of the chloral; it made me feel alive.

"I'll admit the thought crossed my mind." His voice was equally pleasant. "But I've never seriously suspected you."

"I'm glad to hear it." I swirled the whiskey in my glass and wondered if he meant it. My judgment where men were concerned apparently wasn't very good. I'd made a drastic, terrible mistake marrying Charles. As discerning as I thought I'd been when considering my suitors—and I'd had more than a few—somehow I'd chosen a man without a conscience. The candle on the table made the amber liquid glow. "And if I had done it, what then? Would you have written about it? 'Society murderess' would have made a nice headline."

David drank like a man who knew how, taking measured sips without wincing at the burn. He was already halfway through his glass and he seemed looser, his gaze even more direct than usual.

"It would have." The thudding in my chest increased its tempo. "But I like you. Even though we've only begun to get reacquainted. Honestly, I don't know what I would have done."

I had begun to get used to the whiskey, and I drank deeply. The knowledge of Charles's wickedness was still raw.

"I'm sorry, by the way. You probably feel pretty rotten."

I laughed, and it was genuine. If only Charles were guilty of nothing more than an affair. David couldn't begin to guess just how confused and betrayed I truly felt. "That's an understatement if I ever heard one. But you were right about the drink. It's helping a little."

"It will help even more once you get to your second glass."

I smiled at him. I felt daring, and the edges of the room had started to blur. "I do believe you mean to get me drunk."

"It's the best thing for you right now."

"I've never been drunk before." It was true. At the dinner party, I'd been drugged, not drunk. On other occasions, I'd experienced a pleasant buzzing in my body after drinking champagne, but I'd never gotten wild or sick. I wondered what it felt like. I desired nothing more right then than to be just another young woman out on the town in pursuit of a good time—no black-hearted husband to worry about. In fact, no husband at all. "So. Who did that to your nose?"

David often maintained a journalist's careful control of his features, which made it hard for me to guess what he was thinking. But now he raised his eyebrows, crinkling the schooled smoothness of his forehead, and smiled. Surprising him pleased me. "Let me get us another round."

My curiosity was piqued by the time he returned.

"Are you sure you want to hear this? It's not exactly a . . . respectable tale."

"We just returned from the apartment where my husband met his dead mistress. I don't think you can shock me." It was a blunt statement, even for me, but I was so tired of artifice. With David I was tempted to let my guard down. He certainly seemed genuine, and principled, and whether he really was or wasn't, the impression he gave probably made him very good at his job.

He chuckled.

"Fair point. All right." He swallowed deeply from his glass. "I was young, seventeen, and I got talked into a bare-knuckle boxing match in this joint on the Bowery. It was a real hellhole, sawdust on the floor, gangsters in the crowd, that sort of thing. Before I went into the ring people were betting on ratting matches."

I pressed my gloved fingers into the condensation of my glass and hid my expression behind another sip. I'd thought he reminded me of a boxer the first time I had seen him again. And he was right—being part of that sort of exhibition was very, very far from respectable. But I could picture him, with his jacket off, sleeves rolled up, knuckles raw. "And you lost, I take it."

"No, I won." He swigged again from his glass. "Celebrated after by getting good and roaring drunk. There was this woman—if I'd been sober, you understand, I might have realized what she was. But I was young, too, remember."

"She was a prostitute?" I whispered the word.

"I didn't realize it. I thought she was just taken with me. We went upstairs, and before—well, a man burst in and clocked me. Broke my nose. He'd lost money on the match, and they picked my pockets."

I blushed. Of course I knew David was no virgin, even if he was unmarried. He was a man, after all. But his story prompted all sorts of indecent imaginings. I couldn't help being curious as to how many women he'd been with. I watched him spin his glass around and pictured him touching women with that same hand.

"What an exciting life you lead, David."

"Not so exciting anymore. I stopped going to the Bowery after that."

I smiled at him. "I don't believe you."

"It's true. I prefer the Tenderloin now."

We both laughed. The Tenderloin was New York's other famous nightlife destination, located to the west of Times Square and the illuminated stretch of Broadway nicknamed the Great White Way. It was home to Little Africa, and just as full of sin and vice as the Bowery.

"Thank you. For cheering me up." I finished my second drink, and by now the blurred edges of the room had moved inward, so that the world looked like a warped mirror.

"Come on, I'll show you. If you're game for a change in scenery."

I sputtered my drink. "In the Tenderloin?"

"I know a place that's perfectly respectable. It's probably different from what you're used to, though."

"I imagine everywhere in the Tenderloin is different from what I'm used to."

"I imagine you're right."

He held out a hand, and I hesitated for only a moment before taking it.

CHAPTER 20

David hailed a hansom cab after we left the bar and directed the driver to Marshall's Hotel on Fifty-third Street. His thigh pressed against mine in the small carriage, and we looked out the window at the streaks of light blurring together as we clattered up Broadway. I enjoyed having a warm male body next to mine. I didn't feel guilty for thinking it. My marriage was certainly over.

"Do you think I was foolish? For not realizing sooner about Charles?" My words slurred, just a little, and I leaned into him as I spoke. I didn't just mean the affair, but that didn't matter.

"I think we're all a little foolish where love is concerned." He directed his unflinching gaze at me, and my stomach tightened. I could be merely a source to him, the entire evening a ruse to get me to spill my secrets. But maybe he liked me. I was used to men admiring me, and he had to have noticed me that way, at least a little. It sounded like he knew what he was doing when it came to women. I didn't care too much about his motives just then as long as he could distract me from my pain.

David seemed relaxed, and after we checked our coats he led us to a table near a small stage, where there was a Negro pianist and a small band. The music they were playing was like nothing I had ever heard.

"Amazing, aren't they? That's Scott Joplin at the piano." At my blank look, he continued. "He wrote the 'Maple Leaf Rag'? He's a famous ragtime musician."

As I scanned the crowd, I realized two things: first, the place was in fact perfectly respectable; and second, the audience was mixed race. It also contained celebrities. David pointed out the heavyweight boxer Jack Johnson, who was drinking with a white woman. At the table next to them was Diamond Jim Brady, famous for the girth of his person and his accounts, sitting with his girlfriend, actress Lillian Russell.

David left me for a moment to get more drinks at the bar, and as he returned to the table, I saw him say hello to several people. One colored man clapped him on the shoulder, and they laughed at something together, like old friends.

"So what do you think of the music?"

He had brought me a beer this time and a plate of sandwiches for us to share. I was grateful; I wasn't sure if I could manage another whiskey. I went for the sandwich first, and I listened, considering as I ate. It was unusual, unpredictable, the rhythm often interrupted by surprising notes. "It's strange. And intoxicating."

"I hoped you'd like it."

"Do you come here often?"

"All the time."

I was amazed that such a place existed and also that I hadn't known about it. Charles held nativist views, and believed in the purity and superiority of his bloodline. I'd never agreed with him—after all, I didn't come from an old family like he did—but being here made me ashamed I'd never argued with him about it.

"How does one dance to music like this?" The upbeat tempo made me want to move, only I had no idea what steps would make any sense.

"Here. I'll show you."

"What, now?" I was still drunk enough that I let him lead me to the dance floor.

"They call this one the bunny hug." He leaned his torso over at an angle and put his arms around my shoulders, and the silliness of the pose made me laugh. I did the bunny hug with him, and soon other couples were joining as well. It looked ridiculous, and that was the point. It was wild and fun, and made the stately waltzes I'd danced at Sherry's seem boring. After we bunny-hugged, he showed me something he called the turkey trot, and then the grizzly bear. Each was more ridiculous than the last, and I loved it.

We danced for at least an hour, until I was warm and winded. I hadn't expected I could have so much fun after everything that had happened. In fact, I couldn't remember the last time I'd had as much fun as this.

"You're a fast learner." We sat back down at our table. It was loud, so David moved his chair nearer to mine.

"You're a good teacher." I patted David's hand and then let my fingers linger. I'd taken my gloves off at some point, I couldn't remember when, and I traced the outline of his knuckles. David stiffened and watched me, not moving an inch. I wondered how Charles would react if he could see me right now. He already wanted to kill me, but I liked the idea of bruising his ego. He assumed every woman wanted him, and he was usually right; I wished I could show him how revolting I found him now.

David might be poor, but he was handsome and capable and a terrific dancer. I was grateful for the distraction he offered. My mind kept wandering upstairs, to the shabby little hotel rooms, and I was almost drunk enough to ask him up. I'd never been with a man besides Charles, and I wanted to cleanse him from my system.

I took a large swig of my beer. "Would you have written about me? If it had been me."

He reached over slowly to tuck a strand of hair behind my ear. It had come loose on the dance floor.

"No, I wouldn't have."

The beating of my heart was as riotous as the music.

"So why are you here with me?" I turned his hand over and traced the lines of his palm. I stroked delicately, and I watched his chest heave beneath his vest.

"Are you looking for the answer?"

"I went to a party with a palm reader once. I don't remember how it works."

I stopped tracing and looked up at him with big eyes. He was about as drunk as I was, and inched closer. I thought he would kiss me, but instead he spoke to me in a low voice, his breath tickling my ear.

"Come on, I think it's probably time to get you home."

He steered me out to the street with the same efficiency he'd removed me from the apartment. I fought him and tried to turn back.

"I'm not ready. I want another drink."

But he kept a hand on my elbow, then put an arm around my waist, directing me with gentle pressure. "I know you do. But I think you've had enough."

"You promised to get me drunk."

"You are drunk."

We stepped into the street, and the icy air assaulted us. I turned around. His arm was still around my waist and I burrowed into his chest.

"Let's go back inside. It's warm."

"It'll be warm when you get home."

"I don't want to go home." I stepped back. The cold air chapped my lips. My vision blurred and I blinked. "Why can't I just stay here tonight? You could stay with me."

The words echoed in my ears as if someone else had spoken them, and I was exhilarated by my own boldness. I imagined what his kiss would be like, his touch, and my skin tingled in anticipation. Once, I would never have dreamed of doing something so daring, but my life had become unrecognizable. David stared at me, then ran a hand over his face. The wind whistled between the buildings.

"Jesus."

I snuggled deeper into my coat. The building in front of me doubled. "What? Don't tell me you've never taken a girl to a hotel room before."

"Not a girl like you. And certainly not a girl as drunk as you." He reached out a hand to hail a hansom cab. The horse started slowly clopping toward us from the other end of the street.

"So you're turning me down?"

I hadn't considered that he might. The invitation had been impulsive and now I was mortified. "You're turning *me* down?" I wobbled in my boots and he caught my arm. "But you're just some journalist. A nobody."

I hadn't meant to say it. I couldn't focus my eyes well enough to make out his expression, but I guessed that there probably wasn't one. He would have hidden his feelings behind his journalist's mask.

"I didn't mean—"

"It's all right." The carriage pulled up beside us, and I let him help me inside. "Drink a glass of water when you get home."

I winced. "Wait, David—"

But the carriage had already begun to pull away.

CHAPTER 21

❦

My head throbbed and my mouth tasted of sour whiskey as I paced outside of my father's study. It felt as if I'd had a strong dose of chloral, only more painful. I'd been back late and must have reeked of booze when Duffield helped me into my nightclothes. I hoped my condition wouldn't be too obvious. But there was nothing I could do about it now. It was Saturday, and I couldn't avoid my father forever.

My fist hovered in the air. I drew a breath and knocked, and my father's voice boomed through the door. "Come in."

I ran my tongue over my teeth, as if I could sharpen it and make it form the words it needed to. Words that could make my father understand.

"Father." I opened the door and smiled at the pile of books on his desk. He had a habit of quoting texts when he wished to make a point, often from memory. His study was smaller than Charles's, cozy even, and I'd interpreted it as a subtle rebellion of sorts against my mother's ostentation. The smell of his cigars infused the space, and the familiar clutter—a Brownie camera, a globe of the world tucked into the corner, framed lithographs of satirical French scenes that he'd picked up on one of our trips to Paris—all of it brought on a wave of girlhood nostalgia that put me more at ease.

I debated where to begin. After my mother's reaction I knew I'd have to play this carefully. Everyone else already seemed to think I was crazy, and I couldn't bear for him to as well.

"Millie." The voice came not from behind the desk, where my father sat, but to my left. For a moment, I couldn't move. My heart beat painfully in my chest, and the throbbing in my head intensified. My dry mouth turned drier still and the back of my neck tingled. I turned, slowly, unable to draw breath.

Charles had his hands braced against the back of a chair, and now he sat in it, crossing his legs and looking indolent, as if he hadn't a care in the world. I licked my lips. I longed for a glass of water. I sat as well, only because I was afraid my legs would give out. What had Briggs told him? Had she been acting on his orders? I studied him carefully, waiting for him to betray some sign of what he knew, but he only gazed at me with loving concern.

Panic coursed through me, but I fought hard to keep it at bay. I couldn't let him see that I was afraid. It would be better if he believed me a weak fool.

"Darling. So good to see you." I suppressed a shudder and forced a bright smile.

"I've been so worried, Millie. Briggs said you left without sharing your plans, and when you didn't come to our house in town—" He touched a long finger against his lips, as if suppressing a strong emotion. "Thank God you're safe here."

I exhaled slowly and clutched the velvet arms of the chair. I marveled he could make such a declaration with a straight face. "Yes, I'm quite well, and quite safe."

My father studied us with his usual shrewdness. His ability to read people had helped make him a success. He was the only one who'd never taken a shine to Charles, and I had to hope he could sense his falseness now.

"Millie, you know how I feel about hiding from one's problems. If you and Charles are having difficulties, you'll never resolve them if you're not under the same roof." His voice was a low rumble. My mouth tightened in disappointment, and fear. I desperately needed sanctuary here. And telling some version of the truth was out of the question with Charles present. I'd need to be as cunning as he was. More so.

"I quite agree, Father." I spoke sweetly and calmly, determined not to show a trace of the wildness featured in Charles's slander about me to our friends. "Only Charles is trying to have me committed to an insane asylum, so we wouldn't be under the same roof there, either." I spoke quietly and somberly, and heaved a sigh. "I didn't like his doctor, so I came to the city to see Dr. Thatcher. Mother's doctor, you know. An asylum seemed so terribly extreme that I thought it prudent to get another opinion."

"An asylum? Charles, what's all this?" My father's voice rose and his cheeks turned blotchy. My father was usually slow to anger, but I knew exactly what would provoke him. I didn't know how much Charles actually cared about institutionalizing me, given Briggs had been willing to make an attempt on my life at Rose Briar Hall, but it would lend credence to his pretense about my melancholia. Something flashed behind Charles's eyes, only for an instant. Had it been annoyance? Anger? He probably came here today to speak to my father about my medical care and I'd undercut him by revealing his plan before he was ready.

When Charles spoke, though, he was completely composed. "I'm afraid Millie has been suffering from hysteria. Fits of rage and forgetfulness. She actually attacked her own maid before she left Rose Briar Hall." Charles's voice cracked. "It's gotten to a point where it's more than I can manage. I want her to get the very best care."

His characterization of what happened between me and Briggs infuriated me, and I dug my nails into my palms but kept my expression placid. My father's bushy eyebrows shot into his forehead. "Hysteria? She seems perfectly herself." His jowl quivered. I kept my expression carefully neutral.

"I am, Father. Like I said, this doctor has things all confused. I only want to stay here until we can get another diagnosis. I'd like us all to agree before any drastic steps are taken, and Charles was prepared to have me committed without even telling you."

My father scowled at Charles. His eyes darted back and forth between us as he considered my request, and I could tell he was thinking quickly. "Millie can stay here while we get this sorted out. But, Charles, I'm very concerned by your report. Millie, you seem well to me, but a husband would know better. Whatever . . . disagreements Charles and I may have had, I know he cares about you. I'll choose a doctor personally to do a thorough evaluation."

My pulse quickened. I could scarcely believe what I was hearing. My father, the great judge of character, thought Charles had real affection for me. Charles had fooled everyone—all of our friends, my mother, apparently even my father. His charm hid his lies too well. I'd never succeed in leaving him so long as everyone trusted him. His version of events would always win out over mine.

Somehow, I had to show the world who he really was.

Charles shifted his gaze to me as he answered. "I only want to do whatever is best for Millie. Please let me know what the doctor says." His green eyes anchored me in place. In the past, a single look had been all it took to compel me to do anything. His presence pulled you toward him, strong as an ocean current, only now I understood that I could drown if I failed to break free. "If both doctors come to the same conclusion . . . well. Millie, you may not want to go to an institution, but I'm afraid at that point it would no longer be up to you. Legally speaking."

I gaped at him. I thought I'd been smart to recommend getting another opinion, but he had probably foreseen that, and my request aligned neatly with his own plans. The ruse of the institution had probably mattered less when I was trapped at

Rose Briar Hall, but now that I was in town and my parents could observe me for themselves, it might make things simpler for him. An overdose in a mental institution would be easier for everyone to believe, and it would allow Charles to distance himself from what happened. There would be fewer questions.

Surely the doctor would be able to tell that I was well, though. His confidence confused me.

"A sound compromise. Thank you for your wisdom, Father." There was nothing else I could do, at least not yet. I stood and kissed my father's cheek. Then, inspired, I bent over and kissed Charles's as well. I caught a whiff of perfume, almost certainly Lily Applebee's, given the woman stank like a French bordello. His skin was cold as marble. I swallowed my disgust. I wanted to shake my father by the shoulders and force him to recognize the monster sitting in our midst, but Charles was so clever to have accused me with hysteria. If I tried to tell my father everything that had really happened, he'd only see it as evidence of Charles's claim.

My father smiled at my affectionate gesture and stood. "That's the right spirit. I should give you two a moment alone."

When he left, it was as if the temperature in the air dropped. I hugged myself. Being alone with Charles scared me, but I reassured myself that here, in my parents' house, there was little he could do.

"I'm sure I don't need to tell you how unhappy you've made me," he said, and recrossed his legs. So he was continuing the charade, even without my father present. He must not know just how much I'd uncovered, and I'd be safer to keep it that way.

"I can't imagine. It isn't fair to you. Having me as a wife. Don't you want to be free of me? I wouldn't fight it, if you wanted a divorce." I squeezed my eyes shut and flicked at the corner of one, as if I were wiping away a tear. The words were wine on my tongue, intoxicating, and the rush of them made my cheeks flush. I needed to see for myself how he'd react. Surely divorcing me would be preferable to having me murdered in an insane asylum. I still struggled to accept that he could be so completely evil. "We could do it quickly, and quietly. Out of state, maybe." Even if we stayed in New York, sometimes the judges sealed the divorce papers to keep the details from the press, especially for the upper classes.

Charles was silent, and I peeked at him from beneath my eyelids. "Going out of state wouldn't matter. Everyone would still know we'd divorced. I'd lose half my clients, maybe more." He spoke so softly I had to strain to hear. His honesty startled me.

"But we've weathered so much scandal already. And"—I feigned wiping away another tear—"you could remarry. Find someone more worthy of you. Look at Genevieve Folsom. She remarried, and she seems quite happy."

My words hung between us like a haze of smoke. He waved them away.

"Enough. You're going to get better, Millie, and everything will be like before. We won't speak of this again."

I stood, overcome with anger and dismay. I knew he was ruined, but he'd been so successful in the past that surely he could recover, even with the ignominy of a divorce hindering him. My offer should have tempted him, but he hadn't even considered it. He was still determined to have me locked away. "We both know I'm not sick. Whatever doctor my father chooses will see it, too."

I thought I detected a hint of a smirk. "We'll see."

I frowned, bemused. And then I inhaled sharply as comprehension dawned. Charles knew my father would pick a doctor in our circle, someone who he knew personally and who certainly would have already been poisoned by rumors about me. He thought he'd already won.

But I'd learned from Charles. He was masterful at manipu-
lating people, but now I saw what he'd done and how he'd
done it. I was like the audience member who suddenly could
spot all of the magician's tricks. I just had to find a way to
make everyone else see them, too.

I hurried out of the room, not bothering to say goodbye.
Then I called for my mother's carriage.

I was going to see David.

I didn't know where David lived, but it was easy enough to
find out the address of *The World News*. It was near its com-
petitor, *The New York Times*, on Longacre Square. I hadn't
quite gotten used to its new name. They had rechristened it
Times Square a few years ago after the *Times'* new headquarters, an impressive twentysomething-floor building where they
launched fireworks from the roof every New Year's Eve. This
year they would be lowering an electrically lit ball down the
flagpole, which I had to admit sounded rather spectacular.
The World News headquarters was decidedly less impressive.
It was shorter and dingier, and I was glad I was spared the
errand of actually having to go inside when I spotted David approaching on the sidewalk in conversation with another man.
A colleague, probably.

I approached tentatively. I'd behaved so abominably last
night and I was thoroughly ashamed of myself. After my
meeting with Charles, I couldn't help but compare the two
men in my mind. David's confident, purposeful stride was
so different from Charles's affected gait, always slow and refined, as if he were conscious of the eyes that might be on
him. David looked a little worse for wear today, his brown
hair wilder than usual under his homburg and his face sporting the stubble of a man who hadn't bothered to shave. It
only made him more handsome. Charles's features were more
striking, but had a feminine, almost beautiful quality. David's

were more unassuming at first, but the more time I spent with him, the more I wondered if David was actually the better looking of the two.

When he saw me, he stopped short, and his friend had to look over his shoulder for him. David looked surprised, and maybe a little annoyed. I couldn't blame him.

"Mrs. Turner."

I flinched. His formality hurt. He'd started calling me Millie at some point last night, and the intimacy of hearing my Christian name on his lips had thrilled me. He obviously hadn't forgiven me for my behavior. Some of the details of the evening were fuzzy, but I remembered my faux pas before we parted. I couldn't bear what he must think of me now.

"Do you have a moment to speak privately?"

His friend doffed his hat. He looked me up and down appreciatively. "I know when I'm not wanted. Your tastes have grown finer, eh?" He laughed at David before entering the building, leaving us alone. I blushed.

"I only have a minute. I'm on deadline." He squared his shoulders.

"I just wanted to apologize for last night. I'd never drunk whiskey before."

He shrugged, his features neutral. "You had a rough day. You were feeling pretty low."

I hated how distant he sounded. "Yes, I was. And it would have been a mistake. So thank you."

I cringed. It had come out wrong. He studied me and I pinched my purse tightly between my fingers. His friend's comment a moment ago made me wonder if he preferred earthier women. He'd had no trouble resisting me, anyway.

"Whatever you may think, I'm a gentleman. Most of the time."

"Of course." I looked down at our shoes, mine shiny black leather, laced tightly and peeking out under my burgundy skirt, his street-worn and brown. I'd thought that because he was a brawler and a housebreaker that he would be equally as unscrupulous when it came to women. I'd been wrong. If anyone had taken advantage of the situation, it had been me. I'd treated him as no more than a diversion, and he deserved better than that.

"Is that all? I have to get back to work."

I didn't want our conversation to end just yet, but I also needed his help. "I was wondering if you knew anything else. About that night. About my husband."

It was the wrong thing to say. I sounded desperate, and his mouth twitched when I mentioned Charles. He fidgeted, adjusting his vest, checking his pocket watch. "It's not the only story I'm pursuing, Mrs. Turner."

His tone, unemotional before, grew chilly.

"I see." I clutched my purse even tighter. Picked some particles off my gloves. "It's Millie, by the way. Not Mrs. Turner. We're still friends, aren't we?"

He didn't answer me right away. The pause stretched on too long, my cheeks growing hotter with each second.

"I will always admire you, Mrs. Turner, but time changes people. You're different than I remembered. It was foolish of me to expect otherwise."

I pressed my lips together to suppress a whimper. I hadn't thought I could feel worse, but now tears threatened. No one of his class had ever spoken so boldly to me before.

His class. The words snagged in my mind. When had I become such a snob?

"Well, if the story still interests you, I have some things you might want to see." I reached into my purse and pulled out the bundle of papers I'd taken from Charles's desk. They'd seemed reasonably incriminating, and I had no doubt David would understand them even better than I. I'd hesitated to trust him before, but the conference in my father's study that morning made it clear I had no choice. And after last night, I did trust David; he'd shown more character than I had.

He took the papers and his fingers brushed mine, making my breath catch.

"I'll take a look. No promises it leads to anything." He touched the brim of his hat as a parting gesture and walked into the building. I watched him go, my feet rooted to the spot, utterly humiliated.

CHAPTER 22

My stomach jolted forward along with the carriage. I wore one of my favorite afternoon dresses, in a rich purple with black embroidered flowers. I'd sent one of my parents' footmen for my clothes on Long Island, and Briggs hadn't been able to refuse him. At least I looked well. I'd waited only until the day after seeing David to embark upon the next step in my plan: winning back my friends. I couldn't count on David to publish something about Charles, and even if he did, it might not be enough to sway opinion against him. If I truly wanted to redeem my reputation, I needed my friends to see for themselves that I wasn't the hysterical madwoman Charles had claimed. That I wasn't suicidal. If I could make them see that, I'd be safer.

I knew some of my acquaintances would be out or wouldn't receive me, but at least I could leave my card, and they could ask their butlers for details on my demeanor and appearance, which was better than nothing. My mother was more optimistic about my chance for success; in her view, I was a curiosity, and everyone would be eager for the gossip I could deliver.

I mentally tallied my list of stops. The Carters, Evansons, Wainwrights, Richmonds, and Phippses had all been there that night, but I hardly knew if that made them more likely to receive me or less. They had seen my outburst at the dinner, and Gertrude's death. I didn't remember the part of the night that followed after I fainted, but could easily picture the hushed exclamations, the hurried retreats.

There were those I knew for certain wouldn't receive me, among them the Daltons, the Rutherfords, William Vanderbilt II and his wife, Virginia, even though William and Charles had bonded over their love of cars and yachting. I would still leave my card, since I had little to lose. And sometimes people surprised you.

Then there were those who I considered intimates: Arabella and Percy Burton, of course, as well as the Kents, Marcuses, and Stocktons. I would visit them last, I decided, to help make myself feel better. Under normal circumstances, my friends might have called upon me when I returned to town rather than the other way around, but these were hardly normal circumstances.

I decided to visit the Daltons first; I didn't believe in procrastinating unpleasant tasks. Better to have them over and done with. Their house on Fifth Avenue was as grand as my parents', without being as gaudy, and I couldn't help feeling a little nervous as I walked up the stone stoop, flanked with statues of lions. Rich as my father had become, and as prominent a man as I had married, I still felt like the daughter of the owner of a dry goods store whenever I attempted to mix with my social betters. Once I would have laughed off a snub, but being married to Charles had made me more sensitive; I had allowed his social ambitions to matter to me. Because he had mattered to me. David had reminded me how little I used to care about that sort of thing, and it made me braver. Christina Dalton was just a false, pretentious, mean-spirited gossip who happened to be from a very old and wealthy family. I rang the bell.

The butler who answered was as old as the hills, and as unmoving.

"Millie Turner. Is Mrs. Dalton in? I'm back in town and thought I'd call to say hello."

He took my card, his arm extending at a glacial pace, and then studied it as if it held the answer to some great mystery.

"Mrs. Dalton is out," he said. I had expected as much. Odds were she truly was out, since he didn't even have to go and check; I received the same answer any visitor would. She usually didn't have as many engagements as my mother—she had no need to exhaust herself by trying that hard—but it was more than likely she had somewhere else to be.

My next five calls had the same result, and I wondered if perhaps they were at the same gathering together. I was growing bored, my back stiff and my throat dry. I longed for tea. As I arrived at Anna Carter's house, I saw an acquaintance leaving after her own call, and sat up straighter. At last, I knew one of my friends was home.

The butler was a friendly man in his forties, not as stiff and distant as many of the butlers one encountered, and even smiled at me when he took in my fine clothes. I looked like the sort of lady who should be calling on his mistress, and when I gave him my card, he closed the door and said he would go and see if she was in. He was gone only a moment, the space of two breaths, and when he reappeared, his face was stony.

"I'm afraid Mrs. Carter is out."

"I see."

I swallowed and lingered on the stoop a moment before turning away, embarrassed. Of course, people pretended to be out for all sorts of reasons—I'd done it myself many times, and it wasn't always meant as a snub. But this time, I knew it almost certainly was, and it stung. Anna Carter and I had attended the theater together with our husbands, had dined together countless times, and even shared a few secrets. I knew that her husband snored, and she knew how desperately I had hoped for a child. I had always found her warm and funny and genuine. But now she wouldn't even allow me into her home.

My hand shook as my driver helped me into the carriage. It astounded me how easily my friends had believed the worst about me. They actually thought I'd killed a woman, never mind that there hadn't been any kind of official inquiry. Society had acted as my judge and jury, and found me guilty. I hadn't even been given the chance to defend myself.

I took a deep breath. I wanted to give up and go home. But I knew I had to force myself to soldier on. I only needed for a few calls to go well—just a few and the gossip would begin to spread. She looked so well, so calm, I imagined them saying. I pictured Anna Carter and Christina Dalton in conference together, looking contrite as they admitted there had been a terrible misunderstanding, and that they had been too quick to cast blame.

At the next house, I was turned away again, and at the one after. I consoled myself with my daydreams of how sorry everyone would be. Then my thoughts turned to David, and how pretentious I'd been. I'd treated him the way my so-called friends were treating me now. Even though I'd propositioned him, I'd never seriously considered him as a true romantic prospect, and he knew it. I could hardly blame him for turning me down and scorning my company.

As I nestled into my cushy velvet seat, humiliated, it seemed absurd that I had once cared more about friends like these than a man like him. His good opinion was worth a thousand times more than Christina Dalton's. And his rejection hurt a thousand times worse. The swoop in my belly when I thought of him had nothing to do with the rocking of the carriage, and I chastised myself again for my behavior. He'd probably never even been interested in me romantically, and I'd allowed myself to confuse his professional attention for flirtation. And what had I wanted from him, exactly? Someone to make me forget Charles's treachery for a brief while? Something more? I hardly knew.

I forced myself to push him out of my mind. I tried once more at the house of Florence Dewy, a virtuous widow who I'd never liked much, but at the very least it was my last stop before I went to Arabella's house. Florence lived in a handsome row house, modest compared to my parents' home but scrupulously maintained, the black iron stair rails on the stoop perfectly shined. I was turned away, as I expected, and as I descended the stairs, I spied a young woman rounding the corner toward the servants' entrance who I'd seen before. Sophia Lester, who had been Gertrude's personal maid.

"Lester." I spoke before I had time to process that I had, and she paused and turned toward me. My tongue stalled.

"Mrs. Turner."

Lester was a pretty brunette, bosomy and pert. She turned and examined me, a wary look in her eyes. I approached her, unsure of what precisely I meant to say. *Did you know that your mistress was having an affair with my husband? Did she confide in you?* By her expression, I felt sure she had.

"I'm so sorry for your loss." I wondered if she believed, as so many did, that I had killed Gertrude. It was impossible to tell, and given our class difference I doubted she would accuse me outright. I'd never given much consideration before to how often servants must have to restrain their opinions and feelings.

"Thank you." She stared at me, as if gauging my sincerity. "Mrs. Dewy was very kind to offer me a position. Afterward."

Mrs. Dewy was known for her charity work, which I'd always thought merely provided cover for her sanctimony. Now I softened toward her. I doubted anyone else had bothered to remember that Gertrude's maid would need new employment after Gertrude's death. I hadn't.

"I'm glad."

My fingers were frozen stiff inside of my fur-lined kid

gloves. Lester shifted in her shoes and looked back toward the house. If I wanted to know what she knew, I'd have to speak soon. And the words tumbled out, awkward and too sharp.

"I know, you know. That Gertrude was having an affair with Charles."

The bare branches of the linden tree shook in a gust of wind. Lester sucked in her breath but didn't break my gaze.

"It wasn't right. I told her so." She pointed her chin up, a half nod. "But she didn't deserve to die that way. And it just breaks my heart about their poor unborn baby."

I gasped, a strangled noise that the wind carried away. I was so overcome that I couldn't breathe for a moment, and then choked when I finally inhaled, wheezing and coughing. Gertrude was pregnant. She was pregnant with Charles's baby, and he had killed her anyway. I closed my eyes, my head suddenly aching, and hid my face behind my glove. For the briefest instant I doubted whether he really could have done it. His wickedness seemed to have no bounds.

"You didn't know? That's why she was pushing so hard for him to divorce." Sophia Lester had an easy, direct way of speaking, and unusual gray eyes that bored into me. "She was planning to tell you about the baby. She told me so."

I couldn't find my voice. It had frozen in the cold air. And I didn't want Sophia Lester to see me cry. So I turned and hurried toward my carriage, too ashamed to look back and see Lester's face, filled with either judgment or pity.

Once inside, I let the tears slip down my cheeks. Gertrude hadn't only been planning to tell me about the affair the night of the party. She'd planned to tell me about her child, so that I'd leave Charles, or let Charles leave me for her. Charles might have been able to salvage our marriage and his good name if it had been only an affair, but a baby was another thing entirely. He wasn't prepared to ruin his reputation, so he'd killed her.

There was absolutely nothing Charles wouldn't do to protect himself: that much was abundantly clear. I was both angry at the unfairness of his lies and terrified of the power he still held over me. The consequences of my social failure struck me afresh. I wasn't merely trying to save my reputation; my very life was at stake. The seriousness of my mission was both awful and surreal. If I couldn't convince my friends of my innocence, I'd die, just as Gertrude had. But first I'd be locked away in an asylum where no one would hear me scream.

CHAPTER 23

Arabella would know what to do. I'd never seen her discomposed by anything, and she was as smart as anyone I'd ever met. She was a bit fast, but almost everyone liked her, even some of the stodgier women in our circle. She had that effect on people. She was always in good humor, and she made everything more fun.

When I finally arrived at her house, my tears had dried, but I was emotional and weary and relieved that I would finally be received by a friend. I longed to tell her about Gertrude's baby. About everything. If anyone would believe me, it was her.

There was another carriage stopped out front, which meant she was in and had another caller. Even though it meant I would be able to squeeze in a second social call, just then I wished only to see Arabella. But it couldn't be helped.

The butler opened the door. I had called here often enough in the past that he knew me on sight. I smiled at him and unbuttoned my coat.

"I'm afraid Mrs. Burton is out." He wouldn't meet my eyes. Hurt swelled inside, feeding a well of tears, but I pushed them down.

"I'm sure she's not, Rogers. I see a carriage right there."

Arabella, who smoked like a chimney and played cards for money, was not the type to shun someone because of a bit of gossip. She delighted in anything salacious and liked to do things that raised eyebrows. I stepped inside without invitation and handed him my coat. It was impossibly rude, but I was sure there had been a misunderstanding. I barged into the drawing room, where Arabella was laughing hard, her signature bray that made some cringe but I adored. She was pouring tea for Christina Dalton.

When she saw me, she shot out of her chair.

"Arabella, dear, I'm so glad to see you." I expected her to embrace me, but to my surprise, she didn't even smile. Her dark eyes flashed with something like annoyance.

"Excuse us, Mrs. Dalton. We just need a private word."

She placed a hand on my arm and carefully steered me back toward the hall. Christina sniffed. Her expression was easy to read. She was scandalized. "Thank you for the tea, Mrs. Burton, but I really must be going."

Her dress whipped about her ankles as she passed us, and she maintained a careful distance, as if I carried a disease.

"But you've only just arrived. Do stay."

Christina Dalton only sniffed again, looked down at us over her straight and elegant nose, and accepted her coat from the butler. "I apologize, but I quite forgot I have another engagement."

And then she was gone.

"Good, now we can catch up properly," I said, my voice light. Arabella must have turned me away because of Mrs. Dalton. But her features remained expressionless.

"It's such a surprise to see you." Her manner was formal, reserved.

"Arabella, do let's sit down. I've missed you terribly."

Arabella didn't move. She was as beautiful as ever, in a stunning red afternoon dress that complemented her shiny dark hair. She normally had a cigarette between her fingers and its absence surprised me, until I remembered that Christina Dalton abhorred the smell.

"I'm afraid you can't stay." Her eyes softened the slightest bit, but she wouldn't meet my gaze.

"Don't tell me you're cutting me, too. Because of some absurd gossip?" My voice was too high.

"Mrs. Turner, I know we were friendly in the past, but even I have to draw the line somewhere. Surely you couldn't expect things to be the same, after what you did."

I heaved a breath. She looked like Arabella and sounded like Arabella, but surely this cruel creature was not actually her. We had been the closest of friends, and she dismissed our history as merely "friendly"?

"I didn't do anything. How can you believe it?"

Arabella considered me. I had always admired her haughty confidence, but I'd never before been on the receiving end of her disdainful stare. "Charles told everyone you weren't well. That he couldn't even bring you into company. Of course we all assumed . . ."

I clenched my dress in a fist, struggling to contain my anger. Charles had been thorough in his work. I knew he had a silver tongue, but I'd never imagined even Arabella would be susceptible. I'd expected her to be my ardent defender, insisting as my mother had that Gertrude had choked on her tea. I thought she'd listen to me when I told her about the affair, and the baby, and the lengths Charles had gone to in order to protect himself from ruin.

"You assumed the worst. After everything we have shared together."

A tear slipped out of the corner of my eye and I wiped it away. Arabella looked uneasy, but not sorry. She'd always liked Charles and been proud of my marriage, as my mother had. My place in society had always been a couple of notches above hers, but she'd never been the jealous type. She'd always liked having influential friends. My father's wealth and my marriage had brought all kinds of false hangers-on flocking to me, but I'd always thought I'd been able to spot them. Now

I questioned everything. I'd aimed high in choosing Charles, and those who had been so eager to bask in my ascent were apparently all too eager to watch me fall.

"You as good as accused your own husband of having an affair. I was there. And then Gertrude—well. You know, of course."

"He *was* having an affair." More tears spilled out. I had wanted to appear poised and instead I was on the verge of losing control.

"No one believes that. Charles is devoted to you. We have all felt so sorry for him." She smoothed her skirt. She motioned to the butler, who held out my coat, but I didn't take it right away. I could picture all too easily how Charles had spread rumors about me after the dinner party, currying sympathy from our circle. Poor Charles, with his deranged wife. They all trusted him so implicitly that even his outward flirtations with Lily Applebee hadn't been questioned.

Or maybe they did know and didn't care. He was from a better family, and richer than me, so they thought. So they'd take his side, whatever he said. They were leeches.

I prayed that David would make them see the light.

"Whatever Charles told you was a lie. I thought you were my friend."

Arabella took out a cigarette from her little jeweled case, her face impassive. I watched as she lit it, breathed in the smell that I had come to associate with her. I had been as mistaken in her character as I had been in Charles's. I took my coat and left, and didn't allow myself to look back.

CHAPTER 24

The elevator creaked and clattered. I hadn't gone straight home, even though my neck was stiff and my heart bruised.

A little more mortification wouldn't make much difference. I couldn't feel any worse than I already did.

"*World News*, ma'am." The elevator operator appraised me with unprofessional interest, his buttoned jacket looking a bit grubby at the neck and cuffs, a far cry from the shiny buttoned men with averted gazes at my father's department stores.

"Thank you."

A haze of cigarette smoke hovered over the newsroom and I coughed. Dozens of scratched wooden desks crowded the space without any apparent order, piled high with newspapers. Exposed pipes ran along the ceiling, and brass pendant lamps dangled. Men shouted over the din of clacking typewriters, shirtsleeves rolled past forearms, cigarettes dangling precariously from open lips. I watched for a minute, intimidated but fascinated, too. There was a reception desk, but it was currently empty of its occupant, and I had no idea how to find David. I turned around, but the elevator had already gone back down.

A whistle whizzed by my back, then another.

"You lost, ma'am?"

A tall, mustached man with a wide smile and blocky teeth approached, hand outstretched.

"John Ratchet. Something I can do for you?"

The frenzied activity behind him didn't cease, but a few men looked up to watch the exchange.

"I'm looking for David Hannigan. I'm a source."

"Uh-huh. David!" He bellowed without even bothering to turn around. And then I saw him. He'd been hidden behind one of the stacks of papers and now he strode toward me, energetic and purposeful.

"Mrs. Turner. I'm surprised to see you here." His eyes darted down, then up again, inspecting me. I got the impression sources didn't just drop in like this very often, or perhaps just not ones like me. The intrusion probably wasn't welcome. I was wrong, I decided; it was possible to feel worse than I had before. I hadn't yet reached the bottom of my well of shame and I was more embarrassed than I'd been after being turned away by butler after butler. I couldn't bear to remember how we'd last parted and didn't expect this encounter to go any better. But I was desperate. And he was a decent man, who would at least listen to what I had to say. Whatever else he thought of me, he might be the only person I knew who would actually believe me.

"Is there somewhere we can talk?"

"Who's the broad, Hannigan?" a reedy, balding fellow shouted from the back of the room.

"Sure. This way." He led me to a tiny office housing a single battered desk, a hard-backed chair, a table lamp. A window faced Times Square below, which was even busier than the newsroom. He closed the door, muffling a catcall behind it.

"This is my editor's office. I'm not sure when he'll be back. I don't have tea or anything to offer. There's probably whiskey somewhere, but I think we can both agree that's not a good idea." I winced. He gestured toward a chair in front of the desk and I took it. I wouldn't have the strength to stay standing for what I'd come to say. He sat on the edge of the desk, facing me, so close in the tiny office I could have reached out and touched him. "Look, Mrs. Turner, I'm sorry for yesterday. I was rude." His words were as stiff as mine had been. "That night—I know you were blotto, but you weren't wrong about what you said."

"Don't say that. I was awful."

"You and I live in different worlds. I needed reminding. Things were simpler when we were younger, weren't they?" His smile was wistful and a little crooked.

Even as a girl, I'd known he was an idealist. I liked that about him, that he believed the world could be fairer than it was. "Perhaps they only seemed so."

"Perhaps." He paused, then took off his jacket, tossing it over the chair behind him. The radiator was pumping out steam and it was stifling. After suffering without heat for so long at Rose Briar Hall, it didn't bother me much. I watched, entranced, as he rolled up his shirtsleeves. "About the documents you gave me yesterday . . . Do you understand what was in them?"

I twisted my gloves in my lap. "More or less. Charles is ruined."

David rubbed his jaw. "It's worse than that, actually. He's been swindling his clients. He lost a fortune in the Bankers' Panic, and the returns he's been reporting are fake. He's been signing new clients to pay dividends to the old, but he won't be able to keep it up forever. His whole business is a house of cards."

A spark of hope ignited. If it became public that Charles had cheated his clients—including many of our friends—I might stand a chance against him. "I hadn't realized it was that bad."

"Look. I know you're angry at him right now, because of

the affair. This is a great story, and I want it, but I don't like taking advantage of people if I can help it." He crossed his arms, and worry creased his brow. His concern took the sharp edge off my pain. Perhaps he cared a little. "If I publish this, it's going to destroy him. I don't want you to do something you might regret."

I let out a breathy laugh. "I won't regret it. That's what I want you to do."

He studied me, apparently gauging my sincerity. "Showing you that apartment . . . maybe I overstepped. I wasn't using my best judgment. It was selfish of me." I almost laughed again, but his face was so serious that I couldn't. He was so good. Whatever his motives had been, I knew they weren't selfish. If anything, I wished his reasons hadn't been purely professional, and that he'd brought me there not for a story but because he wanted me to understand the truth about my marriage. The idea made my hands sweat inside my gloves and my heart increase its tempo. I knew better now than to hope he harbored any romantic feelings for me, but even if our only relationship would be a professional one, I'd still cherish it. Maybe in time I could regain his good opinion, and we could be friends again.

"The first time I saw you at Rose Briar Hall you gave me your card and said to call you if I remembered anything. Well, I remembered something. Everything, in fact."

He uncrossed his arms and braced his hands against the desk, as if preparing himself. His attention was absolute. He said nothing, letting the silence hang between us as he waited.

And I told him. About Charles killing Gertrude, and drugging me, and trying to have me committed. About Briggs's attempt on my life, and Gertrude's pregnancy. I knew it was an incredible tale, and I prayed he'd recognize the truth when he heard it. While I spoke, his expression transformed from interest to astonishment to alarm.

"Good God." He stared at me so hard I worried I had

something on my face. His eyes swept up and down, as if assessing for damage. Was he anxious for me, or just surprised?

"It's all right if you don't believe me. No one does. I don't know what to do." I hid my face in my hands, momentarily overwhelmed.

"Why on earth wouldn't I believe you?" His voice was velvet soft, and his words made my stomach flutter. He reached over and spun the radiator knob closed. I could tell he was thinking, his journalist's mind picking apart the information. "Why does he want you dead? Is it because of money?"

I tapped my fingers against my lips, considering. "My trust is controlled by my father. I've nothing to offer Charles in that regard. He would inherit Rose Briar Hall, I suppose." My father had gifted us a generous sum upon our marriage, but Charles had always wanted more, expected more. My father had disappointed him time and time again. "I think he wants to marry again, someone with more money, but he doesn't want the scandal of a divorce. Or the delay—they can take ages, can't they?"

David walked around to the other side of the desk and rifled through the drawers, retrieving a half-full bottle of whiskey. He uncorked it and took a swig, not even bothering with a glass. A man in my circle would never have done that. But there was little artifice with David, even if I couldn't always guess what he was thinking. Now that I understood the depth of my husband's deception, I appreciated David's straightforwardness even more.

"The chloral hydrate. He probably didn't intend for you to take it so early. He wanted you to forget Gertrude's death so that he could make you doubt your own sanity, but he didn't want you to sleep through the party. He got lucky that the drug took time to work." He seemed to be speaking mostly to himself, but I nodded. It made sense. We never served that sherry to guests, and Charles knew I liked it after dinner. "Do you think he planned to make you jealous, so that you'd cause a scene? He couldn't have known you'd overhear him speaking to Gertrude."

I thought about it and nodded again. "He would have found a way to provoke me." He'd wanted me disgraced. He could have killed Gertrude more quietly, perhaps an overdose of chloral, as he'd intended for me. Instead he'd turned her death into a show for our friends, one meant to incriminate me. Or maybe it was only that the wolfsbane was so fast and untraceable. If he'd used a sleeping potion there might have been more questions.

David loosened his tie. It really was hot in the office. "Gertrude's pregnancy. I might be able to get her maid to go on the record. But if we publish it, some might see it as giving you more of a motive."

I shrugged. It didn't change anything. Everyone already treated me as if I were guilty, so what difference would it make? And if everyone knew about Gertrude's pregnancy, they'd have to acknowledge Charles wasn't the perfect husband he pretended to be. Everyone knew Gertrude and her husband had lived under different roofs, and I certainly didn't get her pregnant. I thought of Arabella's pity for my poor devoted husband and imagined her reading the news with grim satisfaction.

"You can publish whatever you want. I'm just grateful to you for listening." I heaved a breath and wiped away an errant tear. "If I'd died, everyone would have believed it was suicide. They would have said it was guilt over what I'd done. I just wanted someone to know. In case something happened."

"You're still in danger." His eyes searched mine, his manner tense. Upset, even. Every muscle had gone tight, as if he were struggling to contain a strong emotion. But what? Anger at Charles? At me, for bothering him with my problems?

"He might—" He shook his head. "Never mind, it's not my place." He stood up abruptly. "I have to get back to work."

"Oh." My fingers tightened on my gloves. He hadn't been

anxious for me, only eager to conclude our interview. Despite my usefulness as a source, our conversation was just work to him, nothing more. "I'm sorry to burden you with my troubles. Forgive me."

"Burden me?" He laughed, without humor. "Yes, I've never been so burdened." He looked at me searchingly while he replaced his suit jacket. I didn't understand any of it, other than that I had clearly offended him somehow. He could hardly wait for me to be gone.

"Good day, Mrs. Turner." His words were strained. I remembered him drunk on the sidewalk outside Marshall's Hotel, handsome and scruffy, refusing to kiss me. My husband's treachery hurt deeply, throbbing through every part of me, but David's indifference was a sharp prick, a wasp's bite that made everything else duller in comparison.

I wasted no time in showing myself out.

CHAPTER 25

The news broke the following weekend. I paced nervously outside the dining room where my father was having his breakfast, waiting for his exclamation as he stumbled upon one of the stories. But it never came. He normally read *The New York Times* and the *Financial Times*, but I'd made sure *The World News* was available for him this morning, too. That didn't mean he would read it. I'd have to tell him myself.

I entered to find him still calmly reading his paper's freshly ironed pages while he cut a piece of bacon and moved his fork to his mouth. It was the *Financial Times*, I saw.

"Good morning, Millie. I meant to tell you yesterday—Dr. Kimpton made room for you Tuesday afternoon at two." He didn't look up from his paper. I'd been lucky that my father's choice of doctor was so renowned that he hadn't had an immediate appointment. By Tuesday, perhaps the visit wouldn't even be necessary. If my father still made me go, at least the news about Charles would have had time to circulate, so the doctor wouldn't be as biased against me.

"All right. Father, do you have a moment? There's something I'd like to discuss with you."

I served myself a plate of eggs from the sideboard and picked at it nervously. Something upstairs banged loudly, and my father didn't even flinch. Tonight was one of my mother's famous Munroe "crushes," and this morning there had been servants everywhere, some I could swear I'd never seen before, all of them hurried, heads bent forward and faces strained. My father was used to my mother's constant entertaining and seemed entirely unfazed.

"I always have a moment for you." He folded his paper and looked up to meet my gaze. His eyes were a duller blue than they once had been.

"I know you want me and Charles to reconcile, but you have to understand—" My tongue stuck in the grooves on the roof of my mouth. "He has been unfaithful."

There were two articles running today. Despite my awkward parting from David, he was a consummate professional, and he'd made good use of the information I'd given him. One article was about Charles's fraud, sporting David's byline, and another was by his colleague who covered society scandals, about Gertrude's affair with Charles and her pregnancy.

My father didn't speak for a long time, and the only noise was the clinking of his silverware against the china. "If he has, he has done you great wrong."

"And that's not all. He's been swindling his clients. It's in the paper today. *The World News.*"

I expected my father to search for the article, but he only exhaled deeply, a throaty, beleaguered rumble. "I suspected as much."

"You did?" I could hardly believe what I was hearing. This whole time, my father had known Charles was deceitful. I thought of their encounter after I'd first awoken from the drugs, Charles's fury.

"He's asked me for a loan, several times. An enormous sum. I could tell he was desperate. Yet my friends claim he's making them money hand over fist. It has concerned me for some time."

He abandoned his breakfast, recognizing the seriousness

of our conversation precluded eating, and slipped his hand halfway inside his vest, resting it on his rotund belly.

"I can't stay with him. You must see that now." I leaned forward, tempted to take his hand, to beg. I examined his expression for a trace of sympathy, but he was only sorrowful.

"You know he wouldn't have been my choice for you, but I let you make your own decision." He picked up his fork as if he meant to eat again, then apparently thought better of it and set it back down. I knew I mattered more to him than his breakfast, but he clearly didn't appreciate the interruption. "You must live with its consequences."

"So this is a punishment, then? For not heeding your advice before?" In his presence I sounded like a girl again, pleading for sweets. I wanted him to take me in his arms and tell me he would make everything all right.

"No." He sighed deeply. "Your mother and I had some troubles when we were first married. But I made a vow to her, Millie. I take that very seriously I'm someone who solves problems rather than running from them. That's who I thought I raised you to be."

Even knowing what I knew about Charles, his words shamed me. I wasn't a child. I didn't need my father's approval anymore, but I still craved it. "He's not a good man, Father. It's not the same as with you and Mother."

I knew my parents weren't exactly the picture of wedded bliss, but they had grown used to each other's habits and learned how to get along well enough. Their marriage was better than many. I knew, too, how much my father valued a promise: in business, his word was his bond, and breaking it was something he would never do. I understood his logic, and if it had been anyone but Charles, I might even have been persuaded by it.

"You can make him a better one, Millie. I'm sure of it. And this whole sordid business will blow over, in time."

"And how will I make him a better man in an asylum, Father?" I asked, my voice raised, sharp. I never spoke disrespectfully to my father, and his mouth creased in disapproval.

"I doubt Dr. Kimpton will recommend something so extreme. But if he does, I'll see to it that we find you somewhere very comfortable. You know Gregsby's wife went away for a time, after the loss of their son. It's not how it used to be. It would be more like a retreat."

"I thought you disapproved of hiding from one's troubles."

Now his blue eyes glinted and he lifted a finger, slipping into his favorite role as the pedantic lecturer. "It wouldn't be hiding. You've been under an enormous amount of strain, and I'm merely entertaining the possibility that you need medical help. However unlikely I think that is. But if that is Dr. Kimpton's recommendation, view it as a strategic withdrawal. Edward Cope wrote of a certain snake, the *Drymarchon melanurus erebennus*, that feigns death to confuse its predators. It would be just the same, my dear, and then you could return triumphantly, ready to strike."

I closed my eyes and suppressed a sob. I considered telling him everything about the danger I was in, but the brilliance of Charles's treachery was that the more extreme his actions, the less believable they were. If I told my father the full truth, he wouldn't only support Charles if he wanted to commit me to an institution, he might even encourage it.

His lessons on animal behavior had saved me before, when I eluded Briggs. But now the same advice was putting me in jeopardy.

My mother interrupted us before I'd formed a rebuttal. I heard her delivering orders to one of the servants with militaristic precision before bursting into the dining room.

"Darling, would you mind terribly showing Goodyear the proper way to arrange flowers? She's quite hopeless." She sounded harried. "After breakfast, of course." She said this breathily, as if it were a generous concession.

"Mother, have you eaten anything? Sit down. You can spare a few minutes."

She sighed, as if she really couldn't. But she followed my lead and made herself a plate. My mother's crushes were well-known for being impersonal and decidedly lacking in cachet, and her Christmas crush that evening promised to be her largest event yet. My mother loved nothing better than her house stuffed to the gills with people. The way she saw it, the more people you entertained, the more popular you were. The timing couldn't have been better, with the news about Charles breaking this morning, as her party would provide the perfect setting for the gossip to spread.

"What will you wear?" I asked, figuring she would welcome the chance to boast about her dress. I was right. She brightened as she described the Worth evening gown heavy with gold beading.

"And what about you, darling? What will you wear?"

"You mean . . . you don't mind me coming?" I had prepared a dozen ways to broach the subject gently. As much as I dreaded going, I knew it was the perfect opportunity to show everyone how well I was.

"But of course you're attending! You are, aren't you?" Her exclamation seemed sincere and relief washed over me. She knew by now, of course, that I was a social pariah, and that no one had forgiven or forgotten my fateful dinner party. And my mother had built her whole life around elevating her social status, so her willingness to risk it for me touched me more than a little. Fortunately, her friends had mostly been sympathetic to her, as they had been to Charles. I was certain that if I acted like my usual self at the party tonight, everyone would be more likely to believe my innocence. I merely needed the chance to charm their suspicions away. And her crushes were the sort of place where rich newcomers on the fringes of society could attempt to improve themselves, where a British lady might find herself in conversation with a Jewish

real estate investor. Where bodies crushed up against one another in the drawing room or on the dance floor, where there
were foreheads dabbed with sweat, voices laughing, music
tinkling, cards thwacking, glasses clinking, gossip swirling
around it all, tying it up like a bow. Some of the people there
would still be scandalized by me and would refuse to talk to
me, but it would be easy enough to be lost in the commotion.

"Thank you."

"Whatever for? I wouldn't dream of you missing one of my
little gatherings."

My father snorted at this description of the event but said
nothing. The greasy sausages I'd forced down settled heavily
in my stomach. Remembering the humiliation of my calling
day made my chest tight, but I'd have to risk bearing it again.
I'd endured far worse, after all. And with any luck, Charles's
scandals would overshadow my own.

CHAPTER 26

Early evening found me sitting at my vanity, outwardly calm as Duffield stood behind me with a pair of curling tongs. The air smelled of singed hair.

Duffield said something, but I was too distracted to hear her, and I smiled and nodded at her like a simpleton, hoping it would serve as a reply.

Finally, she finished sweeping my hair into the Grecian look I often favored, accented with a diamond hair comb. She helped me into my rose-pink charmeuse evening gown, edged with a silver embroidered key pattern and featuring short fringe over the arms that suggested sleeves. I looked demure in it, innocent, but noticeable. It wouldn't do to get lost in the crowd when I needed to be seen.

I heard the first guests arriving downstairs, then more right after, and on and on, but I stayed seated, fiddling with my face creams and brushes. I waited, and waited, until the party was loud and boisterous and the noise floated upstairs, light as champagne. Then I stood, weary already, my legs shaking a little as I went into the gallery. My shoes clacked on the marble floors, and the gilded accents gleamed so brightly in the lights that I blinked. Marble busts of Roman emperors and their wives watched me as I made my way to the stairs.

No one noticed me at first. I had to push my way through a group of strangers to even reach the plush drawing room.

Eventually, though, a hiss of whispers trailed me, and people began moving out of the way when they saw me approaching. In return, I forced myself to smile and bow my head, as if they were doing it out of politeness. Inside, anxiety surged, and my chest trembled. It had been too much to expect that Charles's downfall would be my redemption, and that they'd welcome me back into the fold. I'd dared to hope for it, but maybe the articles had only deepened my notoriety.

It didn't matter, so long as his disgrace outweighed mine. I needed only for the scales to tip slightly in my favor. Then maybe the threat of the institution would disappear, and I could sue for divorce.

I kept moving. I wandered through the party purposefully, as if I had a destination in mind, waiting to bump into someone who might talk to me. I made eye contact with Anna Carter and she pretended not to see me, directing her gaze to a spot over my head. Several other friends did the same— all women I had called on and who had feigned being out. I paused for a moment, resting my hand on the back of a chair, and accepted a glass of champagne from a waiter. The bubbles slipped down my throat and fizzed in my stomach, loosening its knots. I spotted Walter Pearley nearby, a loose acquaintance who was known for his charming manners and less charming wife, Evangeline. He had flirted with me years ago before either of us had married, and when he saw me his eyes widened, and then, miraculously, he smiled. He said something to the older gentleman he had been speaking to and came toward me.

"Mrs. Turner. I'm so glad to see you. I was just being bored to death by Claude Hooper about copper mining. And here you are, by far the most interesting person at the party."

"*Interesting*. What a much nicer word than *infamous*. I quite prefer it."

Walter was rather handsome, despite a weak chin.

"A lot of stuff and nonsense if you ask me. Downright ghoulish what people have been saying."

"You may be the only one with that perspective, I'm afraid."

"I'm sure that's not true. Especially with the news today, which half the party is gossiping about."

I'd forgotten how much I liked Walter. His chin wasn't really so weak, either, and his smile was always genuine. And then another acquaintance approached to join our tête-à-tête. Chester something or other, I couldn't recall his surname.

"Mrs. Turner, it's wonderful to see you. The season has been so much duller without you, you know."

I tilted my head strategically, showing off my long expanse of pale neck. "I would say you are too kind, but I suppose you're right, really. I'm sure everyone will agree my last party was anything but dull."

At this, both men erupted into shocked laughter. Chester laughed so hard he had to wipe his eyes. And it dawned on me that I had stumbled on the right tactic. I had been trying to win over the ladies, when I should have been focusing on the men. I was, after all, a pretty woman, one whose marriage was known to be in shambles. And the men didn't have to shy away from scandal the way their wives did. Plenty of them even had mistresses from the lower classes. I supposed my disgrace made me roughly the social equivalent of a vaudeville actress.

The thought had only just entered my head when Bessie Modell joined us. She had been an actress herself, before marrying a much older and richer man. She was no longer young, but she had the most expressive dark eyes of anyone I knew and a husky voice that carried.

"Mrs. Turner! The society poisoner, they're calling you. Not that I believe a word of it. And the hypocrisy! Half of them just want to know how you did it, if you ask me. Want to get rid of their husbands. The way Claude has been droning on tonight, I'm tempted to ask you myself." She laughed loudly, breathing out smoke from her cigarette, and I laughed along. I took another glass of champagne from a passing tray. My legs were weak now not from nerves but from drink. I was almost jubilant. Being ignominious was strangely freeing. I could say anything.

"I wish I could tell you the secret, truly, but I haven't the faintest notion. I was almost a victim myself, you know. Someone put knockout drops in my drink that night."

The men both exclaimed, and Bessie gasped dramatically and put a hand on her heart. "Truly, Mrs. Turner, this is better than any play."

"But it's a tragedy, I'm afraid."

"Quite so. No arguing that. You know, you could be a very great talent if you ever took to the stage. A very great talent."

The four of us continued in this manner for some time, and our laughter drew attention. Everyone was stealing glances at us. Bessie enjoyed being ogled at and reveled in it. Chester was trying hard not to stare at the neckline of my gown. Walter's charm kept the conversation flowing nicely, and it occurred to me that I was actually enjoying myself, something I certainly hadn't expected to do. In time Arabella passed near us, and though the sight of her stirred up the hurt she had caused me, her obvious jealousy assuaged it. I knew her well enough to understand its cause. She was used to being the center of attention at parties, the most outrageous flirt, the one running with the fast set.

I was stealing her limelight.

In the edge of my vision, I saw her waver. And then push her way through the crowd.

"Millie dear, I hate to interrupt, but could we have a private word?"

She looked distracted, annoyed even. I bristled at her use of the word "dear," as if we were still intimates. "I don't see how anyone can have a private word in this crowd." We laughed, me and my three new friends. "But all right, I suppose we can attempt it. I'll be right back," I told them, and followed her to an alcove where a bust of Octavia was displayed.

"What is it?" I kept my tone light, even though I was angry enough to shout. But to regain my footing in society, I needed her. I'd have to act. Bessie had said I'd be a good actress, hadn't she? And Charles was always dissembling. If he could do it, so could I.

"Nothing at all. I just wanted to rescue you from Bessie Modell. Sometimes I really do wish your mother would be more discriminating with her guest lists." She laughed breathily and lit a cigarette.

I arched an eyebrow. "I suppose you'd want her to leave me off it, too."

"What? Is this about that little tiff last week? It was nothing, you know, I was just in a bad mood after having to entertain Christina Dalton. You'll forgive me, won't you?"

I forced a smile, but I pinched my dress hard between my fingers. "There's nothing to forgive."

Over her shoulder, I glanced several of my former friends watching our tête-à-tête—deciding, most likely, whether to follow Arabella's lead and welcome me back.

Many of them did. The next few hours were a blur of bright lights and crystal and champagne. Those who were speaking to me again acted just as Arabella had, pretending nothing at all had transpired between us. Bessie was right. I was a better actress than I realized, and I played my part well. I said all the right things, laughed in all the right places. And at every opportunity, I dropped little comments about how Charles had seemed so strained lately, that I worried he was working too hard. I said it in front of his clients, who cast dark looks at one another. All the while, I was the picture of poise, and I even heard Anna Carter whisper to someone that I was nothing like Charles had said at all. I almost forgot how false they all were; it was easier to forget when I was being false myself.

Finally, though, I escaped them again to an upstairs dressing room. Alone, I ran my hands under the tap, so hot it scalded me. The pain grounded me. My fingers were red and raw, and I hid my face in them and let out a quiet groan. Then I donned my gloves again and rejoined the crowd, ready to continue the charade.

On my way back to my little group, a flash of pink caught my eye. I turned toward it when I felt a hand on my elbow, and found myself staring into the sickly sweet face of Lily Applebee.

"Mrs. Turner. I've been hoping to catch you. I just wanted to say I think it very brave of you to come tonight, given your . . . fragility. Everyone has been so worried for you." She pouted, and the smile frozen on my face almost slipped. "You really shouldn't tax yourself, being in public this way."

She wore a heavily beaded cream gown that made me think of a confectionary, toothache sweet and overly decorated. I could already imagine telling Arabella that she reminded me of a cream puff. It would make her laugh. I almost had to remind myself that Arabella wasn't my friend anymore, not really.

In any case, part of me actually pitied Lily. Charles had hoodwinked her just as he had me. The rest of me still resented her. Charles no longer had the power to make me jealous, but that didn't mean I wanted to be friends with the woman whose fortune he was willing to kill me for. "Thank you, Miss Applebee. I think you're brave, too."

Her smile stayed in place, but her eyes narrowed. She sensed the trap but was unable to resist. "Why is that?"

She was right; I was brave to come tonight, and the wine made me braver still. "Well, when my husband tired of his last mistress, she ended up dead."

I hadn't known for sure she was Charles's mistress, but her

expression confirmed it. I hadn't only said it to provoke her; I'd meant to warn her, too. I stayed just long enough to register her look of shock before turning away, my dress swirling.

She didn't follow me, and I didn't look back. I padded down the softly carpeted stairs, slowly and elegantly, taking in the crowd that had assembled in the front hall below. No one paid me any attention, even though I cut a rather fine figure coming down the stairs, and it took me a moment to understand why.

Some sort of commotion had broken out, and a small circle of onlookers had gathered around two men. I paused, curious, and then nearly dropped my champagne in surprise. One of the men was Charles.

CHAPTER 27

The champagne rushed through my veins and I clutched the stair railing for support. I'd known Charles would be invited, but I never thought he'd come. After the news broke, I expected him to hide away and lick his wounds. I should have known better. His ego would never allow it. He'd probably come here to try to charm his way out of his predicament, just as I had.

His plan must have gone somewhat awry, because he was shouting at the other man and actually had grabbed him by the lapels. The man's back was to me, so I couldn't see who it was, but I guessed it might be an upset client. I was astounded. Charles looked as startlingly handsome as ever, but he never lost control like this, and certainly not in public. I would have expected him to have a polished smile and slick hair and lies as smooth as his suits. No wrinkles in either. But now a piece of his dark hair had come loose, and he was angrier than I'd ever seen him.

"It's libel. You'll be hearing from my lawyer, do you understand? None of it is true. Do you all hear me?" Now he turned his attention to the crowd. The man before him had stood his ground, apparently not intimidated by this display. Charles was putting on a show, I realized. He wanted everyone to see him forcefully disavow the article. I saw some of Charles's clients whispering to one another. Some appeared angry, as if they wanted to jump into the fray, while others were only alarmed.

The man brushed off his jacket where Charles had grasped it. "If it's libel, your investors wouldn't be having so much trouble recovering their funds, would they?" The man turned just enough so that I could make out his profile and I gasped. It was David.

Charles took a swing at him and David ducked, expertly, hardly even moving to avoid the blow. Charles stumbled, and David stepped farther away and grabbed a glass of champagne from a footman standing in the surrounding circle, handing out drinks to the onlookers. He raised it in mock salute and disappeared into the crowd, as if such altercations were a commonplace affair. Perhaps for him they were.

I rushed to follow him, and to disappear into the crowd myself before Charles spotted me. David was a few feet ahead of me and seemed completely at ease. He even stopped to speak to a few people briefly. He didn't look out of place at all, and looked rather spectacular in his dinner jacket. I'd thought that his ready-made suits became him, but now that I'd seen him in evening wear, I couldn't decide which I liked best.

I saw David go into the coat closet and ducked in behind him.

There was no one else in there—at the height of the party, no one was likely to come for their coats. It suddenly struck me as foolish, dangerous even, to be alone with the man who my husband had just tried to punch in the jaw. What if someone came upon us? What would they think?

"What are you doing here? Were you invited?" I asked, and the words sounded accusatory and too blunt. I chastised myself. After our abrupt parting before, I'd hoped to find a way to smooth things over between us. David didn't seem offended, though. He gave a half smile.

"Not technically. But I was curious. I had a professional

interest in seeing how the story was received. I was starting to get the feeling I may have outstayed my welcome, though."

I laughed. "Whatever gave you that idea?"

David shrugged on his overcoat. Any of our other guests would have asked a footman to fetch theirs for them, but it didn't surprise me David preferred to do it himself.

"So were you enjoying the party?"

I wasn't imagining his surprise, and I thought I understood it. I'd told him in his office how all my friends had shunned me, and he was really asking why I was still bothering with them. "It will be harder for Charles to have me committed if my friends see that I'm well." I bristled.

David stiffened and paused buttoning his coat. "That's clever. And what's your plan after that? Will you sue for divorce?" He asked it almost offhandedly, but he stared at me intently as he waited for my answer.

The question forced the air out of my lungs. Of course I knew I'd have to do it, but the prospect daunted me so much that I hadn't allowed myself to face it fully. "Yes, but my father won't approve. He's allowed me to stay here only temporarily." My father had always been so proud of me, but then, I'd never disobeyed him before. Losing his respect, and love, would crush me. I closed my eyes, suddenly dizzy from the alcohol and the questions crowding my mind. I was safe here, but I couldn't stay here forever, and what then? "I thought I might go to Genevieve Folsom's lawyer."

David resumed his buttoning. "I remember that case. She proved her husband was cheating and the judge decreed he could never remarry." He placed his hat on his head.

The coat closet, which was enormous by closet standards, suddenly seemed suffocating. I grasped the door behind me for support. "Oh my God." I suddenly saw everything with perfect clarity. Gertrude's murder, Charles's determination to kill me rather than divorce me. He couldn't risk the outcome that George Folsom faced, not when marriage was the only way to obtain the windfall that he needed. David understood only a moment after I did. I grabbed for the knob, desperate to be out of there, to escape the party onto the wintry street, and put as much distance between myself and Charles as possible.

David, who had been so unfazed by the scuffle earlier, looked agitated.

"Wait." He grabbed my wrist, gently, before I opened the door, and then pulled me toward him, less gently. The surprise of his coarse hands on my skin paralyzed me for a moment. We were only an inch apart, and the remaining air between us was charged. "When you came to see me at my office I was a bit brusque, before you left. It was because I was upset. I don't like you being in danger."

"No?" I was breathing hard.

"No."

He touched my cheek. His fingers carried the zing of electricity and a current ran through me, lighting me up inside.

"What you said, the night we danced. I minded more than I should have. Because I don't want to be a 'nobody.' Not to you."

My terror over Charles faded to the back of my mind, and hope swelled behind my breastbone. He did care. It meant everything to me just then. "You're not. You could never be."

Suddenly his hand was behind my head, and he kissed me, fiercely, a shocking, astonishing kiss that traveled through me, electrifying every filament until my whole body buzzed. I kissed him back, tasting his warm lips, his mouth, my body arching into him, neither of us pausing to draw breath. I forgot everything for a moment, everything except for his lips on mine, sure of themselves, exploring, and his hands running along my back. I didn't think about my cruel former friends, or about Charles and how perilous it would be to leave him.

We broke apart, gasping. He stared at me, his expression still hungry.

"I thought you said you were a gentleman," I said lightly, catching my breath.

"Most of the time." He stepped back as if to see me better, and jostled a woman's fox stole. "So. The Upper East Side heiress and the lowly journalist." It was more of a question than a statement. He eyed the door to the coat closet, the only protection between us and the dazzling party, the monied guests.

But I no longer viewed David as a mere diversion, as I had when I'd propositioned him at Marshall's Hotel. The class difference that had once seemed like a great chasm between us, impossible to bridge, now struck me as trivial. I was ashamed that it had ever mattered to me. "Sounds like a nice headline."

"It does, doesn't it?" He cocked that crooked smile and kissed me again. His mouth moved along the curve of my jaw and his lips reached the lobe of my ear. "He's a dangerous man, Millie. You'll have to be careful." His voice was rough and warm.

"I'll try."

The closet, which had been closing in on me only minutes ago, now seemed like the coziest of havens. I wished I could stay forever in that moment, snug in the coats, in David's arms.

Safe.

CHAPTER 28

❧

My father still insisted I keep my appointment with Dr. Kimpton. I wouldn't have complied, only he made it clear I could not continue to stay in his house if I didn't go. If he witnessed how determined Charles still was to commit me, even after my success at the crush, he might finally realize how little Charles cared about my well-being. He might come around to the idea of divorce, or at the very least continue to grant me succor.

After luncheon, my father walked with me to the front hall, and I asked a footman to call for the brougham.

"Let's take the coach," he said, and I looked questioningly at him.

"You mean you're coming?" This had never been part of my understanding of the plan. But apparently my father wanted to hear the doctor's diagnosis for himself. Did he think I would lie?

"Of course. I thought we should all go."

I didn't have to wait long to understand what he meant. We emerged onto the front stoop to find Charles waiting for us. My stomach clenched. I should have guessed Charles would attempt something like this.

"I don't want him to come," I said, shrilly.

My father heaved a sigh, resting his fingers in between the buttons on his vest. "It is a husband's duty to oversee his wife's medical care. He has been worried about you."

I closed my eyes and forced myself to pause before replying. My father loved me, but he was infuriatingly traditional.

"Darling, it's so wonderful to see you," Charles said. "You look a bit pale. I hope you haven't been overexerting yourself."

I had to hide my scowl. "You do, too. I hope work hasn't been too trying." I smiled sweetly at him and his mouth tightened.

"Now, now. This visit is about you, Millie. Let's put aside any unpleasantness," my father said.

The coach pulled up to the sidewalk and the footman helped me inside. To my chagrin, Charles sat next to me, his body close to mine. I thought of David kissing me in the coat closet and how furious Charles would be if he knew, and the secret warmed me against the chilly winter air. I could make it through this. If the doctor was as good as my father thought, whatever Charles told him shouldn't matter.

The alternative was almost too terrifying to consider. If he recommended commitment, I would be in grave danger. Now that our friends had seen me well, Charles probably needed the doctor to commit me to lend credence to my supposed instability before he could make another attempt against me. At least, that was my guess. It was hard to know exactly what he had planned.

Perhaps I shouldn't go to the appointment. When we arrived at our destination, I could flee. Would they chase me? Charles could overtake me easily, and my father might view running as proof of my insanity. He could be a powerful ally if I could make him see that Charles's attempt to commit me was self-interested, and that there was no hope for us to reconcile.

I looked out the window and knotted my fingers together. It would be better to see the doctor. I'd have to take the risk.

Given his renown, Dr. Kimpton's office was surprisingly simple. It comprised two rooms located over a hat shop: a waiting room and examination room. The waiting room had a rather worn green velvet sofa with a plain wooden table in front of it. A slender, curly-haired female secretary took our coats and offered us tea, which we declined, and minutes later the doctor came out to usher us all in.

The inner room was so cluttered it was a miracle there was room for us all to sit. The doctor's books, instruments, and personal photographs crowded the shelves and desk. Dr. Kimpton himself was burly and blond, and would have made a plausible lumberjack. He greeted us all with cheerful zeal.

"So." He clapped his meaty hands together and faced us all. "Tell me what brings Mrs. Turner here today."

Charles and my father both started speaking at once, and I frowned. "Perhaps the doctor would like to hear from me, first?" I interjected. I had to speak forcefully to be heard, and regretted it afterward. I knew I should avoid showing strong emotions.

Dr. Kimpton smiled genially, his teeth shiny and white. "That's a good idea, Mrs. Turner."

"Well." I pulled off my gloves and sighed heavily. "There's nothing at all the matter with me. My husband and I have been having marital difficulties—do you happen to read *The World News*, Doctor? If so, I'm sure you know all about it. And he's trying to have me committed as a punishment."

The argument was one I'd chosen with my father in mind. If he could be persuaded that Charles had no interest in saving our marriage, I might be able to get somewhere with him.

"Now, Millie. You know that isn't true," Charles scolded, gently, as if he were speaking to a child. "She saw a friend of hers die recently and it was a terrible shock for her. She has been suffering severe melancholia, and I'm concerned she might be a danger to herself. And to others—she swung a fireplace poker at her own maid."

Dr. Kimpton peered inquisitively at me. "Is this true, Mrs. Turner?"

"Not a bit of it. My husband ordered the maid in question to give me sleeping medication, against my wishes, and I saw that she had poured out a lethal overdose. She's careless that way. I had to fight her off to prevent her from forcing it on me."

My father exclaimed at this, and even Charles looked so shocked I almost believed it was genuine. But surely he knew what Briggs had planned, and had instigated it. Hadn't he? I quickly pushed any doubt to the back of my mind. His claim of melancholia mirrored hers so closely. It would have helped preempt any questions if I were to never wake up from a drugged slumber.

"Are you quite sure, Millie? Her other doctor—Dr. Wendell—believed she suffered from paranoia. Delusions. She also experienced an extended period of amnesia." Charles squeezed my hand, as if reassuring me, and I flinched.

"I'm quite sure."

"Hmm. This is a perplexing case." Dr. Kimpton scribbled something in a notebook. "Mrs. Turner, are you often anxious or excitable?"

"No." I squeezed my hands together in my lap. Then I stopped and smoothed my dress. All of my actions were being observed, so I had to be careful. Charles gave an elaborate sigh, as if he disagreed.

"Have you ever had a convulsive fit?"

"No."

"Any unusual headaches or muscular pain? Vomiting?"

"No."

"Mr. Munroe, have you observed any of the melancholia or paranoia that Mr. Turner has described?"

My father harrumphed. "She has seemed quite herself, to my eye."

Hope swelled within me. My father was on my side. The doctor scribbled another note.

"Mrs. Turner, would you mind going to the waiting room? I have a few more questions for your husband and father."

I balked. "Surely I should be here? This appointment concerns me, after all."

"Yes. Quite. But I worry the gentlemen may not be as forthcoming in your presence as I need them to be."

I turned toward my father for assistance, but he only shrugged. I pursed my lips in displeasure but complied. I waited for five minutes, ten. The secretary watched me nervously as I paced the tiny room. I considered leaving. I thought the appointment had gone reasonably well, but I couldn't be certain. If things hadn't gone my way, this might be my only opportunity to run.

The door squeaked open and the three of them emerged. The doctor and my father laughed over something and shook hands. They were social acquaintances, so it made sense they were friendly, and the anxiety in my gut lessened. They wouldn't be joking if the doctor had recommended commitment. Charles looked a little put out.

"Well, Mrs. Turner. I certainly see no reason to recommend an institution. But I'd like to spend more time with you, to more closely consider the question of hysteria." Dr. Kimpton grinned at me again with too many white teeth. His mouth appeared as crowded as his office.

I gave a small smile in return. It wasn't a complete victory, but it was close enough. Charles wasn't quite as disappointed as I expected by the news, or perhaps he was only hiding it well.

"We look forward to seeing you again, Dr. Kimpton." Charles took my hand in his and steered me back toward the coach. Inside, he spread out beside me, seemingly relaxed, and placed a hand on my knee. My father noticed the affectionate gesture and his eyes twinkled. I swallowed.

"Did you want to dine with your parents tonight before we go?" Charles patted my leg.

"What?" My stomach churned.

"Well, you'll be coming home now, of course."

I closed my eyes and turned away. I'd been counting on Charles outwardly pushing harder for the institution at the appointment, and turning my father against him. I'd under-estimated his cleverness. I knew what would really happen once I left my parents' house. Charles would find some other doctor who agreed with him.

"I'll need a few days at least. To get all my things ready." A lie, of course, but fortunately Charles didn't press the issue. He looked smug.

They were both so pleased with themselves. My father's mouth twitched in a suppressed smile. As much as I loved him, in that moment I saw him not as my father, but as an old man with a big gut and white hair, proud and uncompromis-ing. He was another man who thought he could control me.

I couldn't count on him to help me. I'd have to save myself.

In the morning, I'd go and see a lawyer.

CHAPTER 29

⟡

After the decadence of my parents' house, the lawyer's office seemed cheap and spare. The rug was the inexpensive ready-made sort, with a common geometric pattern I'd seen before. Once I might have sought another lawyer, one who adorned his office with hand-knotted Turkish rugs, but he had done good work for Genevieve. Besides, I appreciated that his fees weren't as exorbitant as some of the others. I didn't know if my father would help me financially, once he caught wind of what I was doing.

Everything would have been so much easier with my father's support, but I finally acknowledged that he wouldn't come around on the issue. I'd have to risk his displeasure.

"And on what grounds will you be suing for divorce, Mrs. Turner?"

The lawyer's name was Ted Thistle, and he was a string bean of a man, tall and jumpy. I'd shown up the moment his offices opened in the morning, and luckily he'd accommodated me without an appointment. I recognized that I didn't have time to waste.

"Grounds?" I reached for the glass of water he had provided me and wetted my lips. "What are the choices?"

My mind had gone blank. I hardly knew where to begin with explaining the many wrongs my husband had committed. Just showing up to the office had been a tremendous act of bravery, especially now that I fully understood the lengths Charles had gone to in order to avoid this scenario.

"Well, cruelty or abandonment would suffice for a limited divorce—essentially, a separation. In New York, the only legal grounds for absolute divorce is infidelity. Has he been unfaithful to you?" He had a pen in his hand, poised ready on a piece of paper, then paused to inspect it. Placed it on the paper again. His hands were always moving, like those men on the street who did the trick with the cups and balls.

"Yes."

"So will you be naming a co-respondent in the suit?"

He smiled at me, trying to be reassuring, but his eye teeth were so pointy that it seemed more like he was grimacing. My thoughts were sluggish, after rising so early. It seemed as if he were speaking a different language.

"A what?"

He waved the pen. "The woman your husband was having an affair with. You'll have to prove he was cheating."

I paused to consider. I knew he was pursuing Lily Applebee, but I couldn't be absolutely certain that they'd gone to bed together. And Gertrude—well, Gertrude was dead. "I'm not sure. She has since passed away, you see."

Mr. Thistle dropped the pen. "Good heavens. That may complicate matters considerably."

Anxiety surged through me, engulfing me and making it difficult to breathe. Gertrude's willingness to speak about the affair was the reason she was dead. She probably would have testified. I had no idea if Lily Applebee would, if she and Charles had been intimate. She seemed too enthralled by him to do anything that went against his wishes, but I couldn't be sure.

"Don't despair. I said difficult, but not impossible. If we can find a witness who saw them together, that should suffice. We don't need a name that way."

I took a deep breath. No one among my friends would

have seen them because everyone had believed Charles's lies about me. Perhaps Gertrude's maid would testify. "What if I can't find anyone?"

Ted Thistle bounced in his chair. "We must try."

David—David would know what to do. The desire to see him hit me forcibly. I wished he could be with me right now. He would know what to say to the lawyer. An impossible thought, of course, and besides, I needed to learn to handle things myself. With luck, I would be a single woman soon.

"What did you mean by 'absolute divorce'? That would mean a complete severance?" I wanted to be sure that Charles wouldn't have any scrap of power over me.

"Yes. If your suit succeeds, it will be lawful for you to marry again as though your husband were dead."

"And what of Charles?"

Mr. Thistle shrugged. "It's not unusual for the judge to decree that the unfaithful party cannot marry again until their former spouse is actually dead."

"I see." It was what I'd suspected, but hearing him confirm it sent a shiver through me. Charles cared about the stigma of divorce, certainly, but having the freedom to remarry was something he was willing to kill for to protect. I'd read in the paper how judges were becoming stricter as a means to curb the increase in divorce cases of late, and newspaper columnists bemoaned the deteriorating moral fabric of our society.

"I will file the suit as soon as possible, since it may be some months until there's room on the docket for your case. We will have plenty of time to sort out these details." He smiled at me again and it was warmer this time, less toothy, but his words punctured all the same.

"Months?" Perhaps I hadn't really expected to make it this far. I hadn't reached the end of my struggle; it was dawning on me that it might only be the beginning.

"Some months, yes."

"Oh." I settled back more deeply into the chair, my eyelids

suddenly heavy. I wanted to sleep, and wake up when it was all over.

"And will you be asking for alimony? If so, we'll need to take a good look at your husband's finances to determine what you may be entitled to."

I shook my head, dumbstruck. Charles might have wanted to avoid a divorce not only to ensure he could remarry but to prevent any scrutiny of his business dealings. "He's ruined. There's probably nothing left."

His toothy smile slipped a little. "And what about you, do you have any assets? In case of a countersuit it's best to be prepared."

"My house. Rose Briar Hall. My clothes and jewels."

"We'll need to have the house appraised."

Mr. Thistle continued on about the things we would need to do and talked a good deal more about money. There were an astonishing number of details to go over, and I tried my best to pay attention and answer coherently as he chirped on and on. Mostly I just nodded and smiled like a dumb puppet, but he found nothing strange in it. Perhaps it was what he expected. I was terribly relieved when we finished at last for the day and I rose, my back stiff, and exited into the cold winter air.

CHAPTER 30

Heiress Sues Husband for Divorce

Fashionable folk of this city are much interested in the news that Mrs. Charles Turner of New York has sued her husband for divorce on the grounds of infidelity. Mr. Turner is contesting the suit.

Mr. and Mrs. Turner figured much at social affairs until the accidental death of Mrs. Gertrude Underhill at a dinner party in their Long Island home last October. Mr. Turner, a stockbroker of some renown, is a member of the Union Club and a graduate of Princeton University.

Mrs. Turner, formerly Miss Amelia Munroe, is daughter of department store magnate Harold Munroe. She and Mr. Turner were married in a grand ceremony at her parents' Fifth Avenue mansion in March 1907. The couple has no children.

My father had the paper folded open to the story on the table between us, and the headline seemed to scream into the silence. One of the most terrifying acts I'd ever taken, the gut-wrenching story of my life, was distilled into seven blunt sentences in black and white.

Unlike many powerful men, my father didn't anger easily. With him, there was no clenching of fists or shouting.

When he was displeased, he merely frowned, but the effect of that frown in his usually placid face was enough to make the room go quiet. I'd witnessed him use it with men who worked for him, and seen how pens would stop scratching and breathy excuses would come rushing out. When he was livid, his skin would turn blotchy.

My father used the frown now, but it was deeper than any frown I'd seen from him before, and his pupils seemed to contract to pinpricks. I thought I saw a tinge of red in his cheeks.

"Millie, if you go through with this, you will not be welcome in this house. I want you to think very carefully."

I felt the blood rush out of my face. I knew he'd be furious, but to be unwelcome in his house? The words boomed from somewhere deep in his chest. I'd known I wouldn't have refuge here forever, but I didn't think he'd cut off ties with me completely. I worried I might erupt into tears, but they stayed just beneath the surface.

Untouched crumb cake sat on the table before us, next to undrunk tea, and my mother fretted over it as if by refreshing our cups she could make this meeting go better. She sent me little exasperated looks but stayed silent—unusual for her, and another sign of how serious the situation was. She knew not to test my father's patience when he was upset.

"Father, I don't have any other choice. I'm not safe with him."

"Has he raised a hand to you?" Now the frown went deeper still, which I hadn't thought possible. I paused, reached for the teacup, after all. I considered lying. A man who beat his wife—that was something my father might understand. What Charles had done was more insidious than that.

"Not exactly, but—"

He held up a hand. "Millie. I won't let you take the easy way out on this. Life's challenges are what build a person's character. You're stronger than this. I'm not just going to let you give up on your marriage because it's gotten hard. You made a vow."

"I understand your perspective, really. But you aren't hearing me. He's a wicked man, Father."

My father studied me, but he didn't soften. "You've been married over a year now and the glow has faded. That's often when challenges start to arise. It's quite normal. Your anger will pass. I firmly believe you two can find a way to get along." Beside him, my mother nodded and opened her mouth as if she wanted to add something. Then she shut it, clearly thinking better of it. My father continued. "You were happy enough, I think, until recently. You have to go to that lawyer and stop this preposterous suit at once."

I sighed. "No." The word slid out of my mouth as a whisper. I had dared to defy my father, who I never disagreed with, and who had grown used to always getting his own way. The word stunned him, and he jerked backward as if he'd sustained a physical blow. I wondered who had been the last person to dare say it to him.

"Darling." Now my mother dared to chime in, to take my hand in hers. "Please don't do this. Charles is everything I ever wanted for you in a husband, please don't ruin it."

I struggled to contain my anger. My mother's words stung even more than my father's. She still believed Charles's façade, although I shouldn't have been surprised. There were plenty who'd fallen for his act at the party and remained in his corner, and evidently she was among them. Either that, or the truth didn't matter to her. Marrying him had been a social coup in her eyes, and she wasn't ready to let that go. She didn't want to trade a daughter with a prestigious marriage for a divorcée.

"He's not what you think he is, Mother."

My father shook his head at me. "I can't abide inconstancy in my own daughter. You do not seem to understand the repercussions if you disobey me in this. I can't support this in any way, and I also can't leave your assets vulnerable. You will no longer gain access to your trust on your birthday, or any other day; I will revoke access completely." He looked steadily at me, unblinking. A grandfather clock chimed the hour from another room, a soft and pretty jangle that seemed to mock us. "You will be without money, without friends."

Even with the tea, my mouth went dry. I had known there was a possibility he might react this way—in the same way someone knows the hurricane might come but is still surprised when it arrives with its gale-force winds that rip roofs off of buildings. I had my jewels and Rose Briar Hall, and that would have to be enough because there was no getting any more. It knocked the breath out of me.

I did the calculations again in my head. I'd done them before, but casually, not really expecting that they would be necessary. Selling my jewels should cover the legal fees and leave me enough to live on, but in a much simpler style than I was accustomed to. Eventually I could sell my most valuable asset, Rose Briar Hall, but a sale like that could take ages. It also pained me to think of parting with it, after how much work I'd invested, and how much of myself I'd put into it.

"I'll die if I stay with him." I said it earnestly, but he interpreted it as hyperbole.

"Don't be dramatic. That's your mother's domain."

My mother bristled beside him and risked huffing her annoyance. But she turned toward me instead, her face tight, as if it were I who had offended her. "Darling, please don't do this to me. I won't be able to help you." She shot a little glance at my father that showed me she disagreed with him about the money, but she knew—or had learned, at least— that in some things she couldn't go against him.

"I won't be his prisoner again. I can't. He drugged me, he locked me in my room—"

"It was a rest cure, Millie, ordered by a doctor." He sighed wearily.

I twitched with barely controlled rage. "He killed Gertrude. He'll kill me." I couldn't keep my composure any longer and my voice turned shrill. Sobs racked my body so violently that I bumped the table, and the crumb cake trembled. Snot dripped out of my nose. My mother softened at my distress, but my father recoiled. I knew what he was thinking—that Charles was right, and I was unstable. I could see it in his eyes. He looked at me like I was a stranger to him. No matter how much I argued, I knew he wouldn't listen. I wiped my cheeks. "I don't know how to make you understand."

My father recrossed his legs. "I never thought I could be ashamed of you, Millie." The words were heavy and round, stones in his mouth.

I felt sick to my stomach. "I suppose there's nothing more to say, is there? It would be goodbye either way, you know. At least this way I'll get to live. I'll be free." My voice cracked. My mother winced as if in pain. She was exuberant when she was happy and distressed over the silliest things, but she was never sad. I'd never seen her weep. She closed her eyes and her mouth, as if she were locking in the sadness and burying it down deep. My father turned away as if unable to look at me. I could barely look at them, either, and fury at their betrayal coursed through me. My mother was superficial and my father was pigheaded, but I'd been able to overlook their flaws because they were my parents and we loved each other. But now that they were abandoning me in my time of greatest need, it was hard to feel anything for them but contempt. This was something I would struggle to forgive.

Without another word, I left. I walked out of the over-upholstered drawing room and through the marbled hall. I bid farewell to the bronze statues and porphyry busts and delicate vases of flowers and the blindingly bright crystal chandeliers. To the maids and the footmen and the disapproving butler. The heavy front door closed loudly behind me, and I felt the thud reverberate through me. I turned to stare at it and it stared back, imposing and fortress-like, hiding a world in which I no longer had any part.

CHAPTER 31

❧

I'd never been so utterly alone before. I walked down the gentle stone steps into the gravel path of my parents' front garden, past the bare sticks of the rose bushes and the green boxwoods, disoriented. I blinked into the gray sun. Beyond the stone wall of the park across the street a lone couple promenaded in the cold.

I'd never arranged accommodations for myself, not even when we traveled. When I was younger, my father had chosen the hotels where we'd stay, and I had fond memories of the Ritz Paris, of the grand shopping expeditions with my mother on the Rue de la Paix, of sipping hot chocolate in elegant cafés. When I'd married, Charles had seen to all the details of our honeymoon, and everything had been a grand surprise. At no point in my life had I been without shelter, a home to go back to, and even though I was proud of myself for my courage, I was also a little lost. It was overwhelming.

I clutched my purse tightly, and even its tapestry design of a romantic castle seemed to mock me. The purse wasn't large, and fit only some money, a necklace, and the Bonaparte earrings. I would send for my trunks once I settled somewhere—surely my parents wouldn't deprive me even of those. Although I supposed nothing was certain.

After a few more minutes' hesitation, I hailed a cab and told the driver to take me to the Waldorf-Astoria. The Waldorf was a familiar refuge, as I'd been there for many a dinner and ball, and I knew that it accepted single women without an escort.

Inside, though, my sense of belonging faded as I approached the curved marble reception desk. The grandeur of the towering coffered ceilings and marble columns felt like a reprimand. I should find a ladies' hotel with cheaper rates, only none came to mind offhand. I reassured myself that a night or two here wouldn't make much of a difference while I got my bearings.

As I made my reservation, I swallowed a surge of anger that Rose Briar Hall should sit uselessly empty while I spent precious funds on a hotel. It was my house, but as long as Briggs and Terry were there at Charles's behest, I couldn't go back. Even if I successfully forced them off the property, the house was too isolated, and Charles would be able to find me there too easily. No, it was better to remain anonymous.

Soon I was tucked away in an elegant room with a brass bed frame, richly patterned wallpaper, and a thick rug. I sank down onto the pristine white bedding and looked around. My fear abated, replaced by a growing awe that I was here, by myself, and nobody knew it. I was done living by others' rules.

Now the only counsel I had to follow was my own.

David's boardinghouse glowed with light and noise against the darkening sky. It hadn't taken long for me to grow restless alone in my new room, and I didn't want to sit still and stew over my parents' betrayal. I longed to be comforted.

It was a three-story triangular slice of a building on the west side near the Hudson, and the air stank of salt and river water and beer. The bottom floor was an all-night saloon, and some sailors loitering outside it whistled at me as I searched in vain for a ladies' entrance. I'd persuaded a colleague at David's paper to give me his address, but actually finding *him* at this establishment might be trickier than I'd imagined.

I steeled myself and entered the saloon, which had sawdust on the floor and a man playing a fiddle while brightly dressed whores danced with the customers. I eyed them curiously and a little jealously. I wondered if David had ever taken any of them upstairs.

Fortunately, David himself was at the bar, nursing a pint of beer and talking to a sailor. When he saw me his eyes widened comically, but then he smiled so big that I tingled with pleasure.

"You shouldn't be in a place like this," he said, his breath hot on my ear. But he ordered a pint for me, too. The sailor appraised me with interest before courteously disappearing into the melee.

"What were you speaking about?" I said, watching him depart.

"This and that. Sailors are shameless gossips."

"Is that why you live here?" I hadn't meant to ask the question, but I was curious.

Journalists' wages may not be a fortune, but they could afford more than this. David only shrugged.

"I'm trying to save a little money. And I miss living near the sea. This is as close as I can get for now."

I drank the beer quickly out of nervousness, and it loosened my limbs. After one more, I let David twirl me around the dance floor—such as it was—alongside the whores. It was scandalously improper, but I didn't care. No one on earth I knew would see me here. Besides, David's hand was warm on my waist, and he was a little drunk and looking at me like I had just done something heroic.

"I really want to kiss you."

"Why don't you, then?"

His face was near mine, almost nose to nose, and I licked my lips, expectant, while my heart pattered against my ribs.

"Not here."

"No?"

His breath tickled my nose.

"I want us to be alone." He tugged my hand and I followed him out of the saloon to a different door in the building, which he opened with a key. We went up a poky staircase to a hallway lined with rooms. The ceiling was stained black with soot from the gas lamps.

Outside of his door, David paused. "You don't have to come in, you know. If you're uncomfortable."

It was he who looked uncomfortable, in a too-big suit jacket, his hand lingering on the knob. I considered him, my heart pounding. But I wasn't going to lose my resolve now. This was why I'd come here, wasn't it? I had left my old life behind and was determined to forge ahead dauntlessly into my new one. Yes, the lowness of the saloon and the dinginess of the boardinghouse shocked me a little, but with David before me, gorgeous and adoring, the rest was easy to overlook.

"I'm not."

He smiled with half his mouth, crooked as the stairs.

"All right, then."

The door swung open into David's little sitting room. It was humble enough, but it smelled like him, of books and clean cotton. A banged-up old typewriter sat atop a small desk, and I could easily picture him there, keys clacking while the music from the fiddle floated up through the floorboards.

"I know it's not much. Not what you're used to by a long mile." He looked self-conscious, which surprised me. He was always so self-assured.

"Anywhere with you in it is lovely." And then I kissed him. He was taking far too long to get around to kissing me, and I couldn't wait. He kissed me back gently, slowing me down.

He pulled away, and I stepped back, too, confused. "What's wrong?"

He was breathing heavily. "I shouldn't have brought you here."

"David, it's fine, really. I wasn't expecting a palace, you know."

"Not that."

"What, then?"

"I want to do more than kiss you, Millie. And you're still married. I don't want to be the reason—"

I kissed him softly, stealing his words. "I thought a newspaperman of all people would know the news. I sued Charles for divorce."

I watched his throat bob. "I heard."

"The lawyer said I'll have to be patient. It could take months before it's all over." I touched the hollow in his neck with my finger, awed that I could. "But I'm not patient, David. Not at all." I kissed him again. When I drew away, his uncertainty was gone, and he was smiling a little wickedly.

"But you're going to have to be."

"What do you mean?"

And then his fingers were on my waist, slowly undoing the buttons at the back of my dress. Nimbly and capably. I gasped. "I'm going to make you be very, very patient." My whole body grew warm and tense with anticipation. He finished, and then slid my dress down over my shoulders, exposing my corset beneath. It slid to the floor, and then his fingers—those amazing, dexterous hands—started loosening my laces. I was breathing fast, little rapid shallow breaths. But then he stopped. "Do you want me to keep going?"

My mouth watered. I could barely speak. "Yes. Oh yes." He loosened a single lace.

"Do you still want me to keep going? I want you to be very sure."

"Please. Please go faster."

He loosened one more lace. I thought of Charles's roughness, how he shoved himself into me. We'd have been done by now, or near to it. We had never gone slow like this. He had rarely even fully undressed me.

"Are you still sure, Millie?"

"Oh God, David, please." I reached for him, grabbing at the buttons on his shirt. He grabbed my hand, stopping me. Loosened one more lace. My whole body trembled. I thought he would never finish, but he did at last, and he stood marveling at me as if I were a work of art. My pale skin glowed in the gaslight. Then he loosened his collar and undressed himself while I watched, and I wouldn't let him stop me from helping this time. He felt strong and smooth. Then he led me to his little bedroom and laid me gently on his bed, and I had never wanted anything in the world as badly as I wanted him to touch me. He cupped a breast and I moaned. He was so careful, so deliberate, and it was like being tortured with pleasure instead of pain. Finally, he ended my agony by kissing me somewhere I had never been kissed before, and I cried out, every nerve pulsing, overcome. When he positioned himself above me and took me, as slowly as he had done everything else, I was lost in sensation. It was like we were adrift at sea together, rolling with the waves, swelling and crashing.

The next day was Saturday and we awoke with the sun on our faces.

"Morning." He smiled at me, his eyes still sleepy. I was tucked against him, his arm draped lazily around my waist, and his skin was warm and smelled of the salt from his sweat. He trailed his fingers along my back, up and down the bumps of my spine, and suddenly I was wide awake, my skin tingling. He snuggled me closer to him, and I stroked his strong chest, his sinewy arms, traced the lines connecting his torso and muscular thighs. The sleepiness disappeared from his eyes, and I felt the hardness of him rising against my belly. "Come here, you."

This time, he didn't make me wait. He kissed me along my jaw, my breasts, my lips, and lowered himself into me. I let out a breath and wrapped my legs around him. He rolled me on top of him, a practiced motion, without unlocking himself, and his face was feverish. Within minutes we were slick and sweaty, the winter outside be damned.

He touched me softly, delicately circling the little knob he'd showed me yesterday, his hips rocking up to meet me. My thoughts circled, too, senseless and delirious, until at last I let out a strangled moan, shaking.

"I'm not finished yet," he said, cocking that impish smile again, and he kept rocking, until my whole body pulsed again, every nerve and fiber. Then he grew stiffer inside of me and released himself, and we stayed that way for a minute, me slumped on top of him, still tangled together.

We stayed in bed the whole day, except to use the bathroom down the hall or to eat salty oysters at his little table that he brought up from the bar downstairs. He explored me like I was a new land he had just discovered, like he had to chart every inch of it, until we were stupid with pleasure.

Oh, I could wait. I would wait however long it took to be rid of Charles, if I could have this.

CHAPTER 32

I slunk back to the Waldorf Sunday slightly disheveled and smelling of sex. I imagined that all the tony guests watched me with judgmental stares, and decided I would check out as soon as possible. David had given me a list of alternatives to consider, at different price points, and I'd already succeeded in sending a porter to retrieve my trunks from my parents when I arrived at the hotel. There was nothing to keep me here.

"Room 347, please."

The clerk, a friendly, refined man with gray hair, smiled reassuringly at me. "Mrs. Turner. How lovely to see you again. We've already checked you out and the bill has been paid. Your husband is waiting for you in the Turkish Salon."

Ice filled my stomach. He motioned discreetly, and I looked across the entrance hall toward the heavily mosaicked room, where I glimpsed Charles lounging in a plush velvet armchair. He'd found me so easily; I felt like a fool.

"I see. Can you please arrange for my trunks to be taken to a carriage, as quickly as possible? And retrieve my jewelry from the safe?"

The clerk smiled toothlessly. "Everything has already been taken to your automobile. I'll go have a porter alert your husband that you're here."

"No." The word came out loud and sharp. The clerk

frowned slightly. Trembling overtook me, but I managed a small smile. Best not to make a scene, or Charles would notice my arrival for certain. "I'll go tell him myself. Thank you."

I turned and hurried through the entrance hall, the back of my neck prickling as I passed the Turkish Salon. If he saw me, he would certainly pursue. He would catch up to me and strong-arm me into the car. Even if I shrieked, what would anyone do? The other guests would deem a public marital spat none of their business, and horribly unseemly. The police, should they be summoned by the staff, wouldn't help. As my husband, he had every right to claim me. I could see the scene unfolding and I knew exactly how it would end—the tense journey home, the inevitable doctor's visit, the sleeping potions. I was away from my parents' house and had lost my father's protection, so he might not even bother with the asylum. Now that I'd sued Charles for divorce, he wouldn't waste time.

I rushed down the stairs onto Thirty-third Street and accosted a porter in his shiny-buttoned uniform and sleek cap. "A cab please, quickly."

He must have been used to the haste of his customers, because he hailed a carriage with gusto.

"Millie. Stop." The sound of Charles's voice from the top of the stairs paralyzed me and I was too afraid even to turn and look at him. I could picture him, though, standing straight and lean and angry, his mustache twitching. A carriage clattered to a stop in front of me, and the porter, bless him, opened the door as if he hadn't heard Charles. Somehow I forced my legs to move, to climb into the carriage. I'd been holding my breath and I released it with a whoosh.

"Just go, please. Hurry."

The horses' hooves clopped away from the entrance and now I dared to look back. I saw Charles in angry conference with the porter underneath the wrought iron marquee, but he glanced up and his eyes locked with mine, turning my trembling into shaking. In an instant, though, we were swept up in the stream of traffic, and I knew that if he tried to follow, he'd be too late.

I placed my head in my hands, still convulsing with shock. How near I'd come to failure. Of course Charles had known to look for me at the Waldorf; it had been a thoughtless and impulsive choice. How clever of him to take all of my trunks. My jewels. I swallowed. I thought I'd have to economize before, but now I truly had almost nothing. At least I had a couple of necklaces on my person—one on my neck and one in my purse—but their weight comforted me only a little.

I selected the cheapest boardinghouse from David's list. The driver had looked at me disbelievingly when I'd told him the address, but at last he took me to a severe-looking brick building that David had said offered rooms on short notice. I paid the driver, anxious at parting with any of the money in my purse, and approached the steps.

The air downtown smelled like coal and horses. The landlady who greeted me was as severe looking as her house, rail thin with a knot of gray hair. She eyed me with shrewd appraisal, examining my blue serge dress, finer than anything in the establishment.

"I only have one room at the moment. It's small, but it's yours if you want it. You'll need to pay for the full week upfront, mind."

I nodded. I followed her past a sitting room with a threadbare rug, up a rickety set of stairs, down a narrow hallway. She opened one of the doors and showed me the plainest room I'd ever seen. There was no rug, just wide and rough wooden boards. A small fireplace with ash still coating its bottom. A single bed with no bedding, though she assured me she could make it up for me before evening. A nightstand with a basin and pitcher. That was all.

My throat tightened. Through the wall, I could hear a woman snoring.

"It will do." My voice was faint. I had grown used to luxury, and this room was a window into my future. I never thought of myself as pampered and sometimes envied the working women I saw on the streets, with their practical linen shirtwaists and wool skirts, gossiping together and carrying lunch pails. I knew about tenements, about poverty, of course, but in my imagination these women had lived in cozy little garrets. I had pictured being one of them and going home to some small, charming flat with a balcony and flower boxes. How naïve I'd been. I breathed in the stale boardinghouse air, tinged with the smell of old wood and unwashed bodies.

I paid the landlady reluctantly, and after she left I sat down on the bed, which dipped and creaked. There was no David here to distract me from its meanness, and I swallowed.

But I had lived a simpler life, once. Somehow, I would adjust. I would be safe, at least, and free.

CHAPTER 33

Mrs. Dewy, the charitable employer of Gertrude's former maid, served a marvelous tea. It surprised me; I'd assumed she'd be the penny-pinching sort, given her widowhood and virtuous reputation, but I bit into a delicious chicken salad finger sandwich with gusto. She pursed her mouth a little, but I didn't care. A few days at the boardinghouse had been enough to make me thoroughly sick of boiled food. Breakfast was always porridge, thin and bland, and dinner was usually boiled potatoes and rubbery chicken, or something equally unappetizing. Once I'd splurged on hot spiced nuts from a street vendor, but my goal was only to buy essentials if I could help it. I'd never had to budget before, and it was difficult.

"We appreciate you meeting with us, Mrs. Dewy," Mr. Thistle said. "As we explained, we hoped we might have some time to interview your maid, Sophia Lester, about her former mistress." He craned his neck, looking for her. I spotted her hovering in the hallway outside the drawing room, her pretty gray eyes wide.

"I quite understood your letter. I run a respectable house here, Mr. Thistle, and I don't want poor Lester dragged into this sordid mess." She turned toward the girl, whose crisp white pinafore strained over her ample chest. Her brown hair was tucked neatly under her cap. "You may come in, Lester."

She curtseyed and then sat where Mrs. Dewy indicated,

perching on the edge of her chair as if she might need to spring up at any moment.

"Lester, I'd like to hear in your own words what you knew about the relationship between Charles Turner and your former mistress Gertrude Underhill," Mr. Thistle said.

She shrank back from Mr. Thistle's pointy-toothed smile. "I don't recall, really." Her eyes darted nervously toward Mrs. Dewy.

"I can issue a subpoena that will compel you to testify in court. And in court you'll have to be truthful." Mr. Thistle turned stern.

"You'll do no such thing. I won't have any maid of mine made a spectacle of." Mrs. Dewy pulled her shawl tighter around her shoulders, and her gray curls quivered as she shook her head.

Poor Lester burst into tears. "I need this position, sir. Please. And I don't know anything, really. Not for certain. I never saw them together, I only knew what Mrs. Underhill told me."

Mr. Thistle frowned. "Which was?"

"That she was with child. That it was Mr. Turner's." Lester sobbed harder and hid her face in her hands. I felt sorry for her and ashamed of what we were pressuring her to do. I wouldn't be the reason the poor girl lost her position. At the same time, I didn't know what we would do without her and my chest constricted.

"But you never saw him come to her rooms? Never saw them kiss, or touch?" Mr. Thistle insisted. Lester was crying too hard to answer and just shook her head.

"I think that's quite enough," Mrs. Dewy said. "This interview is over."

Mr. Thistle's frown deepened, but we didn't overstay our welcome. We retrieved our things from the footman and walked down the steep stoop of the brownstone to the quiet gray sidewalk. I savored being back uptown. Near my boardinghouse, cars blared their horns as they careened around corners, hawkers shouted their prices from behind their fruit and fish carts, and boys had snowball fights with blackened snow, scurrying out of the way of streetcars and horses. It was interesting but a bit exhausting, too, when it constantly surrounded you, and I often thought longingly of Rose Briar Hall, with its peaceful grounds and plush rugs and rich furniture.

"That could have gone better," Mr. Thistle said unnecessarily. "She might fall apart on the stand if we force her to testify. And something she was told by a dead woman may not carry enough weight. We need to find someone who actually saw them together. Or better yet, a mistress who's alive."

I appreciated that Mr. Thistle didn't mince words. He spoke to me like a client, not like a delicate lady whose feelings needed to be spared.

"There has to be someone else." I buttoned my gloves, my hands trembling.

"I'll have someone investigate, but because of the expedited trial date we don't have as much time as I would like."

Mr. Thistle had managed to speed things along because of the public interest in the case. I hadn't requested secrecy around the proceedings: I wanted the world to see Charles for what he was.

"There might be someone. Lily Applebee. I don't think she'll help, but I'll go call on her now." I glanced back at Mrs. Dewy's brownstone, and saw Lester's face flash in the window. "It's best I go alone, I think." It was a conversation that needed to be had woman-to-woman, and Mr. Thistle's smiles weren't as reassuring as he thought they were. Maybe poor Lester would have done better with a gentler approach.

"All right. Let me know if you get anywhere. Does she live nearby? I can drop you off on my way back to the office."

She did, and we climbed into Mr. Thistle's waiting carriage, which clattered along the dozen or so blocks to a brownstone very like Mrs. Dewy's. We said goodbye, and I licked my lips nervously as I gazed up at it. The thought crossed my mind that Charles himself might be here, which made the visit a terrible risk, but the lack of a waiting carriage out front encouraged me. I knew Charles would be looking for me. David had made inquiries at several of the more popular ladies' hotels and learned a man fitting Charles's description had made insistent inquiries after a guest named Millie Turner. Uncomfortable as the boardinghouse was, I felt safe there. It wouldn't have occurred to Charles that I would be living so humbly; such parsimony would be impossible for him to fathom.

I faced an uncertain reception when I rang the bell, but to my surprise, the butler showed me in. Miss Applebee was already seated in the drawing room, but it struck me as mere coincidence. She was dressed too simply to be expecting visitors, and she looked like she'd been crying.

"I wondered if you'd come," she said by way of greeting. She looked so terribly young in that moment, her pink cheeks were even pinker than usual, and her eyes rimmed red. "You want to lord it over me, I suppose."

"I'm sure I don't know what you mean."

"Let's not pretend, shall we?" She gestured toward the pink-and-white–striped settee. The room must have been decorated by her; the cream walls and pink curtains, the porcelain figurines crowding the mantel, the rosettes on the ceiling painted with bouquets of flowers, all spoke of a feminine touch. "I didn't believe a word of what was in the paper about him, at first. But Father's very angry at Charles. He'd invested with him, you know."

She pressed her knuckles to her lips, as if suppressing a sob.

"I'm very sorry. I hope his losses weren't too great."

"What it said about Mrs. Underhill was true, wasn't it? She was having his baby. I feel like such an awful fool."

I wondered how long Charles had been wooing her. Since

before Gertrude died, I supposed. How busy he must have been. "I'm the one who was a fool, Miss Applebee," I said, my distaste giving way to compassion. It was hard to be spiteful in the face of her evident despair. "I'm sure you've seen that I've sued for divorce. I know it's a lot to ask, but I'm hoping you might testify."

She raised her perfectly arched blond eyebrows and opened her rosy mouth. Then she laughed breathily, without humor. "You believe the rumors about me, too, then. I thought you of all people might understand that gossip can't always be trusted. I'm not quite the harlot everyone makes me out to be, you know."

Her directness shocked me, and I found myself rather liking her. I hadn't expected that. "But I thought—"

"He told me he wanted to marry me. But I'm not going to say something happened between us that didn't. People are already so vicious." She wiped an eye. My breath hitched. I hadn't really expected her to agree, but I did feel ashamed for so easily believing the snide comments about her. They'd probably been borne out of jealousy.

"I see. Well, I appreciate your candor. And . . . I'm sorry. Truly."

I stood and smiled sadly at her before showing myself out. She stayed seated and said nothing, apparently lost in her own thoughts.

The day had been a disaster and the trial seemed doomed. I hadn't allowed myself to think much about failure, but now the possibility overwhelmed me.

My life had been so easy before, and suddenly everything was hard. I'd never been tested like this and I wasn't sure I was strong enough to bear it. I closed my eyes and thought of David. If he were here, he'd put his arms around me and tell me that I was braver than I knew.

Maybe not all hope was lost. I could still testify. My own word still had to count for something.

CHAPTER 34

The eyes of the reporters bored into me. My heart kicked against my ribs as I looked meekly down at my hands. Someone was sketching me for one of the newspapers, and I sat as still as I could, as if I were posing for a portrait. I wore a soft dove-gray tailored morning suit, very conservative, but still flattering—Mr. Thistle had impressed upon me the importance of looking beautiful. I'd bought it specially for the occasion with my precious funds. We had asked for a jury trial and been granted one; Mr. Thistle told me the men would all fall in love with a pretty thing like me and feel sorry for me. The eyes of the jurors bored into me, too. It was a strange sensation. Like being an actor in a play.

"Please tell us, Mrs. Turner, what you witnessed between your husband and Gertrude Underhill the evening of October 24."

I clasped my hands together in my lap. I focused my attention on Mr. Thistle, and not the reporters beyond him. The medieval-style courtroom was large and a bit intimidating, with its stone arches, granite columns, and busy mosaic floors. "I was having a dinner party that evening, and I happened upon them on the terrace, arguing. Mrs. Underhill said she planned to tell me about their romantic relationship, and my husband protested. They didn't know I could hear them." I spoke slowly and somberly, allowing my voice to catch. Charles faced me, watching me as closely as everyone else, but I avoided his gaze. Still, I could feel his presence, and I shivered. I hadn't seen him since that morning at the Waldorf-Astoria. I was scared to look at him and see the controlled rage on his face.

"I see. And had you known about their affair before then?"

"No, it was quite a shock. I thought we were happy." I dabbed an eye with my handkerchief.

"And did Mrs. Underhill get a chance to tell you, as she'd planned?"

I shook my head sadly. "She died in a tragic accident."

Mr. Thistle said it was best to be vague on this point; we had to explain only why she wasn't available to testify herself, not the circumstances of her death.

"Thank you, Mrs. Turner." He sat back down, and I braced myself for the cross-examination. Charles's lawyer, Samuel Choate, was what I expected: sturdy and polished. Someone who looked like he could handle himself in a physical fight, but wearing an expensive suit as perfectly pressed as Charles's own.

"Mrs. Turner—are you quite sure your memory of this evening is accurate?"

I'd expected this, and Mr. Thistle and I had prepared for it. "I am."

"Only isn't it true, Mrs. Turner, that you had a hysterical fit that evening and couldn't remember the party for weeks afterward?"

I could hear stirring among the jury, but I avoided turning toward them. "I've been told that temporary amnesia after a traumatic incident is quite common. I was also given a great deal of sleeping medication by Charles's doctor. But my memory is fully restored."

Mr. Choate scoffed, as if he didn't believe it. "Didn't your doctor think that it might even be necessary to commit you to an institution?"

"Charles's doctor, not mine. Charles would have done anything to prevent this trial from happening. But Dr. Alfred Kimpton entirely refuted his diagnosis." I spoke calmly and clearly, knowing that appearing even-tempered was critical. I couldn't display even a hint of the hysteria Charles accused me of.

"How terribly unfortunate that Mrs. Underhill isn't able to be here to defend herself." Mr. Thistle stood up to object, but Mr. Choate spread his hands placatingly. "No further questions."

I exhaled in relief and slowly withdrew to the hard wooden chair beside Mr. Thistle. I'd done reasonably well, I thought, and he smiled encouragingly at me.

We planned to call one more witness today. Mr. Thistle's investigator had been thorough, and he'd discovered Dorothy Huntley, the cleaning woman at the apartment building where Charles had kept his secret flat.

"The plaintiff calls Dorothy Huntley to the stand, your honor," Mr. Thistle chirped. The judge had that flaccid, sagging look of a man who drinks and has for years, and big pillows beneath his eyes.

"He's not friendly to divorce cases," Mr. Thistle hissed when he sat back down. His breath stank of onions. "It's a good thing we asked for a jury trial." The judge still had the authority to overturn a jury verdict, but Mr. Thistle assured me that was rare.

Mrs. Huntley trundled out of her seat and to the stand, looking very coarse and out of place in the ostentatious courtroom. The Tweed Courthouse, constructed at a phenomenal expense, was a well-known city symbol of waste and corruption, but it certainly made an impression.

I finally risked a glance at Charles. To my surprise, he didn't look angry. He looked bereft. Heartbroken. His head was bowed, his face crumpled like the handkerchief in his pocket—usually neatly folded—and his eyes red, as if he'd been crying. I had never seen him cry, not once. It was a show,

I reminded myself, for the jurors. Still, it caused a swoop in my belly, an irrational prickle of guilt. Ridiculous that I should feel anything but contempt for him, and yet in his presence I had to struggle to remind myself of what he really was.

Mrs. Huntley was in her fifties and had a pragmatic, direct way of speaking. She made a good witness, according to Mr. Thistle. After she had been sworn in, he asked her to tell the jurors what she had observed on the twentieth of September last year.

"I was scrubbing the stairs when I saw that man there leave his apartment with a lady," she said.

"You saw Mr. Turner?"

"Yes, if that's his name."

"And did you think that the lady was his wife?"

"No, sir. I could tell she wasn't, by the way they was whispering. Acting secretive-like."

"Objection, speculation, your honor." Mr. Choate lacked Mr. Thistle's flair for spectacle. But he was still effective, the way a hammer is effective at nailing: blunt and forceful and direct. I wondered what sport he had played at university, and whether he had gone to Harvard or Yale. Something violent: football, probably. And Harvard, I guessed; I had detected a trace of a Brahmin accent.

"Sustained." The judge scratched his nose. I squared my shoulders and smiled at him; he scowled in reply.

"Mrs. Huntley," Mr. Thistle continued, as if the interruption hadn't happened, "is the woman you saw sitting in the courtroom here today?"

"No, sir."

"Do any women live in the building where you work?"

"No, sir. It's for men only. Bachelors, mostly, or married men who want to meet their mistresses."

"Objection, your honor, speculation. The witness can't possibly know that the men aren't meeting their own wives."

"Sustained. Mr. Thistle, control your witness."

Mrs. Huntley looked confused. "But who would rent out a flat to meet his wife in if he has a separate house with her? That don't make any sense."

She looked so genuinely perplexed that the jurors laughed. Mr. Thistle beamed at her. He asked her a few more questions, and by the end it seemed crystal clear that she had seen Charles meeting another woman. I flicked my eyes up toward the jury, and a few men stared at me with pity in their faces. I was pleased with Mr. Thistle's advice; all of his predictions had been correct so far. Hope swelled within me.

When Charles's lawyer interrogated her, though, her certainty wavered. Did she wear spectacles? he asked her. Had she ever in her life spotted someone she thought she knew and been mistaken? How often had she seen Mr. Turner before that day? How many times exactly? Would she swear on her life it was him? His questions were fast and piercing, like gunfire. Mrs. Huntley looked entirely bewildered.

"I wouldn't swear it on my life, no sir. I value it too much."

"I see. So it could have been some other man meeting his mistress, then?"

"I suppose so, yes."

"Thank you, Mrs. Huntley, that will be all." I gripped the sides of my chair to keep from shaking. I looked at Mr. Thistle and he frowned slightly and shrugged his shoulders, as if to say, *This is the way things go, sometimes.* Losing wouldn't matter much to him personally, I thought. But for me, it wasn't an option.

"We have to call Sophia Lester, Mrs. Turner," he whispered. Court would be adjourning for the day, but he'd included her on the witness list for tomorrow, just in case. It pricked my conscience, but I knew that whatever Mrs. Dewy claimed, she wouldn't force Lester to violate a court-ordered subpoena, nor would she blame her for it. She was too moral for that.

"All right."

CHAPTER 35

I stood beside a massive Corinthian column at the top of the courthouse's steep, grand steps, and I sensed Charles approaching before I saw him, like a crackle of electricity along my spine. The reporters pooled around us, shouting questions and scratching on their little notepads.

"Why are you doing this to me, Millie? To us?" He approached me, and lovingly took my hand in his.

"Please. You know very well why." I retrieved my hand and hurried down the steps, eager to get away from him. I'd paid a hansom cab to be waiting for me and climbed inside in relief. I spoke into the trap door to the driver in the sprung seat in the back and gave him the address for a tea room near my boardinghouse. I didn't want Charles to be able to follow me.

But for some reason, the driver lingered. Before I had a chance to repeat my instructions, Charles himself climbed in beside me. I recoiled and rushed to climb out, but he grabbed my wrist, hard, and the driver quickly spanked his horse. The carriage moved forward.

My heart raced. I was trapped.

"Please, Millie, I just want to talk to you." Charles let go of my wrist. His expression remained just as heartbroken as it had been in the courtroom, even though there was no jury to see it.

"Let me out at once." He wouldn't, I knew. Where would he take me? We'd have to stop somewhere, and when we did, I could run. If there were people nearby, I'd scream for help. A sob bobbed below my breastbone. Charles must have determined which cab was mine and paid the driver to wait for him.

David would come looking for me, surely, if I disappeared. And possibly Mr. Thistle. Surely it would be suspicious if I disappeared or died in the middle of the trial? I didn't think Charles would risk it, not right now.

I clung to hope, reassuring myself and trying to calm the pounding in my chest. David was so smart and so determined. Whatever Charles had planned, David would find me.

Charles's eyes pleaded with me. "I just wanted to apologize. I betrayed you. It's true that Gertrude and I . . . well, I was an utter fool. But other men have had affairs, Millie, and their marriages have recovered. You don't have to do this. I still love you."

I stilled. Charles never admitted he was wrong. It shocked me. The trial must be going better for me than it seemed, if Charles was trying to convince me to drop the suit. He must be desperate. "It's not just the affair. You killed her. She was going to tell me about the baby, and you killed her." My voice cracked. My body shook. I hated how close he was to me in the snug cab, that his leg was pressed against mine.

Charles lurched away from me, as far as he could in the tight space. "What?"

"I saw you. You put the drug in her teacup, before you told me to pour."

He shook his head, apparently at a loss for words. "How can you think such a thing about me? Millie, don't you know me at all?" He clutched my hands again. I was grateful for my gloves separating my skin from his.

"You claimed to think it about me." I turned away, staring at the street outside, attempting to guess our destination.

"My God. You really mean it." I glanced back at him, and he had a hand over his mouth. He appeared deep in thought. "What you said in Dr. Kimpton's office, about Briggs trying to give you an overdose. Was that true?"

"Don't pretend you don't know." I was getting impatient with this charade. He was still so sure of his charm that he thought he could win me back. After everything. His self-absorption knew no bounds.

"Millie, I don't know. I'm just trying to piece this all together. Could it be that Briggs—I mean, she would have had access to Gertrude's tea. And she found the poison that she said was yours. Maybe you were right about her all along. And I didn't listen." He spoke so passionately that for the briefest moment I did consider the possibility that he was telling the truth. Briggs could have acted alone, in theory—only what could she have possibly had against Gertrude? She lacked his motive. "I know you're angry about the medical treatment, but try to see it from my perspective. I truly believed you were dangerous. I shouldn't have given so much credit to Dr. Wendell. Please, Millie. I'm not a perfect man, but I'm not the monster you seem to think I am."

I closed my eyes, and wished I could close my ears against his honeyed lies. His magnetism and charisma were powerful, but they'd lost the influence on me they'd once had. I didn't feel his usual pull—only a gentle tug. I made myself remember Lily Applebee's red-rimmed eyes. Charles couldn't count on marrying her fortune anymore, so he wanted access to what I could still give him—Rose Briar Hall and its valuable contents. It wouldn't save his business, but I imagined he'd rather get something than nothing.

"Stop the cab, Charles. I want out."

He sighed and squeezed my hand harder. "Just promise me you'll think about what I've said." He turned to the trapdoor and, to my utter astonishment, asked the driver to pull over.

I didn't reply and exited, trembling in relief, onto the crowded sidewalk.

I sat on one of the worn chairs in David's sitting room, trying to ignore the stuffing escaping through a small hole, the discoloration of the green fabric. Normally I looked forward to our evenings together, when we ate cheese and bread and fruit, and drank wine, and talked, before ending up in bed together, the sheets tangled around us. But the beginning of the trial and the cab ride with Charles had unsettled me. I swallowed to dislodge the hard knot in my chest, but it stayed in place.

"I think a hansom cab may have followed me here. I can't be sure," I told him. I hadn't gone back to my boardinghouse at all that day, terrified after parting from Charles that he would have me tailed. I thought I'd spotted the same driver several times throughout the day, but the streets downtown had been crowded, and I might have been wrong.

"You know, you don't have to go through with all of this." His voice was gentle. "We could run away together. Leave all this messy business behind. Go to Europe, I could be a stringer for my paper. I know I'm not rich, it wouldn't be the life you are used to, but we could be happy, don't you think?"

He knelt before me and ran a finger along the curve of my jaw. Then he fixed me with a stare that made me strain against every pinch of my corset. David and I talked often of our dreams for travel. Despite my previous wealth, I'd never been to many of the places I longed to see, and Italy in particular called to me—the ancient ruins, the artworks by Renaissance masters. I allowed myself to picture us at a table at a little café, sharing a carafe of wine as we watched Italian children skipping across a cobbled square. And perhaps—who knew?—there could be a child of our own. Charles and I had been childless for long enough that I'd started to worry, but not so long that I'd given up hope that I could conceive. At least there were no children dragged into this mess between Charles and me. I was grateful for that.

I sighed. "It sounds lovely. But he would come looking for me. He'd find me. I'd always be looking over my shoulder." An ocean wouldn't be enough to stop Charles. It might not be the same as a locked room, but I'd still be trapped. Without a divorce, I'd never be free of him. Gertrude's bulging eyes appeared in my mind, the yellow bile spilling down her chin. Fear gripped me, and my vision for a life abroad with David warped. I saw us checking into hotels under false names, hurried exits as Charles pursued us, never living anywhere, always running. I imagined us at that Italian café, me sipping my tea and wondering, always wondering . . .

Ice snaked down my spine.

"If you lose—"

I put a finger to his lips, stopping his words. "Let's not think of that right now." I sat beside the little table where he'd arranged wine and cheese for us, and tasted a piece to distract myself from the adrenaline still coursing through me. My fingers were tense and clumsy. "He spoke to me today. He said Briggs could have been responsible for all of it. He actually apologized to me."

David stood and poured a glass of red wine. "Did you believe him?" There was an edge to his voice. It was the tone he used with sources, and hadn't used with me since before our first kiss.

"No. I'm sorry. I'm just trying to understand." Tears welled in my eyes. I knew what Charles was, but it was difficult to comprehend using people in the way he did. There was part of me that did wonder whether he'd ever felt anything for me at all, or if it had all been an act from the start. It had been my mother's maneuverings that led us to first dancing together at Sherry's that night, and Charles's confidence and poise had stood in stark contrast to so many of the men who'd tried to flirt with me before, men who were too loud or too dull. And he wasn't the snob I'd been expecting. He was impressed by my father's ascent from his humble beginnings, and listened with interest to my opinions on art, a passion he shared. As our courtship progressed over the month before our engagement, my life gained contour and interest. It was as if my world had been a mere sketch on paper, and suddenly I found myself in the painting of a great master. Charles promised me sleigh rides together through Central Park in the winter, picnics in the summer, his voice low and seductive, stirring my desire. I'd liked the challenge, too, of securing someone so sought after and taking on the great task of being Mrs. Charles Turner. It appealed to my ego. I had become more like my mother than I'd recognized at the time.

But now I remembered other things about that month: his criticisms about my behavior, or my fashion choices, so subtle they were easy to overlook. I'd grown more self-conscious, always worried about making a blunder. He had been polished, intriguing, sensuous, but never warm. Never genuine.

David softened when he saw me crying.

"I can only imagine how confusing it must be. To have been married to a man like that." His voice was still gruff. "I should question Briggs. Her involvement doesn't fully add up for me. And she might know something about Charles that could help with the trial."

I wiped my cheek and nodded. "I suppose it's worth trying."

David pulled me up out of the chair and kissed my cheeks, his lips tracing the tracks of salt on my skin. I turned to catch them with mine, and their warmth ran through me, thawing me from the inside out. Music floated through the floorboards, some lighthearted ditty that people were probably dancing to downstairs. I placed a hand on David's chest. I wanted him, and needed him to pause my spinning thoughts. I stood, then directed him toward the chair, taking my place.

"That's how it is, is it?"

He cocked a smile, but his eyes were still troubled. I longed for our focus to be pulled toward earthier matters. I poured myself a glass of the wine and drank it quickly. It was full bodied but rough, and it rushed into my blood. I felt my muscles loosening, my thoughts growing sluggish. I wanted to pour one more, but instead I pulled up my skirts slowly. David's eyes tracked me closely. I removed my stockings, then my underclothes, and he tensed, every muscle in his body rigid.

"Oh God, you're killing me."

"You're going to have to be patient, David." I smiled slyly at him, and he laughed, understanding the reference. But the reality was, I wasn't patient. I straddled him, felt him stiff beneath me. Once I would never have dreamed of doing something so bold, but I'd been a quick study. The whores downstairs surely had no compunction about straddling their customers, and I was no longer a prim and proper lady of the manor. There was no need to act like one.

David placed a hand on the back of my neck and drew me toward him, tasting my mouth and the vinegary wine. I rubbed his trousers and he moaned. Then I freed him, my fingers quick and sure, fingers that had spent years buttoning boots and dresses, tightening laces. A pair of man's trousers posed no great challenge. He reached a hand toward the inside of my thigh, moving it up, but I clicked my tongue at him and moved it away.

"No, let me." I directed him into me and his breath hitched. I moved up, down, up, down, slow and sure, while his breathing grew ragged. I watched his throat bob, his eyes go wider and wider as he watched me.

"I love you, Millie."

His words burrowed their way into me, spreading warmth and hope. Even with all my damage, all the complications and danger that came from loving me, he did anyway. His love was a bulwark against the pain. Yet, I didn't want to unravel my own confused feelings just then. I didn't want to think at all. "Do you like taking me like this?"

"God, yes."

An image of Gertrude appeared in my mind, and I wondered what she was like in bed. Shy, letting Charles have his way with her, the way he liked? Or did she mount him like this, taking him in a way I'd never dared? Charles cared so little for me that he would rather kill me than stay married to me, and it was a betrayal so deep that sometimes it swallowed me up inside of it.

I moved faster, touching the spot David had showed me, feeling the pressure start to build. I screamed, louder than usual, my rage mingling with my pleasure. The chair knocked against the wall, harder and harder.

David put his hands on my thighs, slowing me down. "Millie, look at me."

I did. His eyes were warm and brown. Charles fled my thoughts. I hated myself for thinking of him when David was sure and solid beneath me. "I love you, too, David," I whispered.

He kissed me, slow and soft, and rocked me gently on his lap, filling me up, healing my wounds. He rocked me until my whole body shattered, and then he gathered me to his chest, putting the pieces back together again.

CHAPTER 36

We were ready to rest our case. Lester had been meek and uncertain on the stand when Mr. Thistle questioned her, so much so that even I doubted she was telling the truth. And she'd fallen apart completely under Mr. Choate's interrogation, dissolving into tears.

Our case was finished, and it would be Charles's turn next. I couldn't imagine what he would say. But what we'd presented hadn't been enough. I was sure we'd lose.

Mr. Thistle prepared to stand, but I grabbed his arm, stopping him. "Wait." He frowned. "I'll find another witness." Mr. Thistle's investigator was good, but we hadn't had enough time. There had to be someone else.

"Can you find one by tomorrow?" He scoffed. He didn't know how desperate I was. I would pay someone to say what we needed if I had to; I'd heard of that being done before.

"Yes." I wouldn't meet his eye.

He studied me carefully. He didn't ask how I would do it or who the witness might be. Perhaps he guessed that I would resort to tactics that it would be better for him not to know about. "All right. I'll see what I can do." He stood. "Your honor, new evidence has just come to light. We'd like to ask for a continuance until tomorrow so that we can evaluate this information."

Charles's lawyer objected, of course, but Mr. Thistle argued beautifully, poetically even, and the judge grumbled about it but ultimately took his side.

"You'd better find something good," he said, after he sat again. He buckled his briefcase with the same energy he applied to everything and pulled the straps tight. I felt stretched in just the same way, my whole body taut.

"Don't worry," I assured him, but as we exited the courtroom my mind jumped. Maybe David would know what to do.

I met David outside of a saloon nearby afterward, taking a meandering route there as a precaution. I didn't like to think what might happen if Charles found out about him. He smiled when he saw me, the corners of his eyes crinkling. I expected we'd go somewhere nearby to eat, but David had a cab waiting.

"What is it? Where are we going?" We climbed in together, and David put a hand on my thigh.

"My father told me Briggs left Rose Briar. She's in the city. I found out where she lives."

I shuddered. The name reverberated through me. In an instant my mind drew me back to my room on Long Island, to the teas that made my mind go blank, to the horror. Briggs's smug grin and cutting blue eyes.

David spoke through the trapdoor separating us from the driver and gave him an address in Brooklyn. He had that determined look he often got when he was working, his jaw clenched. But when he turned to look at me everything softened in an instant, and his eyes searched mine. I could feel the force of his attention, like a weight pressing against me. "You look terrified." I caught the ghost of my reflection in the carriage window and saw that I appeared pale and startled. My heartbeat hammered in my whole body, in my stomach, in my bosom. His eyebrows crowded together. "My God, I don't know what I was thinking, asking you to face her again after what happened. Forgive me." He moved toward the trapdoor again.

"No." I swallowed. My lips were dry. "I want to go." It was a wintery day, and the wind howled outside the carriage, but I was snuggled deeply in my coat, with the heat of David radiating against me. Now, though, my limbs went cold. I pressed up against him and he pulled me close, cradling my head against his chest.

"Shhh. You don't have to. You've already been so brave. Braver than anyone I've ever met." He spoke quietly, reverently, and it warmed me up inside. "I'll take you home. Let me speak to her alone."

"I can do it." I squeezed my eyes shut. Whatever David could persuade her to confess I had to hear for myself.

His hand tightened around me protectively. "Only if you're sure."

"Yes, I'm sure."

When the carriage jolted to a stop in front of a clapboard house, I didn't feel so sure. My legs were numb as we climbed the steps.

"I don't understand—is this a boardinghouse?" The street was lined mostly with stately new brownstones. This house was older, probably from before the Civil War, but in good condition and far nicer than anything Briggs could have afforded.

We rang the bell, and I squeezed David's hand for courage. But it wasn't Briggs who answered. It was her daughter, Maisie, the same sweet, freckled girl from my memory. Except for now, rather than a feather duster, she was holding a squirming baby, who cooed and pulled a tendril of her curly hair in his fist. A baby with Charles's shocking green eyes.

My chest hollowed out and filled with the frigid March air. I felt faint, and there was a strange buzzing in my ears. I clutched David's arm for support, but he hadn't realized what I had and was speaking to Maisie in a perfectly civil tone.

"Does Mrs. Bertha Briggs live here?"

Of course, David didn't know who Maisie was. Maisie considered me, deciding how to reply, and I studied her with new zeal. Sweet, freckled, pale, and so young, maybe nineteen or twenty. Pretty enough in the way young women who blush easily sometimes are. The picture of innocence.

But obviously she was far from it. The baby squealed and waved a chubby hand in my direction.

"Yes! That's right, darling. We have visitors." Her voice was even, more confident than the breathy, laughing girl I remembered. She stroked the baby's sleek head and readjusted him over her cocked hip. The cold air numbed my mind, and it took several moments before I understood. Briggs's grandchild was Charles's son. They were, in a way, family.

"Maisie." I breathed her name softly, hardly realizing I'd spoken it out loud. "Briggs's daughter. My former maid," I said to David. She arched an eyebrow at me and her nostrils flared. She probably saw me as her rival. So did her mother, I realized, as Briggs's motive for attacking me suddenly became perfectly clear.

David made a noise in the back of his throat as he understood what I already had, and he settled a warm hand over mine. Briefly. It wouldn't do to advertise our relationship to Maisie, in case she should tell Charles. "We're sorry to show up unannounced. I'm with Mrs. Turner's legal team. Would it be all right if we had a word inside?"

She sucked on a plump lip, her eyes darting between us. David spoke with such authority that she was persuaded. "I suppose."

She left the door open and disappeared. I hesitated before stepping over the threshold. Perhaps this was part of some gruesome trick. Briggs could be inside, waiting for me. My

heart thudded hard and David touched my hand again, looking at me searchingly. "We don't have to."

He was so good. I clutched him tighter and shook my head.
"No. I can do it."

I had to let him go as we entered—the door wasn't wide
enough for both of us—and I followed him into a snug foyer
with a large mirror and a hat stand. The air was toasty warm,
and I peeked through the pocket doors into the parlor, where
a fire was blazing.

Briggs perched on a settee drinking tea. My pulse throbbed.
But David was right; we had to know what she knew. I longed
to know. To hear it from her own lips, what Charles had
asked her to do.

If he had asked her to.

Now that I'd seen Maisie, and her son, Charles's claims in
the cab yesterday no longer struck me as entirely preposterous. Briggs could have acted alone.

Was it possible that I'd been persuaded of Charles's wickedness as easily as he'd been persuaded of mine? We'd both
suspected each other, but perhaps the whole time Briggs
had been responsible. Suspicion had blossomed between us
so easily. There could never be trust between us again and
our marriage was still over, but I clung to the possibility that
maybe he wasn't quite the villain I'd thought. I was surprised
by how fervently I wished that not everything between us had
been a lie. He was a swindler and a philanderer, certainly, but
perhaps not a killer.

Briggs helped herself to a scone from a tea tray and dabbed
at her mouth delicately. She knew we were here, of course,
but was acting as unperturbed as if the milkman had come
calling. It was strange to see her at home, putting on airs. I
couldn't recollect her ever eating or drinking in front of me,
and certainly she never would have sat in our drawing room,
even as impudent as she was.

Maisie motioned for us to follow her into the parlor. I se-

SECRETS OF ROSE BRIAR HALL   227

lected a chair as far away from Briggs as was possible, but it was a cozy room. The fire snapped.

"I'm sure you know that Mrs. Turner has sued her husband for divorce. I'll get right to the point, Miss Briggs. If you testify about your relationship with him, Mrs. Turner will win her suit, and Mr. Turner will be free. I'd think it's what you both would want."

Neither Maisie nor her mother offered us refreshment, not that I'd have accepted it. "Charles says he'll owe you alimony, if you win. He's going to countersue. And then we'll all be together. Little Charlie needs his father." She jiggled the baby a little too hard, and it let out a wail. Again, my mind moved slowly as I struggled to comprehend. Charles had convinced her that he did plan to divorce me, just on his own terms. A nurse appeared, a heavyset woman with thick eyebrows, and Maisie handed her her son. The idea that my own servants now had servants of their own was slightly surreal. Maisie sat on the settee next to her mother and helped herself to some of the tea. The china was as fine as anything I owned, I noted.

Briggs glowered. She stirred her tea, the spoon clanking against the sides of the too-fine china. Lovely white bone china. Briggs didn't deserve it. "What a cruel joke that such a man should have a wife like you. A madwoman and a murderess. He told me so many times how he wished he could be rid of you, so that he and my Maisie could finally be together." She clanked her cup down in its saucer. I stared at her, assessing her sincerity, but as far as I could tell she meant what she said. If she still truly thought I'd killed Gertrude, then she couldn't have done it.

"Was it your idea to give Mrs. Turner an overdose, or his?" David leaned forward, his feet planted firmly on the floor in front of his chair.

On the mantel above the crackling fire, an elegant gold clock ticked. How handsomely Briggs had profited from her relationship with Charles, and from selling my possessions after forcing me into a drugged stupor. Whatever she'd gotten for pawning my valuables, perhaps Charles had given her a cut. Briggs sat back and considered him. "I don't know what you're talking about."

It was too much to expect her to confess. The wind howled, rattling the windowpanes. I was shaken, too. Whether Charles had suggested the overdose outright or not, I knew how influential he could be, how insidious his little hints would have been. Her belief in my own evil had allowed her to act without remorse.

"I didn't poison Gertrude, Briggs. Whatever Charles told you." My hope for his innocence quickly evaporated. "He's never going to marry her, you know. His business is on the brink of collapse and he needs to marry money. He's using you." Briggs seemed convinced that with me out of the way, Charles would make her daughter lady of the manor, but he never would.

Maisie sat up in her chair as quickly as if a hot coal had burned her back. "I'm the mother of his only child. He doesn't want his son to be a bastard."

I clenched my fingers together. He'd never seemed all that interested in children. He had been willing enough to try for one, but he had never longed for them as I had. "What is Charles like as a father?" The words slipped out before I realized I was going to ask them. But I burned to know. I pictured him bouncing that little boy on his knee, kissing his dark hair. Selfish as he was, maybe he could love a child, at least his own child.

A muscle in David's jaw pulsed. My question had made him jealous.

"He dotes on little Charlie. Adores him. Brings him treats and presents every time he visits."

I nodded. The gifts sounded like him. I wondered when Charles had started seeing Maisie, and how often. Had he been sneaking up to the maids' quarters at night? When I was out calling, had he taken her in his room, bent over the furniture she was supposed to be dusting? Charles adored being adored. Gertrude had never stopped loving him, and Maisie spoke about him with awe. Their devotion would have appealed to his ego.

"Whatever promises he has made to you, Maisie, are lies. Please. Come to the courthouse tomorrow. Help me win my trial. I'm not asking him for alimony; he doesn't even have any money to give."

Upstairs, Charles's son squealed in delight, and I heard his nurse's heavy tread. Maisie's eyes turned up toward the plaster ceiling, where a small crystal chandelier swayed. Whether or not she knew about her mother's plotting, she had tried to steal my husband. And yet I pitied her, as I'd pitied Lily Applebee. They were both so young.

"I'll think about it."

There wouldn't be time to issue her a subpoena by tomorrow, so she'd have to show up willingly. I didn't rate it as likely, but it was at least possible. I stood, and David rose as well. He looked so tenderly at me that I worried for a moment Briggs might sense the current between us. But when I glanced at her, she was looking at her daughter with an expression I didn't understand. It took me a moment to recognize it as affection.

Neither of us wished our hosts goodbye.

CHAPTER 37

I twisted my gloves together in my lap and scanned the court-room, searching for Maisie. I knew she probably wouldn't show up, but I still held out hope. I spotted freckles—but no, it was a thin man with red hair.

And then I saw her. She was really here, wearing a ma-tronly plum dress over her plump frame, looking more like a well-to-do lady in a shop than a maid, or the mother of Charles's son. Little Charlie was here, too, in the arms of the thick-browed nurse.

I couldn't believe my luck.

Mr. Thistle saw the moment I did, and smiled. "The plain-tiff calls Maisie Briggs to the stand."

She walked slowly up the aisle, and I noticed that she looked paler than usual. Charles watched her progress as well. Their eyes met, and her expression changed in an in-stant. She paused, as if having second thoughts. But then she kept walking, and both Mr. Thistle and I exhaled.

"Please state your name for the record."

"Maisie Briggs, sir." Her voice trembled. The room behind me stirred to life, and I saw reporters jostling one another and scribbling notes. The hairs on the back of my neck tin-gled whenever their eyes glided over to me.

"And do you solemnly swear that you will tell the whole truth, and nothing but the truth, so help you, God?"

A pause. Her eyes slid toward Charles. I could tell she was losing her nerve. "I do."

Mr. Thistle bounced on the balls of his feet. "Now, Miss Briggs. It is Miss Briggs, isn't it?"

A flush splotched her cheeks. "Yes, sir."

"And how do you know Charles Turner?"

"I was his maid, sir. For about a year."

"I see. And what was your relationship like with him?"

She looked at her hands. I loved how easily she blushed and how clearly it betrayed her. For a full minute she didn't speak, and I could tell she was wrestling with her answer. "He was a kind employer, sir. Not too demanding."

I sucked in my breath and Mr. Thistle studied her. She'd decided to lie. I'd convinced her to come, but she wasn't strong enough to defy Charles, not with him sitting before her, imploring her with his gaze. But at least she was on the stand, and perhaps Mr. Thistle could still get her to betray something.

"Ah, kind. In what ways was he kind, Miss Briggs?" Mr. Thistle walked toward her as he spoke, casually, but she shrunk back. He smiled at the jurors, as if they were all in on the same joke.

She laughed a little. Nervously. "Nothing much. Just please and thank you, that sort of thing."

"Nothing more than that? No special gifts?" Mr. Thistle persisted.

I sat up straighter. I had told Mr. Thistle almost every detail of my relationship with Charles, so that he understood his character nearly as well as I did. Charles had always given gifts to show his regard, and extravagant gifts I could show off to company pleased him most of all. *Just a little something Charles gave me, do you like it?* I would say, as if the exorbitantly priced jewelry were a mere trinket to us. Maisie reached for her neck, where a pendant on a gold chain dangled. I recognized it—I'd scolded her once for wearing it underneath her uniform. Maids weren't permitted to wear that kind of finery.

"No, sir."

But Mr. Thistle had seen her reach for the necklace, too. "Not that pretty necklace you're wearing?"

Maisie's eyes widened. She wasn't as clever as her mother. She didn't know he was just fishing. She thought he had proof. "Oh yes, he got me a locket as a Christmas present. I forgot."

One of the jurors harrumphed and I suppressed a pleased smile. No one would believe such a flimsy lie.

"Did the other maids get lockets? Or did you do something special for Charles Turner?" He smiled at the jury again.

"Objection! Leading the witness." Charles's lawyer with those broad athlete's shoulders in that fine suit made Maisie shrink back again. Mr. Thistle's skinny, bouncy frame seemed almost friendly in comparison. Maisie faced him with more confidence now. "No, I didn't do anything special."

"Why do you think he got you the locket, Miss Briggs?" Mr. Thistle spread his hands wide.

"I don't know, sir."

"Did you think, at the time, that he expected something in return for such a generous gift?"

Maisie blushed again, bless her. "He is a respectable man, sir. He never would have made me do something indecent."

"So you did it of your own accord, then?"

Several people in the room laughed. Charles's lawyer objected, and the judge's jowls quivered even more than usual when he scolded Mr. Thistle. I stared resolutely at my hands, afraid of what my face might betray.

"Miss Briggs. And we have established that it is *Miss* Briggs. Is it true that you have an infant son? And that he is here in this very courtroom?"

Now several people gasped. Necks craned. Little Charlie, as if on cue, let out a wail. Maisie Briggs said nothing.

"Who is the father of your son, Miss Briggs?" He beckoned the nurse forward with a hand, and she obliged. Now everyone could see little Charlie easily, could see that he was his father in miniature. Surely it would be as obvious to everyone as it had been to me. "Is it Charles Turner?"

The courtroom erupted in exclamations and whispers. "Order in the court," the judge said, fierce as ever, and the whispers evaporated into pin-drop quiet. "The witness is instructed to respond."

Maisie Briggs took in several deep breaths. A fat tear slipped down her mottled cheek. "It was a boy I met at a dance hall on my day off. Nobody of importance." It pained her to say it, I could tell. She wanted to tell the world she was Charles's mistress and that he had sworn to make her his wife. Instead she had to describe herself as a common floozy.

Mr. Thistle snorted. "Did he have green eyes? Only, I can't help but notice that Mr. Turner and your son have the same striking shade."

Little Charlie began bawling. Great, sniveling snobs interspersed with inconsolable screams. The poor little boy was overwhelmed. Every eye turned back to look at him again.

"Objection."

"I retract the question." It was hard to hear him over Charlie's crying, and everyone's attention stayed fixed on the child, studying him, comparing him to his father. Mr. Thistle spread his hands toward the judge again, a placating gesture, and his teeth gleamed as he smiled winningly at the jury, his incisor teeth pronounced and pointy. Teeth designed for attack.

Charles's back was hunched, and he was whispering furiously with his lawyer. For the first time in a long time, the pressure in my chest—the constant aching terror that never quite left, that haunted my dreams—eased a fraction. I could win.

There would be no fleeing into the night with my lover, no living a life of fear that Charles might come to reclaim me.

No, Maisie hadn't admitted their affair, but it was obvious she was lying. Surely the jurors knew. I scanned them, analyzing their faces for the thousandth time, these twelve men who would decide my fate. A man with a bumpy nose and rough hands who looked like a farmer. A man with pince-nez glasses balancing on his nose, glasses that would forever remind me of Dr. Wendell, except this man was younger, sloppily dressed, and had squinting eyes. An accountant, perhaps.

Charles's lawyer questioned Maisie next, short, perfunctory questions that elicited short, perfunctory denials, but the damage was done. The cleaning woman's testimony held some weight, too. She hadn't been entirely discredited, and neither had Sophia Lester. But there is nothing so convincing as seeing a mistress in the flesh, wearing her best clothes, her dress straining against her ample bosom, and her hair scrubbed and shining. No doubt they were all picturing the torrid details of the affair, my refined, Knickerbocker husband shoving himself inside of her and gripping her round bottom.

"Anything else, Mr. Thistle? Or can we eat lunch at last?" the judge huffed.

"No, your honor. I rest my case."

We all disbanded for a while, the onlookers bustling out in a happy, excited clamor, but my stomach was too unsettled for food.

Mr. Thistle pulled a ham sandwich out of his briefcase. I turned to confer with him.

"Well done. That was . . . well. Do you think we have a chance, now?"

I hated how high and desperate my voice sounded. But it couldn't be helped.

He chewed, his eyes twinkling. "Absolutely, Mrs. Turner. Absolutely we do."

CHAPTER 38

Mr. Choate planned to call only one witness: Charles himself. Which is why I was surprised when he asked the judge permission to introduce a new one. A man called Jeb Tarbox. I hadn't the faintest notion who he was.

"Objection, your honor. This man was not included on the pretrial witness list." Mr. Thistle stood so quickly one would have thought his feet itched. He spoke passionately and sincerely, as if the hypocrisy of his objection hadn't even occurred to him.

"And yet, I allowed Miss Briggs to take the stand. The door swings both ways, Mr. Thistle. I will grant the request." The judge sounded weary and, perhaps, a little drunk. His words slurred the tiniest amount. Perhaps he'd had a drink at lunch.

Mr. Thistle sat back down with a thud. "You better tell me who the devil this man is," he said to me, genially.

"I honestly haven't the faintest notion."

Mr. Choate called his mysterious witness, and the man who approached the bench did look familiar, though I couldn't place him. Shaggy blond hair, rough features, and rough character. He looked like he could be a sailor.

My stomach tightened as I realized where I'd seen him before. He was the sailor David had been speaking to at the saloon underneath his rooms, the first night I'd visited him there. Which meant Charles knew about David.

"Oh no."

"You'd better tell me quickly, Mrs. Turner."

But I didn't have the chance before his testimony began. Mr. Choate thudded as he paced back and forth before the witness stand.

"And what was Mrs. Turner doing when you saw her in the saloon, Mr. Tarbox?"

"She was with a man. Irish-looking fellow I know who rents rooms upstairs. Friendly sort. Don't recall his name."

I held my breath. If Mr. Tarbox didn't know his name, perhaps Charles didn't, either. David hadn't told his landlord his real name, a precaution against the angry subjects of some of his stories tracking him down. His boardinghouse wasn't the sort of establishment where those sorts of details mattered much. It was bad enough that Charles knew I'd had an affair, but it would be much worse if he knew it was with the journalist who'd exposed him.

"What was she doing with the man?"

"She danced with him. It was unusual to see a fine lady like her at this sort of place, and everyone remarked upon it. Afterward, they went upstairs together."

"How can you be sure?"

"Well, I keep a room next to his, and I went upstairs myself soon after. I could hear them through the wall, moanin' like."

The room blurred. I reached for a cup of water on the table before us and gulped greedily, my tongue like sand and my face hot with shame. To think that someone had overheard David and me at such an intimate moment was bad enough. To hear that information repeated to the public was almost more than I could bear.

"Thank you, Mr. Tarbox. That will be all."

Mr. Thistle leaned over. "Speak quickly, Mrs. Turner."

"I . . . don't know what to say."

He sighed. "You should have told me about this."

"I'm sorry." I swallowed, my throat still dry despite the water. "What does it mean for the trial? Isn't it just more evidence that we shouldn't be married?" The case had never been about damages.

"Unfortunately not. They are making a case for recrimination. If your own infidelity is proven, it indicates Mr. Turner would have grounds for a countersuit, which means your suit can't succeed. Simply put, you can't be divorced."

My breath snagged beneath my breastbone.

"I would have mentioned this to you sooner, but I had no idea it would be relevant here. I'd assumed, incorrectly, that you would have shared such vital information with me." His words were short and crisp, his incisors shiny.

"I'm sorry," I said again, so quiet I doubt he heard.

Mr. Thistle did what he could to discredit the sailor, but I could tell it wouldn't be enough. The men of the jury, whose faces had shown me curiosity or pity or even admiration before, now looked flat and suspicious. And then it was Charles's turn, and I held my breath as I watched him slink up to the witness stand. He looked out at the room with those startling eyes of his, before locking his gaze on me. I released the air from my lungs in a loud whoosh.

His quarterback of a lawyer swore him in, and the whole time, he never took his eyes off me. When he gave testimony, he spoke directly to me.

"I love my wife more than anything in the world. I would never betray her with another woman." His voice never wavered, and those eyes looked at me with such adoration. The women in the room looked at me with outright scorn. I almost believed him myself.

"Why do you think she is suing you for divorce, Mr. Turner?"

Charles sighed and leaned back in his chair, his legs spread. He looked languorous, sensual, a Greek god posing for a statue. "I've tried to keep this out of the papers, but my wife has been unwell. Not of sound mind. She gets paranoid. I had her under the care of an esteemed doctor in the country, but she fought his treatment. Her behavior, I believe, is a symptom of her condition."

The room was silent aside from the sound of pens scribbling furiously, and I could feel eyes on my back like specks of burning coal popping from a fireplace. My neck itched, my nose, but I didn't dare lift a finger, as if fidgeting would draw even more attention. He sounded anguished and sincere. Only two days ago he'd been willing to blame Briggs for everything as a final attempt to win me back. His testimony now illustrated once again just how convincing of a liar he was. It was as if he truly believed what he said.

"I see. And are you prepared to forgive your wife for being unfaithful to you?"

Charles crossed a leg at the knee, bobbed a shiny shoe. He sat as if he were in the library, sipping brandy.

"I take my marriage vows seriously. And her doctor has given me to understand that female indecency can be a symptom of Millie's particular nervous condition. She never fell pregnant, you know, and he says . . . well, it can have an impact. All I want is to take her back into my care and help her get better."

Mr. Choate nodded sadly. "Thank you, Mr. Turner."

Mr. Thistle challenged Charles's assessment of my condition, but Charles made a wonderful witness. The very best.

After he concluded his questions, things happened quickly. The lawyers made their closing statements, and the jury left to discuss the case. I had the awful, sneaking suspicion that I had lost, and the sharp, coppery taste of fear filled my mouth. If only Maisie hadn't refused to admit to the affair.

Still, there was Charles's son, a miniature version of himself displayed for the whole courtroom, all the proof anyone with two eyes should need. It allowed me to kindle the smallest ember of hope.

And then the jury returned. They had deliberated more than an hour. I watched as they walked back in, their eyes not meeting mine, their pace slow and deliberate. One man limped.

"Is it a bad sign that it took so long?"

Mr. Thistle spread his hands. "Could be good or bad. Even odds, I'd say."

"And has the jury reached a verdict?" the judge drawled. He sounded annoyed, as if they should have deliberated more quickly.

"We have, your honor."

CHAPTER 39

I gripped my chair and tried to breathe. By their faces, I was fairly certain I had lost. I hadn't allowed myself to consider that I might lose and now I bemoaned my foolhardiness. I needed a plan. I wasn't prepared.

The lead juror stepped forward. "We find in favor of the plaintiff, Mrs. Charles Turner."

A woman behind me gasped. Clothes rustled as people turned to talk to their neighbor. My head was light and my eyes welled with tears of relief as comprehension dawned. I slumped over in my chair and Mr. Thistle grabbed my elbow, steadying me.

"Congratulations, Mrs. Turner." He beamed at me.

I laughed through my tears, giddy. I was free. Charles no longer had a hold over me. I dared to look at him and he looked back, the picture of grief. But his posture was rigid and despite the creased forehead, the broken frown, his eyes smoldered. I had to hide my hiccupping laughs behind my gloved hand. The manipulation, the potions, the terror, all of it was over. He could never order me to go back to the house, back to bed, away from our friends. He couldn't threaten to send me off to an asylum. Charles, who never lost at anything, had lost.

And I could marry David. We could travel Europe together, and Charles could do nothing to stop me. No one could. I couldn't wait to see him and tell him the good news, and imagined how we'd celebrate. Economizing be damned; tonight we'd have fine champagne and discreetly rent a fancy hotel room where we could make rapturous love on the feather bed.

"Order. Order in the court." The gavel banged, the wooden thump echoing, swallowing the conversations. The judge frowned at all of us, and at the jury, his saggy face trembling. "I am shocked that twelve honest men should have been so bamboozled by a pretty woman." His voice boomed even louder than the gavel. The smile slipped from my face. "It is not often that I have cause to overturn a jury verdict, but in this case, I must. Not only did the plaintiff fail to meet the burden of proof, but her own fidelity was reliably called into question. The marriage stands."

The world tilted. I slipped out of my chair. Mr. Thistle grabbed me before I fell, but I disappeared into my mind, the courtroom dissolving, replaced with a cold, dark place. Mr. Thistle shook me, until I saw the red backs of my eyelids and the chilly courtroom air rushed over me. The respectful quiet had turned clamorous. The gavel banged again, jolting me fully back to the present. The dread spreading through me weighed me down like silver in my veins. I couldn't move an inch.

My emotions had soared and now they plunged, and the breathtaking quickness of it gave me vertigo. My stomach somersaulted. I was still Charles's wife. It shouldn't have shocked me, really. I knew that he always found a way to win in the end.

I thought of my bare boardinghouse room, of the money and jewels hidden under my thin mattress. David and I could get steamer tickets tomorrow, today even, if we were lucky.

"I'm not finished." The judge sounded peevish. "It is no secret that there have been a scourge of divorce cases in the state of New York. Fortunately, to help us combat this immorality, the law has very recently made adultery a misdemeanor offense, punishable by up to a year in prison and a fine not exceeding five hundred dollars. The Police Court Magistrate has seen fit to issue a warrant to hold Mrs. Turner until her criminal trial. Captain Lewis, please take Mrs. Turner into custody."

I watched him form the words, heard their slightly slurred consonants, but the meaning eluded me. I sat stunned, bewildered.

"What . . . what did he say?"

"Mrs. Turner, prepare yourself. I need you to be very brave." Mr. Thistle looked very sorry, his fangs tucked away and his eyes woeful.

A thick-chested police captain descended the aisle, his build sinewy and solid. He was expressionless, his eyes not meeting mine. Then he grabbed one of my arms, forcing me up out of my chair.

"I don't understand. What's happening? Where am I going?"

Mr. Thistle stood and placed a hand on my shoulder. "You're being taken to the Tombs."

The captain had to half drag me out of the courtroom, because my feet refused to work properly. My mind, at least, had revived at last. It worked as quickly as my feet did not.

I was being arrested. I floated, as if I were outside of myself, looking on impartially, or perhaps that was only my feet gliding above the floor as Captain Lewis strong-armed me through the door to the courthouse's dizzying octagonal rotunda, down the stairs and toward the courthouse's Chambers Street entrance. "The prison is just a few blocks away," he said, surprisingly kind. I gave up on the little effort I'd been putting into walking and sank downward, making my body heavy, thinking of silver and gold and iron. Iron. Iron bars, which I would soon be locked behind. I remembered too well the horror of being locked in my room, and the courthouse walls seemed to close in on me.

I must not become hysterical, I scolded myself, even though the air seemed to suffocate me, muffling my cries. I sobbed big, fat, wet tears. Just a hysterical woman, after all, as Charles had said. And now the state of New York concurred. A woman like me, who dared to defy her husband, must be punished. His infidelity didn't warrant criminal investigation, apparently—he was a man, after all. I seethed at the injustice. I hated that judge, I hated Charles, and I hated Mr. Thistle and his pity. I hated the police captain, whose hand squeezed my arm, bruising my flesh.

"If you could walk a little it would make this easier," he said. "Don't worry, a society type like you will get your own cell."

I found my feet. Somehow I made it the few blocks to the prison, where I was turned over to the warden and then to the matron. I was assigned a cell and taken through corridor after corridor, through locked door after locked door. The prison was new, having replaced the first building nicknamed the Tombs, a notorious Egyptian monolithic building, a handful of years before. But the neat brick walls and shiny iron bars and lights penetrating the dim did little to improve the overcrowded cells and the hollering of female inmates who I passed. Some of them were bruised and drunk, others wearing the raggedy, scanty clothing of whores, bright and festive and out of place within these gloomy walls. At last, I was placed in a small cell with a wrought iron twin bed and a table. I sank exhausted onto the lumpy mattress, still sobbing. The matron told me something about dinner, but I couldn't have said what. My ears were ringing. I'd never be able to eat here, anyway.

"What happens now?" I asked, faintly.

"There'll be an arraignment where they decide your bail.

Tomorrow, probably." The matron clanked the door closed, scraped the key in the lock.

Tomorrow. I gulped the thick air and wiped my face.

I stood up and grabbed the bars, shocked at their cold sturdiness and that I should really be behind them. Locked up once again. I peered down the corridor, but this section of the prison was quieter. There were no overcrowded cells here. The captain hadn't lied about me getting special treatment.

I could survive a single night here. I prayed it would be no longer. I lay back on the bed to wallow in self-pity, and bunched up the thin blanket in my fist. Hours passed, and the matron brought a tray of food, which she arranged neatly for me on my little table. I couldn't bring myself to thank her.

Eventually, my tears dried and turned to anger. The injustice of it all sent fury shooting through me, making my blood hot despite the chilliness of the cell. While I was in prison, Charles was free. And Briggs and her daughter had returned home to their cozy little house, with all the elegant things they shouldn't have been able to afford—the fine china, the crystal chandelier, the gold clock on the mantel.

I jolted up from the bed and a cockroach skittered across the floor in surprise. The clock had suddenly appeared in my memory in detail, the little cupids leaning against its face, its elegant scrollwork. I realized it was the same clock that had sat on my own mantel. I'd been too preoccupied with the discovery of Charles's son to notice at the time. I cursed myself for not remembering it sooner.

Because the clock had once belonged to a prince of Versailles. Meaning it had a provenance. It was unique, and if the police found it in her home, it would prove that she'd stolen from me.

It had been foolish of Briggs to keep it. Maybe she just hadn't sold it yet for Charles, but I didn't think so. She had always liked that clock, and after the staff had been reduced, it was one of the only things she'd bothered to dust.

Charles wouldn't come to her rescue, especially not after the trial—he couldn't claim to have a relationship with her that would have included her pawning his possessions. Even if it weren't for the trial, his pride wouldn't have allowed such a confession.

"Hello!" I stood and wrapped my fingers around the cold iron bars. Instead of the matron, a police officer arrived, and it felt like fate that he should be here just when I needed him.

"Officer—you need to send someone to the home of Bertha Briggs at once. On Washington Avenue in Brooklyn. The clock on her mantel was stolen from my house, a priceless antique. Sotheby's will have a record of the sale."

The words rushed out in a single breath, without introduction and too quickly. The officer only raised his eyebrows. I knew at once how I sounded, and how he saw me. Frantic and unstable. I repeated it again, more slowly.

"Uh-huh. We'll be sure to look into that, ma'am." He sounded insincere. I wanted to scream with frustration.

"Why are you here? Is it to take my statement?" I would make him listen.

The officer smiled, but there was nothing kind about it.

"No. I'm here to tell you the good news. The charges have been dropped. You're being released."

"What?"

And then I heard another pair of footsteps, lighter than the officer's, clacking on the hard floors in a way that his had not. I saw his finely pressed trousers emerge first into the halo of light, then the rest of him, trim torso fitted neatly into his Italian-made suit. Green eyes that flashed at me, seeming to glow themselves.

"Hello, darling."

CHAPTER 40

❧

The estate loomed ahead, the white stone of the house turned gray under the overcast sky. The dark windows seemed to watch us approach, and I shivered. In the distance, the water of the harbor chopped in the wind. The little pond halfway down the grassy slope, where a giant heron stood nobly in warmer weather, had crusted over with ice. My dream home, once. My dream life. Now terror filled my throat.

"What are you going to do to me?"

I wasn't completely sure if he still wanted me dead, or if he'd abandoned that plan now that Lily Applebee wouldn't have him. I spoke quietly, and Charles didn't answer. He hadn't heard me over the roar of the engine. But then he pressed a long finger to my cheek.

"Do to you? Why, love you. You're my wife. I'm going to take care of you, and prove to you that we belong together. I want us to put all this unpleasantness behind us."

His words were sweet with honey, his accent posh and stiff. He added another finger, two more, and caressed my skin. I swallowed my revulsion and smiled. I'd be safer if I went along with this ruse, I decided. The carriage ride with Charles during the trial convinced me he might be vain enough to still value my opinion of him. How rapturous my love for him had once been, how worshipful. Maisie had re- mained obedient to him, unlike Gertrude. So she'd been rewarded, while Gertrude—well. If I stroked his ego enough, would he let me live?

"I thought you'd be furious with me."

His green eyes turned woeful. "How could I ever be furious with you? I neglected you. I see that now."

Months ago, those words would have warmed my heart. Now my stomach churned, choppy as the bay. I couldn't tell if he meant to taunt me with this charade, or if he believed he still had a hold over me.

"Everything is forgiven, truly?" I would have expected him to be furious over my affair, which would have wounded his pride. And anger did flash in his eyes, but only for an instant.

"I don't know who this low man was who shared your bed, nor do I ever wish to. I want to pretend it never happened. You only did it to take revenge on me." He spoke as if convincing himself. If he could view my relationship with David as being only about him, rather than about me caring for someone else, apparently he could bear it. It was a great comfort that he didn't know David's identity, at least.

"Yes, I was so hurt. It was nothing. A moment of stupidity."

He nodded, and his pinched expression turned smooth. "I made mistakes, too. And I let Briggs go, of course. She came between us. All of this was her fault. I see that now." He spoke with such conviction that I doubted myself, just for a moment. I questioned again whether he could be guilty only of the affairs. I shook my head, as if the motion could dispel the idea.

Tom Hannigan emerged from the gatehouse, and Charles watched him methodically scrape the key in the lock and swing open the wrought iron gates, the bars curving at the top to form the letter *T* for Turner. Tom moved slowly, steadily, and I wished I could speak to him and get a message to David. The engine rumbled beneath us and Charles opened the car door, his shiny shoes crunching the gravel.

"Hannigan. Your services will no longer be needed here. I'd like you to be packed and ready to go by the morning."

Hannigan looked at him stoically and my heart jumped. Charles must have learned he was David's father. Even if he didn't know David was my lover, he did know that he'd written the article that exposed his fraud.

Or perhaps he only knew I was fond of Tom, and wanted to punish me. I stepped out of the car behind Charles and placed a hand on his arm.

"Charles, this is so sudden. Surely we can discuss this. At least give him more time."

"He's getting too old for this sort of work. I've made my decision." He climbed back into the car, but I stayed outside of it, breathing the frosty air and trying to communicate to Tom with my eyes the depths of my sorrow. He nodded at me once. His throat bobbed. He'd found comfort and solitude here, and he'd have a hard time finding work at his age. I knew David had been saving so that he could take care of him, but the injustice of how little they had when we had so much filled me with shame. Charles's thoughtless dismissal of him—an errand barely worth the effort of getting out of the car for—disgusted me.

"Don't make a fuss, dear. It had to be done." Charles patted the seat beside him.

"I'm sorry. I'll make it right, somehow." I gripped Tom's hand with mine and wished I could kiss his weathered cheek. The man who might have been my father-in-law, if the world were a kinder place.

"Seems to me you've got troubles enough of your own," Tom said, low and gruff. Quiet enough that Charles didn't hear. "Don't worry yourself. I'll be just fine."

We exchanged one more meaningful look and I got back in the car.

"We should have done asphalt for the driveway instead of gravel," Charles said, as if he hadn't just upended a man's life. "The dirt is a nuisance."

"Charles, what are we going to do without a gatekeeper? We can't let him go before we've found another one."

Charles had meant to show me who was in control of running the house now. I shouldn't challenge him, not when I might still be in danger, but I wanted to understand his schemes.

"Nonsense." He flicked a handkerchief against his shoe. "I don't imagine we'll be getting many visitors out here until the season starts. And with Terry and the dogs we'll have plenty of protection."

I didn't feel protected. I knew too well what Cerberus was capable of. Even Charles's greyhounds intimidated me. They seemed docile enough, but were trained to course deer, to use their speed to overtake them and pin them down, gripping their delicate necks between strong jaws.

"But what if I want to go to the city? To see my parents?" I guessed what the answer would be, but I needed to hear it from his own lips.

"I think it's best if we both stay here for a while. We need time and space to work on our marriage. Besides, your constitution is still delicate, even Dr. Kimpton thought so, and I don't want you to do anything too taxing."

Gooseflesh rose on my skin. So I would be a prisoner once more. "I see."

"You've been troubled. Lonely. But I'm back now, darling. I won't leave your side. I can conduct my business from here for a time."

I swallowed. The prospect of being locked up here with Charles made my limbs turn cold. I considered bolting toward the road, but I wouldn't make it far, not when Charles had the car, and the dogs. I'd have to be cleverer than that.

But so would he, surely? If something happened to me right away, it would seem suspicious. At least, that's what I tried to tell myself, to quell the panic spreading through me, making it hard to move, hard to breathe.

"How wonderful."

The car stopped for us near the front door and we climbed out again. As if on cue, Cerberus ran over, snarling at me. The sleeping medication I'd given him apparently hadn't caused any lasting harm. Duke and Prince, who could run faster than our car, were lazy when they felt like it and took their time on their way over, stretching their elegant legs.

"Down, boy," Charles said, and Terry whistled once, using his tongue, a short *zweet*. Cerberus stopped snarling. Terry stood behind him and glared at me.

I trembled. Charles saw, and gazed lovingly at me, but instead of reassuring me, it felt like he was mocking me. No one would blame him for a dog attack: a tragedy, they'd say. I was completely at his mercy. Tom Hannigan's steadying presence had been my last bit of armor, and he'd be gone soon.

I had to do something, and quickly.

CHAPTER 41

It was a strange sensation to eat breakfast across from a man who might be plotting to kill me. And surprisingly peaceable. He read his paper and chewed a piece of sausage, and I raised my teacup to my mouth and wondered about poison. He wouldn't use the same method again, would he? Too obvious. So I ate fluffy eggs and decadent fruit off of shining china and a perfectly starched tablecloth, still scared but also marveling over the luxury. After my time in a damp boardinghouse, eating rubbery eggs or porridge at a communal table, the wealth of my own home overwhelmed me.

Charles finished and patted his mouth delicately. Stood. "I'm going to take Duke and Prince out for a while. Let them chase some rabbits. They could use a little exercise."

I always pitied the rabbits, no match to the stylish speed of the greyhounds, their fine muscles bunching. "Enjoy yourself."

I lingered at the table, listening to his tread as he walked toward the gun room, and imagined him opening one of the gleaming cabinets as he located his shotgun. A few minutes later, the door to the back veranda thudded shut, and my heart leapt. While he was away, I could sneak out to the road.

As soon as I had the thought, a loud thud sounded at the front door. One, two, three more thuds. Charles was wrong about us not getting any visitors for a while. Whoever it was

hadn't bothered with the bell. It sounded like they were trying to batter the door down.

I scooted my chair back abruptly, upsetting my teacup,
which sloshed brown liquid into its saucer.

I ran to the front of the house. I flew through the hallway,
feeling as fast as Charles's greyhounds.

I threw open the door to find David before me, looking
like hell. And also like the most beautiful thing I'd ever seen.
His hair was wild, his mouth serious, the pouches beneath
his eyes purple from sleeplessness, and his eyes themselves
luminous at the sight of me.

"Hurry. I have a carriage waiting."

I didn't hesitate. I rushed down the steps into his arms and
we crunched across the gravel. The gate hung open. I knew it
must be a parting gift from his father.

And then Cerberus careened into view, spittle flying. He
growled at both of us, his dark eyes devoid of feeling, and we
slowed our pace.

"Just hold still."

"Millie, we have to go. I don't care if the beast rips my
limbs off."

"But I care."

David inched backward, and Cerberus lurched forward.
David jumped and teeth grazed his pant leg.

David turned to me and there was a desperation in his eyes
that I'd never seen there before. "Has Charles hurt you? You
coming back here with him—God, I've been sick over it."

"No, not yet."

I stared at Terry's ugly, horrible dog. When Charles named
him Cerberus, after the dog that guarded the gates of Hades
to keep the dead from escaping, I'd found it funny.

I wasn't laughing now.

We kissed, a heartbreaking, untamed kiss, one that traveled to my belly, my legs.

"Come on. The dog wants me gone, doesn't he? We have to try." David held my hand as he backed up slowly away from Cerberus, toward the gate. Cerberus growled and followed him, but this time didn't lunge.

Terry appeared from around the side of the house, squinting into the gray sunlight. He didn't whistle to call Cerberus back to him, but he walked toward us quickly with a heavy, athletic stride.

"If we run, Cerberus will attack for certain," I said. I didn't have any sleeping medication this time, nothing I could use against him.

"Would he attack *you?*"

I could see him calculating, his forehead creased in tender concern. He wouldn't give a second thought to running if he were the only one bearing the risk. "Yes."

And so we stayed still, watching Terry approach. I wouldn't have been able to run, anyway, not when my legs were weak with fear. The wind whipped a strand of my hair across my cheek. I squeezed David's hand tighter and wondered whether I dared to kiss him again, in front of Terry.

I didn't. Instead, as Terry neared, I let go of his hand. Terry remained expressionless, but I knew he'd seen it, and wondered whether he would tell Charles. I assumed he would, and my teeth clacked together as I tightened my jaw.

"Is this man a friend of yours?" He spoke with a deep voice and flat New York vowels.

"Yes. Please, call off your beast."

But Terry didn't. He assessed us both carefully, and I could see him thinking, the effort of the activity plain on his face. His eyes lingered on David's scuffed shoes and the sleeves of his jacket, which protruded a few fractions too far beyond the bones of his wrist. He had surmised he wasn't the owner of a neighboring estate, a friend of Charles's.

"You know Mr. Turner has forbidden any visitors."

Cerberus growled continuously, his fangs bared. David squared his shoulders. Even in danger, his stance was confident, cocksure.

"Terry. The dog," I snapped. I was, after all, still mistress of the house.

"He senses danger. He knows when visitors aren't welcome." He rubbed his thumb and forefinger together and my breath stopped in my throat. A snap of his fingers and the dog could rip David's neck open. He wouldn't dare. Would he? What instructions had he been given?

In the distance, I heard the rooing of Charles's greyhounds, the explosion of his shotgun. Some poor, frightened rabbit had met its end.

"He was just leaving. I'm headed back to the house now."

The words scraped my mouth. David stiffened. He turned to me, looking like I'd just knocked the breath out of him. With my eyes, I implored him to understand. We were out of options. The safest thing right now was for me to play Charles's game.

I couldn't be sure if David understood. I almost wept at the heartbreak in his face.

"I'll come back for you." David grabbed my hand. I made my wrist limp, let my fingers drop away.

Terry nodded at me, then whistled, and Cerberus trotted toward his heel. He grabbed my arm, too hard, and turned back toward the house. I had no choice but to follow. I glanced over my shoulder to see David standing still, watching me retreat, his eyes focused intently as if he hoped to pin me down with his gaze. It destroyed me that I couldn't run into his arms and explain what I had to do.

David couldn't rescue me. Not with Charles, Terry, and the dogs to guard me. If he tried again, he'd fail.

I just had to hope Charles would give me a little more time. I had to make him think he still needed me. And then I'd find a way to escape.

CHAPTER 42

Charles spent the day hunting and then in his study, but at breakfast the next day he behaved as if nothing had happened. He seated himself in front of his newspaper, unfolding his lean form artfully, his face flushed from the exercise of a morning hunt. But I'd seen him speak to Terry the day before and his eyes glinted with a hint of malice. His words never betrayed him, but his expressions sometimes did.

I stared at my plate. Wedgwood bone China, gold edged, showing a bucolic country scene: a couple sitting on a grassy slope gazing toward the water. It had reminded me of our estate, when I selected the pattern.

Terry could have killed David yesterday if he'd wanted to. Charles could have already killed me. And yet he hadn't. Perhaps my guess had been right, and he'd surmised I could still be useful to him. Or maybe he was only waiting for a more opportune moment.

Another thought snaked its way into my mind, a twisted wish that he wasn't actually a killer. His manner toward me was so gentle and caring that my uncertainty grew. I still loved David, and wouldn't have forgiven Charles's infidelity and lies, even if they were all that he was guilty of. But of course I didn't want to believe he was completely without conscience.

My heart still galloped in my chest and my thoughts were

full of David. What was he thinking? Did he hate me for not trying to run? The minutes dragged on. Charles read and chewed. My thoughts battered against my skull.

Charles set the paper down and considered me. "You know, I've been thinking. Perhaps once the weather is nicer we should throw a big party. We can show everyone how well you are. How well we are."

I gazed at him with an expression I hoped was loving. It made my cheeks hurt. "That's a splendid idea." My confusion only increased. Did he truly believe that things could just go back to how they were? At least it indicated he didn't have imminent plans to harm me—unless he was trying to trick me into a false sense of security. "Some of our friends might not want to come," I said carefully. As far as many of our friends were concerned, we were a swindler and a murderess. We made quite the pair. I hadn't spoken to him directly about David's article and his eyes darkened, a forest before a storm.

"Anyone who believes that libelous article is no friend. I have no doubt you'll plan something marvelous."

I stared at my plate to hide my feelings. I wasn't sure if his statement was a compliment or a challenge. It would be no easy feat to do what he asked, but maybe I could arrange for a less exclusive affair, something more like my mother's crushes.

"Thank you." I stood. "I'll go phone Sanders now. We should call for some of the servants, since we won't be using the city house. And arrange for some more part-time help. We can begin getting things here in order."

It was a test. I wanted as many servants about as possible. The more servants, the more witnesses.

"That's a wise idea."

I forced my brightest smile to hide my bewilderment. But I didn't wait for him to change his mind. I walked purposefully toward the telephone and picked up the earpiece with firm fingers.

I kept my directions succinct and exhaled in a whoosh after I hung the earpiece back in its cradle. I considered ringing David's newspaper to leave a message to him, but Charles might hear. I had to hope that David would trust me and not attempt anything rash before I found my chance to escape.

As soon as I returned to the table, the phone let out a shrill ring that made me jump. It was probably Sanders calling me back with a question. I turned to go back and retrieve it, but Charles stood.

"I'll get it."

My false smile slipped a little.

"As you wish."

I sat back down to continue picking at my food. I'd hardly eaten; my stomach was already full of fear.

Charles had left his newspaper beside his empty plate, I noticed, and cold crept down my spine as I recognized it as David's. Charles had never read *The World News* before.

I picked it up, yearning to see David's name. But it was something else that caught my eye. A headline screaming at the top of the page made me gasp.

Arrest in Elaborate Knickerbocker Theft
Former Maid Held on $20,000 Bail on the Charge
of Grand Larceny

A woman known as Bertha Briggs was arrested yester-day outside of her home on Washington Avenue in Brooklyn on the charge of grand larceny. Her former mistress, Mrs. Charles Turner of New York, accused Mrs. Briggs . . .

I couldn't believe it. The officer at the Tombs had listened, after all. For once, someone had actually believed me. I let out a strangled noise somewhere between a laugh and a sob.

The story continued to explain what I already knew: that

Briggs had robbed us of valuable paintings and antiques. Multiple items had been found in her home, and a reputable importer admitted to buying goods from her after being fooled by a false letter from her employer to act as his agent. Charles almost certainly *had* written such a letter, though he'd hardly admit it now, when he was determined to hide his financial problems.

But there would be more questions. He'd have to face another trial.

Now my smile turned genuine.

I read the article three times, squeezing it for every detail. It wasn't long, only a few paragraphs.

Charles's shouting into the telephone interrupted my thoughts, and I crept to the hallway to listen.

"No, as I told you, I didn't know anything about it. Nothing at all. No—look, I can hardly hear you. This damn connection. Yes, all right. I'll come in tomorrow."

Charles slammed down the mouthpiece into its cradle. His head snapped up and he saw me hovering, but I remained calm.

"Is everything all right?"

"Fine." He stroked his mustache. "I just have to go into the city tomorrow, that's all."

At once, I understood. The police wanted to get his statement about Briggs. The woman who had nearly murdered me might end up saving me. If I had a better sense of humor, perhaps I would appreciate the irony.

"Oh." I couldn't feign disappointment, but I managed to keep my tone neutral.

I wondered what Briggs would make of his betrayal. Briggs had been as devoted to Charles as a mother—and expected to be his mother, after he wed her daughter—and I couldn't fathom how she'd react. He'd manipulated her so well that she had been willing to kill for him. Of course I'd always known that eventually Briggs would realize he never planned to marry Maisie and make her mistress of the manor. I'd never imagined this outcome, though. Briggs deserved to be in prison, but Charles's cruelty in leaving his son's grandmother, and his accomplice, to rot surprised me. I shouldn't be shocked anymore by what he was capable of, and yet I was.

That other possibility hovered persistently on the edge of my thoughts: that her plots had been hers alone and now he understood what she'd done. In that scenario his actions would be understandable.

"Don't worry, I'll be back in the evening. I won't leave you for long."

I swallowed. *I won't leave you for long.* He made it sound affectionate, but it rang in my ears like a threat.

Charles left the next morning. For an entire day, I'd be free. I could escape. It seemed too easy, and suspicion nagged me. But as soon as he was gone, I did the only sensible thing: I sneaked into his study and stole his handgun from his desk drawer.

Then I retreated to my room, the gun cradled in my arms like a newborn. The servants hadn't arrived yet, so there was no one to see. I slipped it into my beaded cream purse, which was just large enough to hold it. It rustled the crisp bills I'd already stuffed it with, and clinked against the metal of my jewelry.

Then I left. I walked through the French doors leading to the veranda, with the idea that I'd head through the trees along our dirt trails and exit somewhere near the road. We had nearly forty acres, more than enough to hide in, should Terry or Cerberus come looking.

I half walked, half ran along the West Lawn, the greenhouse glass reflecting the sun to my right, the water of the Sound stretching beyond it. The trees straight ahead.

And then a deep bark vibrated the air, followed by peals of barks as all three dogs ran toward me. I wouldn't make it to the trees, so instead I bolted toward the greenhouse, shutting the glass door tightly behind me. They all stood just outside of it, staring at me, tails wagging excitedly, as if this were a game. As if I were a deer or a rabbit.

I swore. I never used to swear, but I'd picked up a few things in my time living independently. It helped only a little. The barking continued incessantly and I pressed a finger to my temple, hoping to pause the headache now splitting open my skull. I had to think.

I opened the purse and touched the cold metal of the gun. This was why I'd brought it, hadn't I? I knew Cerberus might find me and attack. But this didn't feel like self-defense, with them facing me through the glass. Just the idea of it made me queasy. I closed my purse. I didn't have the heart for it. It wasn't their fault, what Charles had made them become. They were just poor dumb beasts.

And besides, Terry would be here soon. Eminently capable of overpowering me all by himself. He'd make me return to the house.

No sooner had the thought crossed my mind than I heard Terry's whistle, and the dogs stopped barking. If he saw my purse, he'd know I'd been trying to escape, and I didn't want him telling Charles. I certainly couldn't risk him looking inside. I hurried to the potting bench and stuck it hastily in one of the drawers, its silk and shining beads out of place against the splintering green wood, alongside a pair of dirty shears. When I returned to the glass door, Terry stood in front of it, his dark brown eyes just as empty as Cerberus's. He was also Charles's pet. His weapon. He rubbed his nose with a hairy-knuckled hand.

"What were you doing?"

"Gardening, obviously." I wondered if he'd seen me put my purse in the potting bench. He considered me. Blinked.

"Charles doesn't want you to leave the house. For your health."

"I see."

"You should come with me now."

And so I did, with as much dignity as I could muster.

But I wouldn't be a prisoner forever. One way or another, this would end.

CHAPTER 43

❧

The warm sunshine streamed through my window, and I rolled over lazily, still half dreaming. I heard the clanking plates and rose, slow and comfortable, to watch my new maid, Delaney, set up a breakfast tray with cranberry scones and clotted cream. I let her help me into a dressing gown before I sat. The roses crawling in my wallpaper looked warm and cheerful.

"You're an angel, Delaney. I don't know what I'd do without you." She was sweet and blond and pretty, and her naïve cheer made the days more bearable.

I had slipped through the last weeks in a state of languid terror. I'd expected Charles to turn cruel, but I'd been met with only kind solicitousness and tender concern. He treated me as delicately as a wilted flower.

I had stuffed the house to the gills with servants, even more than we'd had in the city house. We'd had to sell a few paintings for cash, as Briggs had been doing, because our funds "weren't liquid right now," according to Charles, which meant nonexistent. But I wanted to never be alone with Charles, not for an instant. And so we had a legion of maids and footmen. A few of the menservants were Charles's creatures, burly fellows like Terry with nothing behind their eyes who looked more suited to a boxing ring than our dining room, but I steered well clear of them. And after the poor boardinghouse living, I enjoyed being pampered again. My freshly starched linens, my lavender-scented handkerchiefs, the divine clotted cream. I took a generous bite of my scone. The comforts of home had nearly lulled me into complacency.

There were moments where it almost felt like it had before. Yesterday Charles had made me laugh by reading a humorous article aloud from the paper and doing silly voices. He'd taken to leaving me little presents and notes on my pillow to surprise me. I knew better now than to trust any of it, but some days it was easier to let myself pretend. And he repeated so often that Briggs was a villain, that she'd tried to kill me and Gertrude based on an outlandish idea that he'd marry her daughter, that I questioned more and more whether he might be right. I'd learned that repeating falsehoods could make them take root in your mind, and remembered that he'd done the same thing before when he insisted to all of our friends that I was unstable. But Charles was so passionate that he couldn't help saying what he was thinking. And he always truly seemed to believe what he said.

But just as often as I found myself tempted to give in to his version of reality, something would come and shatter the illusion. For one, I wasn't allowed to leave. Charles had started letting me on the veranda, where I could watch the boats on the water and let the breeze tickle my cheeks. The crocuses had started peeking through the soil, and the hyacinths and tulips would soon follow. It wouldn't be long before the estate was bursting with blossoms. He'd found a new doctor to come visit me, to continue the pretense that the restrictions were for my health, but at least there were no more sleeping potions.

And although he tried to hide his moods from me, Charles had grown more stressed and erratic. He spent hours in his study, and often went to town to send cables to the city. He hadn't even noticed that some of his papers were missing until last week, and when he'd questioned me casually about it,

I'd feigned innocence. I'd almost never left my room when I'd been unwell before, I said, and would never dare enter his study. He'd scowled and blamed Briggs. It seemed that somehow he'd placated enough of his clients, or brought on enough new ones to delay the inevitable, but I sensed it was only a matter of time before things became truly dire. He asked often about how the plans for the party were progressing, and I began to understand its true purpose: to fool new prospective clients into believing that all was well. He was desperate, and unable to accept his defeat.

Delaney helped me into a powder-blue dress with black trim and buttons, suited to walking outdoors, not that I'd have an opportunity. Still, you never knew, and I hadn't given up on my hope of escape. Delaney went into the city once a week on her day off, and she'd been delivering messages to David for me. I'd asked him to be patient and told him that I seemed not to be in any apparent danger. Delaney glowed with the deliciousness of the secret, her pale skin almost luminous. She shot me a meaningful look as she refreshed my tea and giggled.

After she finished getting me ready I descended the stairs and paused as I neared the bottom. Voices drifted from the drawing room. We had company. I couldn't imagine who it might be. I squeezed the stair rail.

Charles emerged through the pocket doors into the hall.

"Darling. Your parents are here."

My stomach contracted and my cheeks turned hot. I didn't want to see them.

"What on earth are they doing here?"

As soon as the words passed my lips I realized the answer: Charles had asked them here. Of course.

"I thought it was time for you to make amends. Let bygones be bygones."

I remembered my father's unyieldingness, my mother's cowardice. I'd been in danger and they'd abandoned me.

"Tell them I'm unwell." I turned to go back up the stairs and Charles closed the distance between us in a few lean strides and gripped my arm.

"Millie, please. It's the perfect opportunity for you to apologize."

"Me?" I opened my mouth to argue. When I saw the expression on his face, I closed it again, my reason returning. He needed them. Which meant I needed them. "What is it you want from them, Charles? Tell me quickly." He frowned at my abruptness and I forced a smile. "So that I can help, of course."

His frown disappeared, replaced by solicitude. "I only want you to make up. They're your family. I care about your happiness."

I nearly groaned. It was exhausting to constantly play his game.

"And?"

"I'd hoped they'd help us out financially. Just a little gift to tide us over until I organize my affairs."

"I see." I pressed my lips together and squeezed the stair rail more tightly. My anger and my pride made me want to refuse him—I couldn't bear the thought of groveling before them—and yet I also knew I had no choice. This was probably a key part of the reason he had granted me clemency. With some of their money, I could be useful to him for a short while more.

The party, suddenly, came into focus in my mind, the shining motorcades crunching over the gravel in our driveway, the beaded dresses, the dancing. If we sold too many valuables, people might notice, but a gift from my parents would allow us to keep up the appearance of wealth and fool potential business prospects. Not to mention women he needed to woo. I wondered if he would try to win back Lily Applebee.

"It's best if I speak to them alone. You'll give us privacy, won't you, dear?" I pecked his cheek and didn't wait for his answer before brushing past him and into the drawing room.

I nearly fainted at the sight of my mother smoking. Smoking! A cigarette perched between the middle and pointer finger of her gloved hands and a tendril of smoke snaked toward the ceiling. My mother laughed guiltily at the sight of my evident astonishment.

"I know. But these last few months have been absolute agony on my nerves. Seeing your name splashed about the paper like that." She took a luxurious drag. My father coughed, obviously disapproving. His posture was rigid, and he wouldn't meet my eyes. "He's sworn he's not speaking to you, just so you know. It took some doing even getting him here, believe me."

I balled my hands into fists. It was mulishness, that's what it was. For all his renowned gravitas, he was acting like a petulant child. But I forced myself to look contrite.

"I completely understand. But he should know that he was right, and I know now one can never run from one's problems." I sat delicately on a wingback armchair and looked at my father somberly. He still avoided my gaze, but there was something in his eyes, a flicker, that encouraged me to continue. "Charles and I have reconciled. We hope that in time we can do the same. I've missed you."

My mother stubbed her cigarette in a silver ashtray. "I've missed you terribly. It's been awful not speaking to you and reading all the stories. He's missed you, too, but he won't say it."

I'd avoided most of the newspaper stories. It had taken enormous willpower, but really, I didn't want to know the impression my most recent scandal had made on society.

"I hope that's true."

"It is. But you know how stubborn he is."

"Georgina, I'm right here."

"Yes, Harold, but if you're going to refuse to join the conversation, you're really leaving me no choice but to speak about you in your presence."

He harrumphed and placed a thumb in the buttonhole of his vest, stretched over his ample belly.

I could easily picture it: my mother's frenzied breakfast table conversations about me, my father refusing to engage. He preferred to eat breakfast in silence, but she rarely obliged him. She truly did look strained; her frown lines were deeper than I remembered. I knew she cared. And yet they'd left me to face one of the most difficult challenges of my life alone. All I had wanted was for them to take my side and to believe me.

"She's just after money. He made her do this."

It was very like my father to cut straight to the truth of the matter, at least where money was concerned. My pulse ticked in my throat as I decided what to say. I did what he'd always done, analyzing the conversation like a game of chess, evaluating what this remark would make him do, or that. Reading the man as well as the board.

In the end, there was only one thing to do.

"I don't care about money. We will find a way to get by. Somehow."

He studied me, searching for the lie, and I held perfectly still and finally managed to catch his eyes.

"Georgina, we have to get the eleven o'clock train." He stood and left the drawing room, not once looking back.

My mother gave a raspy, exasperated sigh. "I did what I could. He'll come around." She grasped my hand, then pulled me into a hug, squeezing me so that I couldn't breathe. "I love you, Millie. We both do."

And then she was gone, leaving only a whiff of cigarettes and perfume.

When I exited the drawing room, Charles was waiting right outside the door. "Well?"

"Give it a week."

"A week." Charles considered this, rolling the word over in his mouth as if it were sour.

A few feet away, a maid dusted the Rococo table topped by the Qing dynasty vase. She was beautiful, like all of the new maids I had hired. Charles hadn't noticed. I'd tempted him deliberately, and he had resisted. He hadn't attempted to touch me, either, thank God.

"Very well. One week." He pronounced this with an official, formal air, like a sentence.

Which it probably was. I swallowed and went upstairs to ask Delaney for a cup of tea, to wash the taste of shame out of my mouth.

Luckily, my guess had been exactly correct. I knew my father well, and one week later, I received a check in the mail. There was also a letter from his bank, printed on stiff ivory paper, with details about my restored trust. I would once again gain control on my twenty-fifth birthday in August, as my father had originally planned.

There was no letter from my father, no phone call, and I saw this for what it was: a test to call my bluff. He wanted to know if I truly wanted to make amends or only wanted the money.

I called for Charles as soon as the check arrived, and my heartbeat drummed slowly as I watched him read the amount.

"Excellent." He touched it almost reverently.

My father would be smug about the trap he'd laid and how I'd fallen right into it, but it hardly mattered. When all this was over, when David and I were safe and snug in some little flat in Europe, I wouldn't come asking for more. I'd make my own way, and eventually, *I'd* try to forgive *him*.

"I want the party to be grand. Something people will talk about."

My chest expanded, as if there was suddenly room for twice as much air. The party would provide the opportunity I needed to flee. Money was a funny thing, wasn't it? Strange how it could save you and imprison you at once.

"Naturally."

I turned and climbed the stairs with light steps, almost floating. I had another message for Delaney to bring to David. An image formed in my mind, perfect and clear: David in a rowboat approaching our little beach, lanterns on the deck and oars slicing through the black water. The dogs would be in their kennel at the party, and with all the commotion, it would be easy to slip away unnoticed. It would be the perfect opportunity to escape.

It might also be my last.

CHAPTER 44

The party was just how I'd always imagined it. Before we built the house, I had pictured this: a warm, humid night relieved by a breeze from the water; fat moths fluttering drunkenly, their white wings glowing; candles dancing on the veranda; the harbor bathed in moonlight. Music from the ballroom floated down over the lawn, and the hydrangeas bloomed gloriously, visible in the warm light pouring through the mullioned windows. I hadn't known, of course, that the party would be a ruse. Merely a way to cover my escape.

I watched from the drawing room as the gate opened for a flashy roadster. I'd considered trying to escape through the gate, of course, but the new gatekeeper chosen by Charles was surly and overzealous in his duties. Charles might expect me to leave that way. The drawing room swelled with the guests I should have been greeting, but instead I lingered at the window, avoiding them. I wished I had a view of the water from this room, and wondered where David was right now. Had he arrived at the beach already?

I hadn't run yet. I wanted to make sure David had enough time to find his way in the dark. I was grateful for the full moon. Besides, if I waited until guests were departing, those not staying the night, the house would be full and merry and drunk. My absence wouldn't be remarked upon then. No one would come looking right away.

Anna Carter sashayed toward me and touched my elbow. "What a fierce specimen," she said, gesturing at the taxidermic lion prowling near the fireplace, its teeth glistening. I shrugged. I'd never paid it much attention before. I included hunting trophies in our decor scheme only to please Charles. "We were just remarking upon it. Did Charles shoot it on safari in East Africa? With the Applebees, wasn't it?"

I remembered Charles's expedition to East Africa but had forgotten he'd gone with the Applebees, or maybe I'd never known. I refused to let Anna see my discomfort and the tightness of my smile strained my cheeks. "Yes, I believe so." There was an awkward pause. Charles had said he wanted us to show our friends we were reconciled, but it was all too easy for them to taunt me. I stared at the lion, paying closer attention now. It was well preserved: I could almost hear its furious snarl. I had to suppress my own.

"Will Lily be here tonight? I'd wanted to say hello." Anna smiled blandly, but there was a spark of mischief in her eyes. I sighed, remembering another dinner party, another mistress. This was just as humiliating as before. More so, because everything was out in the open now. Even though I'd lost the trial, it had been enough to start the rumors swirling. Everyone had learned the details of Charles's philandering, and the insults were less veiled. Perhaps that is why so many of our friends agreed to come: to see what spectacle we would treat them to this time.

"No." I hadn't invited her. I wouldn't make that mistake twice. "I hadn't realized you were such intimates."

"We're not, really. But she's such a sweet, pretty little thing, like a doll I'd like to dress up."

"Oh! That reminds me. I must go attend to preparations for the tableau vivant." I strode away, glad to be rid of her.

I didn't have to worry about impressing them anymore. I'd be gone after tonight. The thought made me giddy, as if I'd drunk a bottle of champagne, though in truth I hadn't touched a drop.

The tableau vivant had been Charles's idea. It was the sort of pageantry that would help ensure our party would be well attended. I had enlisted a number of our friends to participate, and we would bring scenes by Vermeer, Raphael, Titian, and a dozen other masters to life.

I nodded hello to a few people as I headed toward the ballroom. Until last week it had sat forlorn and dusty, our occasional chairs hiding under cloths. Now it was blazing from the light of no fewer than four crystal and gold French Empire chandeliers, and every mite of dust had been banished by our maids. The windows faced the water, but at night, I could see only the dazzling reflection of the room itself.

"There you are, darling." I heard Charles before I saw him, and his deep voice was icy. I paused midstep, turned. He looked impossibly handsome, of course, and his hair and shoes both shined. "Might we have a private word?" He held out a hand, and I placed mine delicately inside it.

"Of course."

I followed him to, of all places, the butler's pantry, currently devoid of butler or footmen, a shocking state of affairs given the party was now well underway. Charles must have ordered them out.

"I want this to be a new beginning for us." He flashed his teeth. There was something wild in his expression, and his green eyes sparked. Then he pulled me toward him and kissed me, rough and insistent. I was too shocked to push him away and instead grew limp in his arms. His embrace was familiar and foreign at once. My head spun.

He hadn't attempted physical affection since the trial, and I didn't know what inspired him now. I suspected that maybe he was nervous. Everything depended on his success tonight.

On another night, at another party, I'd felt just the same.

"Do you still love me, Millie?" His voice was rough. His skin was cool as marble.

I'd grown so good at lying lately that sometimes it was hard to tell when I was doing it. "Of course I do." It wasn't as hard as it should have been to make myself kiss him again. "The tableau vivant is starting soon. I have to get ready."

I squeezed his hand in a parting gesture and hurried away, back toward the party, my lips still chilled.

Arabella stopped me, looking even more ravishing than I remembered her, a burgundy gown showing off her full bosom and her gleaming dark hair arranged in artful curves and waves. "It's you at last! We'd wondered where you got off to." She looked over my shoulder and held a hand to her mouth to hide a laugh. I turned to see Charles emerging a few feet behind me. "So you really have made up. I'd wondered, you know. But how could you possibly want to divorce a specimen like that?" Her choice of words made me think, fleetingly, of the lion.

"I dare say I'd have survived it." My stomach roiled. His kiss had discomposed me.

"Oh, I see. Have you been quarreling? Really, Millie. I mean half the women in New York would have been thrilled to see him back on the market. Perhaps you are crazy, after all. Or nervous, or whatever they're calling it these days when you shut yourself away in the country and neglect your closest friends."

"Did you miss me, then?" My tone was bitter. I half wondered, given her glowing praise of my husband, whether he'd bedded her, too. It hardly mattered. Her fickleness as a friend couldn't shock me anymore. It would only make it that much easier not to miss her when I left.

"Dreadfully." She tucked my hand in the crook of her elbow and stroked it, as if I were her pet. "Now let's go get some champagne and catch up properly."

"I'm not drinking until later." It was safest, I decided. I couldn't risk it.

"Not drinking! Now I know you've gone mad."

We continued on that way for a while, and I nodded to people as we passed and stopped to say pleasant things to guests I disliked. I disliked most of them, and made a little game of separating out the awful and tolerable ones in my head as we made our way around the rooms. I endured our disgustingly sumptuous dinner, the polite conversation, and the thinly disguised barbs until it was time to prepare for the tableau vivant.

We had erected a stage in the ballroom and turned two rooms down the hall into dressing rooms. I entered the ladies' dressing room, already weary, as women laughed and exclaimed over their costumes, and the chairs were piled with lacy frills, and rich velvet, and beaded gold. It had been hard for me to decide who I should portray. There were so many famous artworks that inspired me: of Persephone returning to light and land after being trapped with Hades, of Judith beheading Holofernes, of Helen fleeing with Paris. But Charles was no fool. The thematic significance would hardly be lost on him, and I couldn't do anything to make him suspicious before my escape. So I'd opted instead for Botticelli's Primavera, a celebration of lush springtime. There were eight of us creating the scene, but I would be at the center, Venus in a diaphanous light blue dress draped with red fabric, my head tilted, my hand held out just so.

Delaney was in the dressing room helping attend to some of the ladies. She looked harried, and the air smelled of singed hair. She set down the curling tongs and helped me into my silk chiffon dress. I studied myself in the cheval mirror. The costume was a good approximation. But the sapphire necklace and earrings I wore would have to go; I gestured and Delaney took them off, fumbling with the clasps in her haste. My neck and ears looked unflatteringly bare, but you couldn't quite see Venus's ears in the painting, because of her hair. I pondered my reflection.

"Delaney, would you bring me my ruby and diamond earrings? I think they'll match quite nicely." I heard the words before I'd realized I'd spoken them, and they gave me a little thrill. My eyes shone and I smiled at myself. It was foolish, I knew that, but an impish part of me couldn't resist. If Charles had noticed their absence from his drawer, he hadn't suspected me. Wearing them would let him know that I had been in his study, after all, not Briggs. I was the one who had stolen his papers and betrayed his secrets. To see the look on his face when he noticed them—oh, it was just the parting gift I wanted.

"Here you go, ma'am." Delaney was out of breath; she must have run up and down the stairs. She fixed them on my ears, and it occurred to me that they had last adorned the ears of a dead woman. I shuddered, but didn't take them off. They would be my talisman against Charles's trickery.

We heard applause as the curtain closed on the scene before ours, and waited a minute while the servants changed the set. As we alit the dark stage, my heart pounded. We arranged ourselves in front of the faux orange grove, and a Cupid doll dangled from a string above our heads. The curtains rose, and the lights blinded me for a moment; it took all of my willpower not to blink.

Once my eyes adjusted, I scanned the audience, looking for him. I spotted him in the second row, close enough that I could make out the pearly opalescence of his vest buttons, but he was chatting with his neighbor and laughing. He wasn't looking at me at all.

It was just as well. I shouldn't have taken the risk, not when I was so close to leaving.

Charles settled back into his chair and turned toward the

stage at last. I felt his gaze rake over me, evaluating. Ever the perfectionist, he would be looking for my errors, the minor ways in which I had failed to do justice to the art.

He jolted forward, his placid composure finally slipping, his smile turning into something like a snarl. Hot satisfaction trickled into my belly. His eyes were wide and haunted.

And then the curtain fell, and I dropped my hand to my side. My exhilaration dissipated, leaving dread and regret behind. It had been reckless to provoke Charles, and I cursed myself for my stupidity. I could no longer wait until the end of the party to slip away. I had to leave at once. He'd come looking for me right away. He wouldn't want a scene, at least not one that involved him; would he try to force me upstairs, where we'd have privacy? Would he drug me and tell the guests that I was unwell? Would he drag me outside and stage an accident? He could task one of the footmen with his dirty work, or Terry, and all at once I was catapulted back to my nightmares of drowning in the briny Sound. Or one of them could murder me and dump my corpse at sea. I grabbed my throat, overcome by the sensation of being strangled. I struggled for air.

"Oh, we looked wonderful, don't you think?" Isobel Weathersfield, one of the most eligible young women in society at the moment, giggled. She had played one of the three Graces. I didn't have time for her.

"Just wonderful, dear," I said, before rushing off the stage.

I ran to the closet underneath the stairs, where I had stashed a purse stuffed with cash and jewels. If I had time, I'd grab the one I'd stashed in the greenhouse as well. I pushed aside a blue shawl and tucked my hand into the pocket of the old automobile coat where I'd hidden it. The pocket was empty. I swallowed my panic and reached into the other, and my palm grazed the soft velvet. I exhaled as I retrieved it and looked down at my dress, clinging scandalously to my legs. There was no time to change. Instead I hurried past the sweeping stairs, past the pocket drawers to the drawing room. The butler wasn't there to notice me pad through the front hall on costume-slippered feet. In the darkness, I doubted anyone would see me rushing toward the Sound. In my diaphanous dress, flowing and ethereal, I would look like a blur against the dark, a ghost.

I reached for the door handle.

A long-fingered hand gripped my wrist, hard. I yelped.

"Going somewhere, dear?"

CHAPTER 45

Charles's fingers dug into my skin, so hard that tears sprang to my eyes. He'd caught me. I'd failed. David would wait and wait for me, and if I never appeared, he might come looking. I didn't like to picture what might happen then.

I couldn't give up yet.

"I'm just going to get some fresh air. It's such a lovely night."

"With your purse?"

I looked down in surprise. "I hardly realized I was carrying it. Habit, I suppose." I'd become such an adept liar. Not as good as him, never as good as him, but competent enough that he released my wrist.

"You're wearing the earrings from our engagement." A statement, not a question. His voice was flat and cold.

"Yes, it turns out I'd never lost them, after all." Because he'd taken them, first from me, then from the ears of his dead mistress. I smiled and laughed prettily, as if it had all been a foolish mistake.

"I would like to speak to you, privately."

I looked anxiously toward the door. "I can't right now. I've a terrible headache. That's why I was going out."

"I'll go with you. Something happened that I need to speak with you about." He was tense, and I sensed the anger coiled inside of him, ready to spring free.

"What is it?"

"Terry was out walking Cerberus and they found a tres-passer on the beach. Cerberus sensed that he was dangerous and attacked. It was that journalist. The one who wrote the article about me."

"No." I gripped the door handle. My whisper scratched my throat. "What happened to him?"

"He bled to death."

The blood rushed out of my face. The floor tilted. It had to be a lie. It had to be someone other than David. David had to be whole and well and waiting for me, his strong heart beating in his chest. I didn't want to picture him cold and lifeless, his blood seeping into the sand, but the images came unbidden. I couldn't breathe.

"Are you quite well, dear?" Charles's lip curled.

"Why hasn't the constable been called?" Surely if it were true, he would have been forced to call the authorities. Charles could have made up the story to test me. I wanted to run until my lungs burned, legs hammering the ground, until I found David. I needed to see him.

"I wanted to wait until after the party. To avoid another scandal."

He jerked the door open with surprising force and steered me out of it and across the lawn. There were a handful of couples strolling about, taking in the view of the moonlit water from afar, and Charles stiffened. Whatever he meant to say, he wanted to make sure no one overheard us.

"The greenhouse. No one will disturb us there." I couldn't feel my face, wasn't aware of my lips forming the words. They echoed as if from a dream. Perhaps this was only some terrible dream, and I was still drugged in my bed upstairs.

Charles gripped my wrist again, vise-like, and the pain was real. My throat was raw. Tears spilled down my cheeks, a trickle at first, then faster. What point was there in pretending anymore? Charles had won. David wouldn't be saving me.

The greenhouse glowed in the darkness, its jungle of plants visible through the glass. Once we were inside, I could see my rose garden blooming spectacularly, mocking my grief. The green wood of the potting bench nearly blended in with the leaves. I walked toward it. Charles followed me and I hurried my pace.

"Millie, stop." I paused and reluctantly turned to face him. Whatever he had to say, I might as well hear it. "You were in my study. You gave my papers to that journalist. I'd wondered where he got his information." He crossed his arms and moved closer, until he loomed over me. I took a step backward. Rage filled his face. I'd never seen him so furious. "Was he your lover, too? Did he come here tonight for you?"

By wearing the earrings, I had ruined everything. They had allowed him to piece together the truth.

They were cursed. After what had happened to Gertrude I should have known better.

"Yes." I didn't see the point in denying it. I was so awfully sick of the charade.

He grabbed me and wrapped his long fingers around my throat. He was shaking. "I thought you loved me."

I laughed through my sobs, a short, high burst. "Love you? You tried to have me killed. You murdered Gertrude."

I closed my eyes. If he killed me, I'd be with David. I'd finally lost my will to fight. His fingers tightened and I was grateful at least that he'd finally revealed his true self to me. I could die knowing for certain what he really was.

My heart was still so full of David that I didn't register fear. I attempted to squirm out of his grasp, and to my surprise he released me. I took another step backward.

"What happened to Gertrude was to protect you, to save our marriage, can't you see that? I'm devoted to you, Millie. We can still be the couple we were before. The envy of everyone."

His startling eyes darted around in their sockets. He was

as delusional as he'd once accused me of being. His perfect life was falling to pieces around him, and he couldn't accept that it could never be put back together again.

I laughed and cried intermittently as I backed up farther. A thorn pricked my hand, gloveless because of my costume, and my elbow bumped the potting bench. I stopped. Dropped my purse heavy with jewels on top and flung open a drawer. I saw only twine and a packet of seeds. No, it was the other one.

"What are you looking for? Wolfsbane?" he sneered.

In the next drawer, the beaded cream purse lay just as I'd left it, perched delicately next to the shears, its belly bulky from the shape within. I snapped it open and then reached in to feel the cold, hard metal of the gun. I pulled it out tentatively, letting it dangle from my hand. Then I pointed it at Charles's chest.

"I want you to confess. I want to hear you say that you tried to kill me. That you killed David." The gun wobbled. I couldn't stop crying. I wiped my nose with a free hand.

"There's nothing to confess. *I* never did anything to you, or to him."

"How very clever of you." My voice was husky from crying.

"What happened with Briggs was all a mistake. A misunderstanding. She's unhinged." His pomaded hair had come loose and a piece fell across his forehead. The hand that had so recently been wrapped around my neck was balled into a fist.

"Funny how it's always everyone else who's crazy, Charles. Never you. But it's all over, can't you see that? You're going to lose everything."

"Millie. Put down the gun. You know you'd never actually shoot me."

His shiny shoes crunched on the gravel pathway between the neat rows of plants. He hardly ever came here. He didn't want to risk getting dirty. He must have made an exception when he planted the wolfsbane. He'd been the one to make the tincture, then to put it on my vanity later for Briggs to find.

Crunch. Crunch.

"Stop. Stay where you are." The gun was heavier than I remembered. I pointed it more deliberately, but still not well. My finger hovered over the trigger.

I pictured David, with Cerberus's teeth digging into him, his shock as he staggered backward. And suddenly I pulled my finger back, and I felt the recoil in my arm and shoulder, heard the *bang* and then a great crash. I'd missed, and the glass of the greenhouse exploded into little tiny shards, suspended in the air, glittering like crystal.

Charles jumped.

"Tell me, damn it. Just tell me you did it."

"What then, Millie? If I told you I did all of it. What would it matter?" His lips twisted into a smirk. "But there's nothing to tell, of course. I would never harm you. It's all in your head," he said, his words exaggerated and insincere. He mocked me with every syllable.

I should have known that he was too arrogant to ever admit his guilt, but in that moment, I also realized that he was right: it didn't matter. I already knew with utter certainty what he did, and what kind of man he was. Manipulative. Selfish. Dangerous.

He held still and then glanced at the gun, as if deciding whether to pounce and try to take it from me. I knew we had only moments before someone burst in on us, moments to decide. It wasn't murder, not if the alternative would be to be killed myself. It was self-defense.

"You're lying. You've always lied."

I stared at the center of his pristine dress shirt. And I pulled the trigger again.

The bullet struck his chest, and a red stain spread across the starched white fabric. He looked down at it in shock and disbelief, then at me, wonderingly, as if he'd never really seen me before until now. He staggered backward and fell to the ground with a thud, and blood flowed outward, into the gravel. A rose petal spiraled downward and landed on top of the growing puddle. I crouched down next to him, my flimsy dress getting stained red, and placed the gun in his hand. He watched me, blood sputtering between his lips, trying to speak. The flicker of fear in his eyes had expanded into horror as he understood that he was going to die. Time felt suspended. I stared back at him, as astonished as he was at what I'd done. The life left his eyes.

Then I screamed.

One of the footmen appeared a minute later, and I rocked back and forth on my knees over Charles's body. I had just enough presence of mind to mutter, "I tried to stop him. I tried."

The footman, a man called Stover with twitchy eyes, dropped his jaw.

"Please, Stover, call the coroner. Tell him to come quick. Tell all the guests to leave at once."

The rest of the night unspooled tortuously slow. I stayed with the body, waiting, until at last the coroner arrived, a man named Dr. Scott, who was as paunchy and rheumy-eyed as Charles had said.

"Good God. This house must be cursed," he said, his voice booming as he took in the scene. I rose, no doubt looking as shaken as I felt. I could still feel the recoil of the gun vibrating in my arm. He studied everything: the body, the gun, the broken glass. "What happened here, Mrs. Turner?" His voice was surprisingly kind.

"He . . . he had a gun. I knew he meant to harm himself and I tried to stop him." I started crying, real tears—for

David, for myself, for the man in front of me who I'd once adored. "We struggled. And—" I cried so hard that I couldn't continue.

"My God. A great man, he was, a great man," Dr. Scott said. "Shocking. Shocking."

"He had lost all of his money. He was going to have to declare bankruptcy within days," I said. "The party was meant to be a last hurrah, but I think it was just too much for him. It reminded him of what he was losing."

Dr. Scott squinted and stroked his luxurious mustache. I clutched the folds of my bloody chiffon dress, my hands shaking.

"Hmm." He stroked his mustache again.

And then I found the right words, and they oiled my mouth. "I'm so grateful for your help. I'm sure my father will be as well. Harold Munroe." The coroner's eyes grew round. He'd heard of him, then. "In fact, I'm sure he would be honored to contribute to your next campaign."

Charles had used this same trick on the coroner when Gertrude died. I looked again at his body sprawled on the ground, his green eyes still wide and staring. Had I become like him? Was I any better?

Dr. Scott cleared his throat. "Would he indeed?"

"Gladly."

He paused, and I twisted my bloody fingers together, holding my breath. "I'm much obliged." He nodded, his neck swallowing his chin. "Everything appears to me just as you said. A suicide, which you failed to thwart in time."

CHAPTER 46

The tombstone was a simple affair. Just a plain slab, no sculptures, no monuments. No special inscription, just his name etched in the gray granite.

Charles Randall Turner

He would have hated it.

But I was not willing to buy a mausoleum of marble to appease the dead. Not for him.

The funeral hadn't been announced to the public, and so he had been buried quietly a few months ago in the Rural Cemetery, only fifty feet from his murdered mistress. My parents had attended. My mother had looked more solemn than I'd ever seen her and squeezed me tightly. My father ended his silent treatment and told me he was sorry for my loss. He had looked truly sorry. No doubt enduring a husband's death was the type of thing he thought would build character. Even more character than a horrific marriage. I hadn't forgiven them, yet, but I found I was glad they came. It was a start.

Charles's business had entered receivership and then been shut down. The receiver distributed money back to the clients—much less than they'd thought they had—and his personal property was seized as well, including the town-house in the city. He'd owned it before our marriage and I didn't mourn its loss. It belonged to a life I was leaving behind.

But Rose Briar Hall was safe. And so was my trust.

The stately manor I had built was transformed. I'd gotten rid of everything that reminded me of him—all of the hunting trophies and the armchair where Gertrude had died. The days spent there filled with gloomy terror felt like a distant memory. Sunlight poured in through the mullioned windows, banishing the shadows.

Briggs had been convicted and sentenced to five years in jail. I had testified at her trial and been there when the jury returned her guilty verdict. I'd watched her smug smile fade away. Somehow Charles had set up Maisie comfortably, probably with stolen money from his clients, so his son would be taken care of. I was glad. He was an innocent in all this.

My so-called friends, of course, were scandalized all over again by Charles's bankruptcy and death, and I doubted many would receive me, should I care to call. But I didn't care to. I would make new friends. I imagined parties with actors and artists, bohemian types and writers. I had no regrets on that score.

Of other regrets, though, I had plenty. Charles's death still haunted me constantly, whether I was asleep or awake. Every instant of it had been preserved in my mind like one of his trophies. The greenhouse glass shining above like the chandeliers the night we danced at Sherry's. The earsplitting bang as the bullet struck, propelling him backward, the thump of his body as he collapsed.

I turned toward the road, where a man in a tweed suit leaned against the car, waiting for me. He held his walking cane as tightly as a weapon. In his pocket were two ocean liner tickets for Rome. There would have been three, but his father had opted to stay behind, in his cozy bungalow by the sea. We would depart on our trip later that afternoon.

David hadn't bled to death. He'd encountered Terry and

Cerberus soon after coming ashore, and when Terry snapped his fingers, Cerberus had attacked. Terry should have recognized David from his prior rescue attempt and known he wasn't an intruder, but apparently he'd been willing to obey whatever instructions Charles had given him. Maybe Charles had expected I'd try to escape.

But David had reacted in a brilliant fashion, and it had saved his life. He'd tackled Terry. Cerberus didn't want to hurt his master and couldn't reach David's neck while they fought, so he'd had to settle for biting his leg. Terry had pulled a knife on David, but David had turned it back on Terry.

Terry had bled to death on the beach, not David. When Charles had come to investigate the source of Cerberus's barking, he'd whistled for him, and the dog had run down the beach to greet him. In the light of his lantern, Charles had witnessed David escape back to his boat. David had a bad leg wound, but the doctor predicted a full recovery. When Terry was discovered later, Dr. Scott had declared that he had died in an altercation with an unknown trespasser.

If it weren't for David, I might not have survived the tormented months that followed Charles's death. I might have gone as mad as Charles had once accused me of being. But his journalistic logic had helped me make sense of the facts and fantasies, the truth and lies.

The papers had printed the news of Charles's tragic suicide. Sometimes, when I lay awake, my mind wired and humming, I imagined what they might have said if Dr. Scott had exposed a different version of events.

Perhaps: **Woman Saves Herself from Murderous Husband.** Or: **Heiress Kills Husband and Absconds with Lover.**

Both were factual, weren't they? Only one was truer than the other. One told the full story, plumbed its depths, and the other laid out the barest of facts that told a different story altogether, a false one. Because Charles and I weren't the same. I'd spent many sleepless nights puzzling over this question—

had he made me like him? Had the web of lies he had made me live in tangled me up so much that the only way to unknot myself was to become a spider, too? But no. I was only a clever moth, one who managed to fly away.

David would kiss my sweaty brow when I emerged from my nightmares, stroke my hair and face. His sturdy presence was the only reality that mattered to me anymore.

I reached into my purse and clutched the earrings, the jewels cold against my skin. I laid them on top of the headstone, where the rubies glinted red in the sun.

ACKNOWLEDGMENTS

Secrets of Rose Briar Hall may not be my first published book, but it was the book that landed me an agent. I'm so grateful to Danielle Egan-Miller, Eleanor Roth Imbody, and the whole team at Browne & Miller for saving me from the slush pile. Danielle, you saw something in this book, even though the first draft ended up needing a major overhaul, and without your guidance this never would have made it into the hands of readers. Thank you.

I truly couldn't be luckier to have an editor like John Scognamiglio, who is brilliant, kind, and incredibly dedicated to his writers. Thank you for making this book the best it could be. Vida Engstrand, I'm in awe of you and all the phenomenal work you've done to help launch my books and my career. Matt Johnson, Alexandra Nicolajsen, Carly Sommerstein, Kristin McLaughlin, Samantha Larabbee, Lauren Jernigan, and the whole team at Kensington—it's truly been a pleasure working with each and every one of you and I'm grateful every day that my books found a home here.

To my writing group: Hannah Howard, Desiree Byker Abiri, Jess Manners, Carolyn Kylstra, Yelena Schuster, Simon Morris, and especially Kate Fridkis Berring, none of this would have happened without you. To all the wonderful fellow authors I've met who have provided encouragement, your support is so appreciated. Making friends in the writing community is the best part of this whole journey.

To my parents, James and Jill, my sister Emily, and my in-laws Ann and Brian: thank you for your endless support and patience. To my husband Steve, and my children Walden, Cecilia, and the little one on the way, you remind me every day of what really matters. I love you all so much.

SECRETS OF ROSE BRIAR HALL

ABOUT THIS GUIDE

The suggested questions are included to enhance your group's reading of Kelsey James's *Secrets of Rose Briar Hall*!

Discussion Questions

1. At the beginning of the book, Rose Briar Hall is cold and dark, without electricity or heat. At the end, Millie says, "Sunlight poured in through the mullioned windows, banishing the shadows." How is Millie like her house? In what ways was she also kept in the dark in the beginning of the book?

2. Toward the end of the book, Millie thinks: "Money was a funny thing, wasn't it? Strange how it could save you and imprison you at once." Why do you think she feels that way?

3. At the first dinner party at Rose Briar Hall, Millie is eager to show off her new house and prove she deserves to be Mrs. Charles Turner. At the very last dinner party, Charles is the one with something to prove. What did you think of the parallels between these two parties?

4. In 1907, a new law in the state of New York made infidelity a misdemeanor. It was enacted as a way to curb divorce cases. As of 2023, this law is still in effect (though a bill is in motion to repeal it). What is your reaction to this law? How did it impact Millie?

5. Millie's experience teaches her how to be more independent, and David shows her another way to live. What was your reaction to David's influence on Millie? In the end, how did you feel about the fact that Millie only had herself to rely on?

6. At the end, Millie wonders, "Had the web of lies he had made me live in tangled me up so much that the only way

to unknot myself was to become a spider, too?" What do you think? Are there any ways in which Millie had to become "like a spider" to free herself?

7. Millie finally remembers the dinner party and also finds some critical evidence. What do you think ultimately convinces her of the truth about that night? How do you decide if something is true? Have you ever struggled to accept the truth about a situation?

8. Briggs tells Millie, "Poor Mr. Turner. To be stuck with a woman like you. A murderess." Why do you think Briggs believes this about Millie? Why do all of Millie's friends believe it?

9. Have you ever been deceived by someone? How did you come to realize it?

Visit our website at
KensingtonBooks.com
to sign up for our newsletters, read
more from your favorite authors, see
books by series, view reading group
guides, and more!

Become a Part of Our
Between the Chapters Book Club
Community and Join the Conversation

Betweenthechapters.net

Submit your book review for a chance to win exclusive
Between the Chapters swag you can't get anywhere else!
https://www.kensingtonbooks.com/pages/review/